Riley's
BIKER

ROYAL BASTARDS MC

ROYAL BASTARDS MC

RENO, NV

USA TODAY BESTSELLING AUTHOR
MISTY WALKER

To Jason, I miss you every day.
"Everything that happens is supposed to be
And it's all predetermined can't change your destiny
Guess I'll just keep moving
Someday maybe I'll get to where I'm going"
—Bright Eyes

PLAYLIST

"New Americans" by Halsey
"Better Off Dead" by Sleeping With Sirens
"Nails" by Call Me Karizma
"Need to Know" by Doja Cat
"Love In The Dark" by Adele
"Black Out Days" by Phantogram, Future Islands
"Dirty Thoughts" by Chloe Adams
"We Belong Together" by Ritchie Valens
"Daddy Issues (Remix)" by The Neighbourhood, Syd
"Freak Like Me" by NoMBe
"Cringe" by Matt Maeson
"FUCK YOU HEATHER" by Boyish
"Glory Box" by Portishead
"Save Your Tears" by The Weeknd
"Tonight You Are Mine" by The Technicolors
"Come a Little Closer" by Cage the Elephant
"Aerials" by System Of A Down
"She Thinks of Me" by Landon Tewers
"W.D.Y.W.F.M?" by The Neighbourhood
"Bad Things" by Cults
"The Other Side of Paradise" by Glass Animals
"Light My Love" by Greta Van Fleet
"Meet Me At Our Spot" by The Anxiety, WILLOW, Tyler Cole
"High Enough-RAC Remix" by K.Flay, RAC
"Don't Blame Me" by Taylor Swift
"Clouds" by BØRNS
"Feel Better" by Penelope Scott
"redesign" by awfultune
"I Can't Handle Change" by Roar
"You Don't Get Me High Anymore" by Phantogram, How To Dress Well

ROYAL BASTARDS CODE

PROTECT: The club and your brothers come before anything else, and must be protected at all costs. **CLUB** is **FAMILY**.

RESPECT: Earn it & Give it. Respect club law. Respect the patch. Respect your brothers. Disrespect a member and there will be hell to pay.

HONOR: Being patched in is an honor, not a right. Your colors are sacred, not to be left alone, and **NEVER** let them touch the ground.

OL' LADIES: Never disrespect a member's or brother's Ol'Lady. **PERIOD.**

CHURCH is **MANDATORY.**

LOYALTY: Takes precedence over all, including well-being.

HONESTY: Never **LIE, CHEAT,** or **STEAL** from another member or the club.

TERRITORY: You are to respect your brother's property and follow their Chapter's club rules.

TRUST: Years to earn it . . .seconds to lose it.

NEVER RIDE OFF: Brothers do not abandon their family.

Dear Reader,

Riley's Biker is a dark MC romance with themes that might be triggering to some readers. To see a full list of these content warnings, please visit my website at www.authormistywalker. com.

XOXO,

Misty Walker

ROMANCE AUTHOR

**Five years ago, she took a piece of me.
Now it's time to collect.**

From USA Today bestselling author Misty Walker comes a secret baby, age gap, dark MC romance.

It was supposed to be a one-night stand. A quick release before Coyote went back to his nomad lifestyle with the Royal Bastards MC.

But it's been five years, and he's still searching for the girl with the owl eyes who disappeared into the night. And not just because she stole his leather cut. He can't seem to get her out of his head.

Until one day, she pops back up out of nowhere. Instead of breaking down her door and confronting her, Coyote does what he does best. He hides in the shadows, watches from a distance, and learns everything he can.

Turns out Riley Renna isn't who he thought at all. Somehow, she's involved with a rival MC—the Sons of Erebus—and has a kid. A little girl who looks suspiciously like Coyote.

When the president of the Sons starts moving in on his family, Coyote knows the time for just watching is up. It's time to step into the light and claim what's his.

Daddy's home, Little Owl.

Riley's
BIKER

xoxo

PROLOGUE

Coyote
Five years ago

"**L**et's do another shot." Loki, the prince of the Royal Bastards, slaps one hand on my shoulder while the other forms a fist and pounds on the bar. The prospect scrambles to do his bidding.

"One more, then I'm out." I swivel on my barstool, taking in the chaos and debauchery going on around me.

I grin and tuck my head when I see Trucker, Prez of Reno's Royal Bastards, making out on a leather sofa with his ol' lady like they're teenagers. Boar, the VP of this chapter, has his face buried in some young girl's chest—who is not his wife, but we don't talk about that—while the younger members are screwing patch pussy like their peckers are going to fall off.

I swivel back around. This ain't my scene. I pick up my shot glass of God knows what and clink it against Loki's.

"Cheers," Loki says, and tosses the shot down his throat without a flinch. When you grow up in the clubhouse of a motorcycle club, booze and women are early lessons learned.

"Cheers." I throw back the shot and set the glass down.

Mmm. Mezcal. The prince has good taste.

"What're your plans when you leave here?" he asks, wrapping an arm around a blonde wearing a shirt low-cut enough to see the tops of her areolas. She blatantly cups him over his jeans, startling a reaction out of him. He leans into her and whispers, "In a minute."

I shift my gaze to the peanut shell-covered floor and scratch at the back of my neck. "Meetin' back up with Dunk and Mac. Gettin' to be cold out, so we'll probably head south."

He quirks a brow. "Or you could patch in here and stick around."

"Nah. You know me." I chuckle as if my inability to stay in one place is a personality trait. It's not, and we both know it. Reno is a fine place to rest, but there's no settling down for a man like me.

"Don't be a stranger. We'll catch you next time." He takes his bottle of beer and leads the blonde over to a quiet corner.

I leave my half-empty bottle and head out to the backyard. The second the door closes behind me, it's quiet and serene. The air is easier to breathe, and my heart rate slows the further I get from the clubhouse and the closer I get to my pup tent.

I strip down to my underwear before climbing inside to lie down. I need some sleep before I meet up with Mac and Dunk tomorrow. My nomad brothers skipped our stop in Reno in favor of hitting up some Vegas casinos, with plans to reunite in Northern California before riding down the coast.

My eyes have almost shut when I hear a sniffing. I scan the area through the mesh walls of my tent, but I don't see anything.

Wild horses, bears, coyotes all live out here in the high desert. Normally, I wouldn't go inspect, except it didn't sound like any of those things. What I heard was more human.

I pull on my faded black jeans and leather boots before stepping outside. At first glance, there's nothing to see. It's dark, and the lights from the house are too far away to light up the area.

Then I hear it again. My eyes scour the fence line until I see it. Or rather, see her. A girl is hunched over on the ground. Her back is leaning against the fence post, and the light of her cell phone illuminates her face as her thumbs work fast and furious to type out a message.

"Hey," I call out. Her eyes grow wide as saucers, her lips purse, and she freezes. I chuckle to myself and shake my head. "I can still see you, little owl."

She rises to her feet slowly. Her jean shorts are cut off at the tops of her thighs, and her tight black tank top is cut low. She's young for a club whore, but I've seen all types show up looking to bag a biker.

"You okay?" I ask because it's the polite thing to do.

"Do you know why every Uber driver cancels my pick up?" she asks, her voice sweet and thick like syrup.

My cock hardens, but I talk myself down. She hangs around the club, so she's probably fucked a few of my brothers just so she can run home to her girlfriends to tell them all about her walk on the dark side. Not into that shit.

"They won't come anywhere near the club. Walk a few blocks away and try again."

Her face falls. "Damn it. Can nothing go right tonight?"

"Not sure what else went wrong, but it's a simple solution." I gesture in the direction she should start hoofing it.

"Do you have a bike?" she asks.

"Yeah." I don't like where this is going. I don't let chicks on the back of my bike.

"Can you take me to the airport?"

My brows lift. "Nope."

"But I have a flight to catch." She walks over to me, and I get my first up-close look at her.

I'm six foot four, and she barely reaches my chest, making her no taller than five foot three. She's tiny, too. I'll bet my biceps are thicker than her thighs.

Her soft, creamy complexion only adds to the beauty of her pronounced Cupid's bow lip, the high arch of her dark eyebrows, and her defined jawline. Her eyes are swollen, and her cheeks are red from crying, but it doesn't detract from her beauty.

"Like I said, a couple blocks that way." I point again.

"It's dark, and I don't know the area." She twists a strand of hair around a finger.

I roll my eyes. "Not gonna work on me, little owl. But go inside; one of my brothers would be happy to service you again."

"Again?" she scoffs, her hand falling to her side. "I didn't go in there, and I wouldn't"—she glances away, embarrassed—"do that with any of them."

"Then why are you here?" I ask.

Her gaze meets mine, and her cobalt eyes go icy. "It doesn't matter."

The little owl has some bite. Maybe she isn't a sweet butt.

"Look. I'll walk you to the street, but after that, you're on your own." I turn and walk back toward my tent.

"Where are you going?" she asks, trailing behind me.

"To put on a shirt." I reach into my tent and pull out my pack.

"Do you live out here?" She folds her arms across her chest, propping up her bite-sized titties.

"Don't live anywhere." I find a black tee and pull it over my head.

"What does that mean?" She watches me closely with a focused interest I don't like.

"Means I'm a nomad."

"Nomad?" Her brows furrow.

I sigh. "I'm a Royal Bastard, like all those guys in there, but I don't belong to a chapter. I'm on my own. I help if someone needs me, then I'm back on the road."

She walks a circle around the tent, taking in the contents inside. My pack. My cut. My bedding. Nothing special.

"Interesting. Why is your tent made from mesh? That can't protect you from the weather."

It's not the question that has me closing my eyes and taking a breath; it's the answer. Something I haven't told a soul, and I'm certainly not going to start with a girl I don't know.

"Have a tarp in case it rains, but I don't see much weather 'cause I ride south for the winter." I tie the laces on my boots to give me an extra second to avoid her scrutinizing gaze on me.

"Don't you get lonely?" She stops in front of me and knocks her tennis shoes against my boots. I look up to see her hands on her hips.

"No." I'm done answering questions, so I turn the table on her. "Why are you going to the airport?"

She tips her head back, the sky suddenly becoming interesting to her. She's avoiding, like me.

"I need to catch a flight home."

"Still not gonna tell me why you're here?" I ask.

"Nope."

"When's your flight?"

"Tomorrow morning at eight." She sinks to the ground in defeat. Guess we're not going anywhere anytime soon. Not that I entirely mind. For some reason, I don't mind talking to her, and I enjoy hearing her voice. My cock's interested, too, now that I know she wasn't in the clubhouse making the rounds.

"Oh, yeah?" I sit down next to her, one leg outstretched and the other bent.

"I didn't plan this out well. I thought I'd show up, and things would be... different." She scoops handfuls of sand, then spreads her delicate fingers wide so it all falls to the ground again. "But that's not what happened, and now I'm stranded in a place where Uber drivers are too scared to venture. How is this my life right now?"

She's talking to herself more than me, and her story is nothing but a garbled, vague telling I don't understand, so I say nothing. Then she hides her face with her hands, and the tears return. I pat her back awkwardly, not knowing how the hell I got myself into this situation.

"You could stay the night here. It ain't much, but at least you don't have to sit in an empty airport all night."

This is my dick talking. Not me. It's been too long since I've found a woman who sparks my interest, and for whatever reason, this one does.

"I'm not having sex with you," she blurts.

"Not interested in that with you, little owl." It's a lie. Now that I have the idea in my head, all I can think about is her tight little body riding me until the sun comes up. But I don't strong-arm women into something they don't want, so if she needs shelter for the night, that's what I'll give her.

She peers over at me, her face pinched in irritation. "Why not? What's wrong with me?"

I chuckle, then lean into her and, in a lust-thick voice, say, "Ain't nothing wrong with you. If it were up to me, I'd strip you down and fuck you so hard you can't sit down on your flight home tomorrow."

"Oh." Her eyes home in on my lips. "Then why don't you?"

I pull away. "You said no, and I don't force myself on women."

"Okay. I guess, in that case, I'll stay here and catch an Uber in the morning."

"Whatever you wanna do." I kick off my boots and stand. "I'm going to bed."

"I'm coming too."

Those big owl eyes watch as I strip off my pants and shirt, leaving me in a pair of boxer briefs. I smirk. She's more interested than she lets on.

She kicks off her Chucks, and we both climb inside. As she pointed out before, the walls of this tent are made of mesh so even though we're inside, it feels like we're still outside.

I only have one pillow, so I offer it to her. Likewise, I only have one sleeping bag, so I unzip it and spread it over the top of us. The blow-up mattress pad keeps us from feeling the rocks underneath, but for us to both be on it, we have to get close. Real close. Close enough, I smell the patchouli and mint from her shampoo.

We lie on our sides, facing the same direction but not touching. It should be awkward. We know fuck-all about each other, but for whatever reason, I don't feel uncomfortable.

"What's your name?" she whispers.

"Coyote."

She flips over, her face within inches of mine. "Your momma named you Coyote?"

The mention of my mom is like a stab through the heart, but I'm used to the pain. "No. What's your name?"

"Way to deflect, but I'll let it pass. I'm Riley. It's nice to meet you." She holds out her hand, which barely fits in the space between us. I shake it slowly and intentionally.

"Nice to meet you too."

We stare at each other for a long moment, our warm breaths mingling between us. The tension builds and builds, neither of us turning away.

"Are you going to kiss me, Coyote?"

"No."

"What if I ask you to?" she pouts.

"Sorry, little owl. I'm a man. I don't just make out with girls anymore."

"What if I want *more*?"

Maybe I'm pussy deprived, but her boldness turns me right the fuck on.

"How old are you?" I assume she's of age, but I make it a habit to ask when there's even a question.

"Nineteen."

"Then all you have to do is ask." I reach over and grip her by the hip, tugging her against me. Those owl eyes widen impossibly big when she feels the result of her words against her belly.

She swallows hard. "Ask?"

"Need your words."

Her lips purse as she makes her decision. "Coyote, will you fuck me?"

The curse sounds wrong in her saccharine voice, but it doesn't stop me from crushing my lips to hers and snaking an arm under her head. I can feel her pebbled nipples through her thin tank top telling me she's not wearing a bra, and thank fuck for that. Reaching under the sleeping bag, I snake a hand under her shirt and am met with bare flesh.

Her tits are barely a palmful, but I love the way they feel in my hand. I pinch her nipple, and she lets out a choked sound that is all pleasure.

"Feel good, little owl?"

"Yes," she says on an exhale. She tentatively places a hand on my chest, then drifts it lower until she reaches the band of my underwear and teases the elastic with the tips of her fingers.

Tossing the sleeping bag off us, I roll on top of her and shove her tank top up. My mouth wraps around her tit, sucking the whole thing in before releasing it with a *pop*. "What about that?"

She wraps her legs around my waist and rocks her pelvis against me. "So good."

I continue to suck and bite on her tiny nipples, working her up into a frenzy.

"Need to taste the rest of you," I murmur, sitting up to help her out of her shorts and panties.

I wish I could see her pussy, but it's too dark, so I'll live with the next best thing. Touching her. Swiping a finger through her bare folds, I find her wet—sopping, really. I can smell her arousal from here, and it's an addictive scent I'll never forget.

Lowering my mouth to her cunt, I lick her up and down,

eliciting soft and sensual moans from her. "How do you like it? Fast and hard or soft and sweet."

The question perplexes her for a moment before she says, "Fast and hard."

"My kind of girl." I flick my tongue against her clit, inserting a finger into her tight hole. It's gonna be a stretch for her to take my cock, but I'm willing to put in the effort.

It only takes a few more minutes before she's coming, her channel pulsing around my finger and her hips grinding against my face. Her sweet cream coats my tongue, her flavor like a freshly picked tomato after it's been sitting in the sun all day.

I've never wanted anyone like I want her. If she changed her mind right now, I'd have blue balls for a month.

I coax her down from her orgasm before reaching for my pack and digging out a condom. Riley watches me intently as I pull my boxer briefs down past my ass and roll the rubber down my cock.

"You ready?" I rub a hand up her pussy, feeling how wet she still is for me.

She doesn't respond, and I can't make out her expression. As much as it will pain me, I'm not about to do this if she doesn't want it.

I lean over her body and kiss her sweet lips. "I'll ask again. Are you ready?"

"I feel like I should tell you something."

"What?"

"I'm a virgin." She locks her arms around my neck, preventing me from pulling away. "I'm not saving it out of some purity culture obligation. It just hasn't happened, and I want it to. With you."

"Don't fuck virgins, little owl." Despite my words, my cock is like a heat-seeking missile, aligning itself at her entrance.

"Please," she begs. "I want it to be you."

I want it to be me, too, but I'm not sure what the right thing to do is. I'm too old to be fuckin' virgins. Hell, I wasn't even with a virgin when I was fourteen and losing my own virginity. That was sixteen years ago, and I don't know if girls still feel the same about their cherry as they did back then.

"I won't be sweet and gentle."

"I don't want sweet and gentle," she spits out, as though I offended her.

My answer is to grip the base of my cock and thrust into her in one fluid motion. God, she's tight. So tight there's no chance of me lasting long. She moans, and her fingernails claw into my neck. The pain spurs me on, so I lift onto my knees, tossing her legs over either shoulder and reaching under her ass, taking two handfuls.

I use her body to fuck my cock, pushing and pulling on her elevated hips. Her chest heaves, thrusting those gorgeous bite-sized tits into the air. If I didn't have my hands full of ass, I'd be pinching those little buds.

Her heels dig into the back of my shoulders, helping me move her body back and forth on my hard length, and to my surprise, she cries out with another orgasm. Her cunt bears down on my cock, strangling me in the best way. Beads of sweat gather on my brow and lower back from the exertion as I work her down from her release. My muscles will be sore tomorrow, but I don't give a shit right now.

"Damn, little owl. Your cunt is so good, you're going to make me come. You ready?"

She nods vehemently, her hands reaching between her legs to dig her nails into my abdomen. The image of the claw marks she's leaving behind spurs me into an orgasm.

I come with a roar, burying my cock as deep as I can get. I don't remember it ever lasting this long or feeling this good, but with Riley, it does.

After she's milked every drop of cum from my cock, I pull

out and toss the used condom outside. I'll deal with it in the morning.

"That was. . . well, it was incredible," she gasps out, her breaths still coming fast.

"Hell yeah, it was." I flop back down onto the mattress and encourage her to her side.

I'm not much for cuddling, but I'm also not an asshole, so I'm going to hold her all night. She melds into me, letting out a satisfied sigh and sweeping her hair off her neck so it's draped over the top of the pillow. With her hair in my face, I inhale, attaching her patchouli and mint scent to this memory.

I don't mean to fall asleep so quickly, but I do, and when I wake the next morning, she's gone. Every trace of her. If it weren't for the used condom I find when I climb out of my tent, I'd think I dreamed the whole thing.

Guess it's for the best, though I wish I could've gotten a look at her in the daylight.

I'm up later than I planned, so I quickly pack up. It's not until I'm walking through the clubhouse that I feel like something's missing. I dig through my backpack, coming up empty-handed. It's then I realize something.

The bitch stole my cut.

Chapter
ONE

Riley
Five years later. . .

Wiping the dampness from my tear-stained cheeks, I blow out a breath and walk inside the hospital room. The vibrant abstract paintings hanging on the stark white walls do little to liven the place up.

Color doesn't hide the smell of sickness. Busy paint strokes don't camouflage the overwhelming feeling of imminent death in the air. They shouldn't even bother.

Crash places a hand on my lower back, propelling me forward. "Best hurry."

Smoothing down my T-shirt, I force myself to put one foot in front of the other, past the blue and pink striped curtain, and to the bedside of the man who raised me from birth until I was eight years old.

Hiding underneath tubes and the pallid skin of a dying man is Wrecker, or as I knew him, Dad. Happy memories flood my mind, and I rush to his side, taking his hand in mine.

"Daddy," I cry, sinking into a plastic chair and clutching his hand to my chest.

He doesn't respond or even wake up.

"Only thing keepin' him alive are those machines, Ry," Crash explains, running a hand through his beautiful dirty-blond hair and taking a seat by the window.

"I know. I guess I just thought—"

"Thought what? That the sound of your voice would perform a medical miracle?"

His brash tone is nothing new, but I thought since Wrecker's on his death bed, he might cut me a break. I should know better. He's always been a dick to me, yet sometimes I catch him looking at me with half-lidded eyes, and I think maybe. . . but then he opens his mouth to insult me, and we're back to square one.

I narrow my eyes on him. "Maybe."

"This might make your head explode, but not even *you* can bring a man back to life." He leans forward, resting his forearms on his thick, jean-covered thighs.

"So what happens now?" I ask, ignoring his jab.

"The doctor has some paperwork for you to sign. After that, they'll turn off all these machines."

"Why me?" It's not like me and Wrecker are related. Not really.

Crash sighs. "He had you listed as next of kin."

My heart sinks. If guilt could eat you alive, I'd be dead next to Dad. But it's not my own guilt I feel; it's the guilt of my mother. She's the one who lied about my paternity and then took me from the only father I've ever known, crushing not only Wrecker's heart but mine too.

Although I've been trying to repair that relationship for the last five years, we'd only just begun to feel like a family again. And now he's gone.

"So, you'll sign the papers?" Crash asks, breaking through my trip down memory lane.

I sniffle. "There's no chance of recovery?"

"He got shot in the head, Ry. No. There's no chance."

"Then I guess I have to." I stand and kiss Wrecker's cold cheek before whispering, "You'll always be my Daddy."

My eyes blur as tears well and drip onto the sheet of paper containing Wrecker's last words to me. I knew he cared about me, but I had no idea how he really felt until now.

Dear Riley,

If you're reading this, it means shit happened and I've been sent to Hades. Don't worry about my soul. After all, I'm not. I deserve everything coming to me but if given a chance to start all over, I'd do it again because every choice I made led to you being born.

And Riley, you were the best part of my fucked up life.

Before I get to the whole purpose behind this letter, I'm gonna tell you a story. One I've told you before, but it bears repeating.

I met your mom in 2000. I remember like it was yesterday. I was in California on a run and there, at a stoplight, driving a BMW, was the most beautiful woman I've ever seen. My heart nearly stopped when she flashed me a smile.

She was so far out of my league, but that smile had me going against my better judgment and I followed her to a restaurant parking lot. She got out of the car, came right up to me and kissed me square on the lips. That kiss changed my entire life.

She agreed to let me buy her lunch at that restaurant and for the next four hours, we got to know each other. She told me all about her family's wealth and how she felt she didn't belong in that world, and I told her all about club life with the Sons of Erebus.

Said she dreamed of having the freedom I did, so after only four hours of knowing her, I asked her to come with me. There wasn't a doubt in my mind that she was the one for me. Not one single doubt.

To my surprise, she agreed to leave her bullshit world behind and take a chance on me. We left that BMW in the parking lot, she hopped on the back of my bike, heels and all, and I took her home.

I'm telling you all this because I see a lot of your mother in you. You don't fit in with all those rich fuckers who only want to use you for your family's money. You tell me all the time how much you wish you didn't have to dress up every weekend for charity balls that cost more to put on than they make in donations.

Now you have a way out.

In this envelope, you'll find my will. I've left everything I own in your name. My house, car, bank accounts, and most importantly, my bike—it's not much, but it's all yours.

But before you decide to sell it all and pocket the money, hear me out.

Give Reno a chance. Pack your shit and move out here. Lean on the club to help. They already consider you family. Get a job and teach Veda—and yourself for that matter—how much more things mean when you work hard for them.

If you decide it's not for you, like your mom did, then you can always go back. But maybe, just maybe, you'll find out who the real Riley is. I see her buried underneath all the fancy clothes and expensive car. You're the same girl you were when you were five, with your tiny hands all greasy from helping me fix motorcycles and talking about how you can't wait to have a bike of your own.

Find that girl, Riley.

I know you're probably crying right now—you've always been a crier—but wipe those eyes because it's time to do work.

One last piece of advice for you. Like everything else in this letter, you can take it or leave it.

Give Crash a chance. I know your mom has warned you off of bikers but you'll never meet a more loyal and dedicated man than one in an MC. My soul would rest easy knowing you're taken care of. And while I don't think anyone is good enough for my baby girl, Crash has earned my respect.

I'm trusting him to take over my club, so it's only right I trust him to do right by you and Veda.

I love you and Veda with all I am,
Wrecker

I set the letter next to me on the bed, wipe snot and tears away with the back of my hand, and scan over the piles of boxes stacked around me. I did it. I moved to Reno. Wrecker would be proud of me.

"Mommy, where are my books?" Veda asks, walking into my new bedroom. The second she sees my tears, her angelic face falls. "Why are you crying?"

I open my arms, and she runs into them. Kissing the top of her head, I say, "I miss Granddaddy."

She pulls away and gazes up at me with the only feature she inherited from me—big, blue owl eyes. "I'm sorry, Mommy."

I circle my finger around one of her springy curls. "It's okay, baby. Actually, I'm glad you're here. I need help unpacking all these boxes."

The doorbell rings before we can get started, and Veda runs over to open it.

"Wait," I call out, rushing to follow her. Before now, there were employees to do things like answering the front door, so the notion that we now do it ourselves is exciting.

Swinging the door open, I'm met with a broad chest clad in a white T-shirt and a leather cut. My gaze slowly lifts until I reach Crash's hazel eyes.

"Hey, Ry." He rubs at the back of his neck, looking uncomfortable.

I try to see what Wrecker saw, running every interaction I've had with Crash through my mind, but I don't see it. This man has been nothing but standoffish with me. I was under the impression he didn't like me at all.

Maybe I'm wrong. Maybe he plays by those misogynistic little boy rules where he's mean to the girl he likes. If that's the case, then I don't care what Wrecker wants for me. I don't play games.

"Crash." I glance behind him to see if he's alone or if any other Sons of Erebus members came along. They didn't. "I didn't know you were coming by."

"Last minute decision."

"Hi!" Veda chirps, always so friendly to everyone. He ignores her completely.

"Need to talk to you." His gaze flitters down to Veda for a split second before he scowls. "Alone."

He's never been comfortable around her. I chalked it up to him not used to kids, but now that we live here, I take offense to it and move Veda to stand behind me.

"Sure," I draw out, curious why he wouldn't just call. "Veda, why don't you go look in the boxes I set in your room. I think your books might be in there."

"Okay, Mommy." My happy girl bounces inside, and I step onto the porch, closing the door behind me. "What's up?"

"Let's take a seat." He motions to the porch swing Wrecker installed when I was five.

He replaced the wood and changed the chain, but the memories I have of sitting here with him at night after he got home from work are still attached to this swing.

"So?" I ask after we're both settled.

"How are you adjusting?"

I narrow my eyes on him. He's not one for small talk, and I've never heard him bother himself with other people's comfort. It's weird, and I don't like it.

"Fine. It was nice of you guys to stock the fridge and clean up before we got here. I was just here a month ago, before"—I swallow my emotion, unable to say the words—"you know, and it didn't look this tidy."

Crash chuckles, running his palms down his jeans. "Wrecker didn't know his way around a mop, that's for sure. But I'm glad to hear the girls did a good job getting things ready for you."

By girls, he means the club whores or the patch pussy or whatever they call them. I should've known the guys wouldn't be the ones to vacuum and dust.

"It was a nice surprise." I push off from the ground to set the swing in motion, but we go nowhere with Crash's worn black leather boots planted on the wooden deck.

If it were any other man, he'd take the hint and pick his feet up. But it's not any other man; it's Crash, and he doesn't move a muscle.

This right here is what I'm talking about. He's so. . . odd.

We sit, staring into the front yard for long, torturous minutes in silence. At least if Wrecker had done some landscaping, there would be something to look at. But the old man didn't have the time or attention to maintain a lawn or plants, so the only things growing are sagebrush and pine trees.

"Guys voted me in as Prez last night." He tugs on the lapel of his cut, showing me the Prez patch under his name.

"That's what Wrecker wanted."

"Wrecker wanted a lot of things for me," he says ominously.

I wonder if that means he read the letter Wrecker wrote. If so, he knows Wrecker wanted us to be together. That's awkward. Honestly, this entire visit is awkward. What do I care if he was voted in as Prez? I'm not in the club life.

Finally, Crash stands and stretches, exposing a sliver of skin between the hem of his shirt and the top of his jeans. My eyes fixate on the V of muscle that leads down. Goddamn. If nothing else, he's nice to look at.

"If you need anything, you got my number," he says, breaking my trance.

I can't be sure because my eyes take way too long to reach his face, but I think I glimpse a smirk before he turns his back to me and strides over to his bike. Pushing his helmet on his head, he straddles his motorcycle and revs the engine before driving away and leaving me wondering what the hell that was all about.

Chapter
TWO

Coyote

"I'm heading out," Lucas says, shaking hands with the casino floor manager.

From the outside, Lucas Orton appears to be a well-known property developer here in Vegas. But me, Dunk, and Mac aren't on the outside. We live in a world where the truths are much more depraved.

This asshole gets off on luring drunk girls off the Strip by flashing money at them and promising a night they won't forget. After they're in his car, he drugs them until they don't know or care what happens to them. Then they're sold off like livestock to the highest bidder who will use them to fulfill their sick and twisted perversions.

Then, after the girls have been used and abused and no longer hold any worth, these assholes toss them back on the streets like garbage. Only now, they're mutilated, addicted to drugs, and so traumatized they're afraid of their own shadow.

My ears perk up at Lucas's departure, and I give Mac a discreet nod from across the room. I get up from the blackjack table I've been playing on, tossing my cards in front of me and grabbing my remaining chips before walking away.

"Sir, you won," the dealer shouts after me, but I ignore him. "Sir. You forgot your winnings."

I don't give a shit about a hundred-dollar chip. I wasn't here to play cards in the first place. The game I'm interested in involves blood and penance.

And that game has only just begun.

I follow behind while Dunk and Mac flank him from a safe distance. Lucas stops at the cage reserved for high rollers and trades a suitcase full of chips for one that I'm hoping is full of cash before strolling out the front door.

He's not stupid; he has two bodyguards hot on his tail. A powerful man like him knows he's a target, but he could have ten men protecting him, and they'd still be no match for the three of us.

When Lucas steps outside, his driver already has the door to his limo open and waiting. While they load into the vehicle, Mac, Dunk, and I hang a right to the front row parking for motorcycles.

Seconds later, we're trailing behind the shiny black limo, keeping our distance as it pulls onto the freeway and heads to a staff-gated estate on the outskirts of town. He doesn't know it yet, but he won't be making it home to his ridiculous mansion tonight.

Once we hit the two-lane road that's mostly deserted this time of night, we speed up. Mac veers to the right of the limo while Dunk veers to the left, and I stay on their tail. In a choreographed move, we pull out our guns and open fire on the vehicle, aiming for the tires.

Screeching rubber pierces the quiet night air as the driver tries to slow down and stay on the road. The second the rims hit the asphalt, he loses control and steers the vehicle right into the ditch. We skid to a stop and hop off our bikes, guns aimed at the limo.

The guards jump out first, their own weapons at the ready. But they didn't expect this, and the adrenaline coursing through their bodies leaves them at a disadvantage as they scramble to figure out what just happened. Two gunshots sound, one from Mac and one from me, dropping the guards like flies.

Dunk reaches the driver's side door and throws it open, his Glock trained on the driver, who immediately throws his hands up in the air. He's most likely innocent, and if he keeps his head on straight, he'll walk away from this.

Without saying a word, I reach into the open back door and grab hold of Lucas's arm, yanking him out of the car.

"Don't hurt me. You can have the money," the sleazy bastard cries.

"That's a given," I say, handing him off to Mac, who pistol whips him across the temple. He falls to the dirt in a heap.

Sliding over the expensive leather interior, I find the briefcase. After a quick check to make sure it is, in fact, full of cash, I get back out and hand it to Mac.

"Empty it. I'll deal with him." I nod to the man sprawled out on the ground.

Mac disappears to divvy up the cash into our saddlebags while I straddle Lucas, crouching down to grip him by the front of his suit coat. I lift him up with one hand and slap his face a few times to rouse him with the other.

He mumbles as he comes to, eyes widening when the realization hits that this wasn't a nightmare.

"What do you want from me?" His voice quavers, and he blinks rapidly.

"I already got what I want."

"Then why are you still here?"

"I wanted to look you in the eyes while I did this." I release him and stand before aiming my Glock at his face and firing a single hollow point bullet. Bone, flesh, and blood explode until there's nothing left but a bloody, gaping wound.

"Let's go. Neighbors have probably already called the cops," Mac shouts.

Jogging back over to my bike, I hop on, and within seconds, we're back on the freeway. Putting the neon lights of the Strip behind us, we ride for over an hour until we reach The Hen House in Pahrump, Nevada.

A smile creeps onto my lips as we approach the brothel. If it weren't for the large neon chicken on a tall metal pole in front of the place, you'd think it was a quaint bed-and-breakfast in the middle of the desert. But step inside, and you'll see it's anything but.

It's as much home to us as anywhere else. The three of us are nomads for the Royal Bastards MC and often travel together, sticking to the West Coast. To earn, we hook up with other chapters, helping them with jobs. Or, like tonight, we find our own way to pad our pockets. This world is full of assholes with more money than sense, which means we're never hurting for jobs.

The Hen House is one of our many stops. Dunk and Mac like to take advantage of the no-strings company for a night or two, and I like a safe place to camp out and chat with the madam of the house, Sonya. We've been friends for years, and she often gets word of jobs that need doing everywhere from Reno to Vegas.

The job we just completed, though, was a personal favor to Sonya.

Lifting my helmet off and hooking it on my handlebars, I open my saddlebag to see stacks upon stacks of hundreds. Even after we make things right with Sonya, this'll last me a long time since my expenses are minimal.

"All in a day's work." Dunk claps me on the back.

"Not a bad payday," I agree, peering over my shoulder to see Mac fanning out a wad of cash.

"Coyote!" a woman's voice calls out, and I turn to see Sonya running out the front door, a huge smile on her leathery face.

"Hey there, woman. How's it going?" I grab two stacks of bills and hand them over to her.

"I don't want his money," she spits out.

"Take it."

"So, it's done?" she asks, her smile fading and her eyes watering. I nod, and she folds the two wads in half, tucking them into her ample cleavage. Her face hardens, accentuating the deep lines around her lips and eyes from years of smoking. "Did he suffer?"

"He paid with his life. That's all you need to know."

For an entire year now, Sonya has been sending money to her little sister, who attends school at UNLV. But three weeks ago, Sonya got a phone call that her sister was found dead in a dumpster behind a casino. That's when she reached out to me. After a few days of recon, I found out her sister was approached by a man on the Strip. She was out drinking with girlfriends and had a little too much. According to the same friends, who knew it was a bad idea but let her go anyway, she got into the limo and hadn't been heard from since.

After talking to them, I found out the man was Lucas Orton. They recognized him because he often made the front page of the newspaper for his hand in big developments all over Vegas. Scared of the ramifications, they didn't tell the cops this bit of information. But after a carefully worded exchange with me, they spilled everything.

The autopsy report showed that the girl had been violated in every way possible. She was so strung up on heroin, there was no way she even knew what was happening to her. The cause of death was listed as an overdose, and since the girl's only family was the madam of a whore house, the cops didn't feel the need to investigate it further.

"Good." Her expression softens in the blink of an eye, and she smiles big. "You guys sticking around a couple days?"

"I'm only staying the night, but these two assholes will be around longer." I nod to Mac and Dunk, who're unloading their packs from their bikes.

"I'll see who we have available to keep them company," she says. "It's on me tonight, boys."

Mac throws an arm over Sonya's shoulder and delivers a smacking kiss to her cheek. "Not tonight, doll. We're beat. But come tomorrow, I'll take you up on that."

"Sure, sure. You guys at least want a room to sleep in?"

"Nah. We'll camp around back if that's okay?" Dunk asks.

"Of course. Actually, one of my night guards called in sick, so that'll work out perfect for me." Sonya pats Mac on the butt affectionately and steps out of his hold. "Holler if you need anything."

"Thanks," I say.

We take our packs around back and set up our tents. The only time I don't feel like an outsider is when I'm with Mac and Dunk. Like me, they don't like sleeping indoors. But unlike me, it's a preference for them. It's a necessity for me.

They're also the only ones who know why I am the way I am.

"That couldn't have gone better," I say, taking a seat next to the fire Mac started.

"Fuckin' asshole deserved that shit," Dunk says.

"You headed to Reno tomorrow?" Mac sits across from me, stretching his legs out in front of him.

"Yep. Sly's got an update on that girl, Riley. He thinks he found her."

"Finally. You can get your cut back and move on with your life. You've been a raging asshole for damn near five years." Dunk hurls a rock at me, nailing me in the chest.

Picking it up, I chuck it back at him. "Tell me you wouldn't do the same if some bitch took your cut."

"Not saying you aren't justified, dipshit."

"You know Loki's gonna try to get you to stay, right? With Roch's old lady knocked up and him getting married, he'll need the backup." Mac removes a joint from the inner pocket of his cut and lights up. After taking a few drags, he passes it across the fire to me.

Loki is the president of the Royal Bastards in Reno, and over the last year, the club has gone through a lot of changes. Including three of them finding old ladies. Now they're all domesticated and shit.

"He's been trying to get me to patch in for years. Not happening," I say with a lungful of the skunky weed.

"What are you gonna do to her when you find her?" Dunk asks.

"I don't know yet." I've thought about this a lot. If it were a man who stole my leather, I'd kill him on sight, no questions asked.

But it's a chick, and even more, it's Riley, a girl whose owl eyes have haunted my dreams almost every night since we met. I need to know her story, why she was at the clubhouse that night, and why she left without saying anything.

Maybe after I have those answers, I'll know what to do. The only thing I'm certain of is that I will be punishing her. Just don't know what that'll look like quite yet.

"You sure this is about the cut and not the pussy?" Dunk accepts the joint from me and takes a puff.

I'm not about to admit a chick has me strung out, so I shake my head. "Pussy is pussy. That cut is my life."

"Good. I'd hate to lose a riding partner," Mac says.

"Not a chance. I'm not built like Loki, Khan, and Roch. I don't want a white picket fence and all that bullshit." I lean back, resting my weight on my hands. "All I want is to sock away enough money that by the time I can't ride or shoot, I can retire on a piece of land of my own."

"Kind of young to be thinking about retirement," Mac says. It doesn't surprise me; he spends his cash as fast as he earns.

"The kind of life we live, we'll be lucky not to be dead by forty-five. If I make it that long, I want to know I have options."

Dunk stubs out the spent joint. "Never thought I'd live this long, let alone have a retirement plan."

"You ever think about patching in?" I ask him.

"I'd think about sticking around in Reno, but not anywhere else."

"If I had to, that's the only chapter I'd consider too," I agree. "How long you guys staying in Vegas?"

"Few weeks," Dunk says. "You be ready to meet back up by then?"

"Yeah. Should be." I stand and dust off my ass. "I'm turning in, gonna hit the road at first light."

"After we have our fill of Vegas bitches and booze, we'll swing by and pick you up," Mac says, turning his attention to the night sky.

"Head north to Seattle before the rain starts up there?" I ask.

"Sounds good." Mac holds out a fist, and I bump it with my own.

"G'night." Before ducking into my tent, I spread out my yoga mat and strip down to my boxers. I push away the teasing taunts coming from Mac and Dunk and move through my poses, clearing my head of all the bullshit of the day.

An image of blue owl eyes pops into my head like it always does, and I stare into them through my mind's eye. It's been five years, and I still can't shake them. A torrent of anger, not only because she stole my cut, but because she disappeared after a night that still lives on in my memories, rushes through me. I let it flow through my blood, red and angry. Then I push it out through my breaths, blue and calm.

After my body and mind are settled, I duck into my tent and slip into my sleeping bag.

Things are about to get interesting; I can feel it.

Sly, treasurer and resident hacker for the Reno chapter of the Royal Bastards, has had leads before, but this one feels different. It's the first time the girl he's found fits the profile of who I'm looking for.

I hope it's her. If it's not, I vow to give up the search and move on with my life. I don't want to live with this unresolved shit poisoning my thoughts any longer.

Chapter
THREE

Riley

After putting Veda to bed, I pour a glass of wine and take it to the back patio. Wrecker's house—my house now—sits on five acres up in the hills overlooking the Reno valley. While Wrecker didn't care much for landscaping, he did care about keeping his view unobstructed. Every year, he'd pull up hundreds of saplings in his backyard before they could grow into trees and block the view.

I guess that's my job now.

The neighborhood is wealthy, and the surrounding homes reflect that. My neighbors must think this small log cabin is an eyesore compared to their multi-million-dollar estates. Still, this land has been in Wrecker's family for ages, and he refused to sell each time he was approached by a developer.

I take a healthy sip of wine, watching the bustling city below and trying to get the motivation to unpack the last of the boxes. We've been living here for two weeks now, and I'm proud of how much I've done to make this place my own. I've changed out the curtains, purchased new area rugs to cover the worn wooden floors, and bought things like plates and bowls to replace the chipped and damaged ones Wrecker left behind.

For the first time in my life, I feel like an adult.

With that thought, I stand up, polish off my wine, and go back inside to do the adult thing and finish unpacking.

I've just plopped down on my bed to begin when there's a knock on the door.

"Damn, Crash doesn't know how to use a cellphone," I mutter, hurrying to the door before Veda hears the pounding and wakes up.

But it's not Crash at the door. It's a tall, curvaceous, beautiful Black woman who I don't know. She smiles at me, showing me all her blinding white teeth.

"Hi," I say in a questioning tone.

"Riley, right?"

"Yes."

"Hey, girl. This is fucking awkward, but my name's Charlotte." She holds out a hand that I awkwardly shake.

Then I notice her leather booty shorts and crop top, which is the look of someone connected to the club. I didn't visit the Sons of Erebus clubhouse often, but the few times I did, I quickly learned the women who hung around there were all drop-dead gorgeous and very scantily dressed.

"Let me guess. Crash sent you?" I guess.

"Yep."

I smirk. "Are you supposed to be my new best friend?"

"Honestly, I have no fucking clue. When one of the Sons asks me to do something, I do it, no questions asked. Just part of the gig."

"Well, this is embarrassing," I say, humiliated that he thought I couldn't make friends on my own. Her eyes dart inside the house and back to me. "Oh, I'm sorry. I've lost my manners. Please, come in."

Her smile returns, and she bounces—literally bounces— inside the house.

"I like what you've done to the place," she says, turning in a slow circle.

"Thanks. Did you come out here often?" I'm curious to know how close to the club she is. Has she slept with Wrecker? I hope not. That would be weird.

"Sometimes." She holds up a hand that has a diamond ring on it. "I'm Cyrus's old lady."

I instantly relax. Cyrus is one of the old-timers I've known since I was a little girl. It doesn't surprise me he has a wife half his age.

"Aw, I love Cyrus."

"Yeah," she swoons. "He's amazing."

"I'm happy for you," I say.

"So, what are you up to tonight?"

"Drinking wine and unpacking boxes."

"Want some company?" she asks.

"Sure. Want a glass?"

"Duh."

We both laugh, and I motion for her to follow me into the kitchen. I pour our drinks and lead her into my bedroom, where the remaining boxes are. She plops down on my bed like she's done it a million times before, and I find myself liking this chick. Since I left my pretentious life back in California, I'm reinventing myself. And part of that reinvention is giving up formalities. Charlotte fits perfectly into my new life.

"So, you're Wrecker's daughter?" she asks.

"Yeah. Well, kind of. My mom was his old lady, but she had an affair and got pregnant with me. She hid it from Wrecker for a long time, playing it off like I was his kid until something happened—I don't know what, neither of them would tell me— and she left."

"Wow. That's a lot." Charlotte thinks for a second. "Did he go after her?"

"I don't think so. According to him, she never even told him about the affair. Even if she had, he wouldn't have turned his back on me. But for whatever reason, my mom was too scared to stick around and find out."

"Where did she take you?" She flops onto her belly, propping her head up with her hands.

"To California. My mom grew up on a vineyard in St. Helena. My family is stupidly wealthy and very uptight, which is why she ran away to be with Wrecker in the first place."

"Why would you leave a vineyard in California for Reno?" Her nose scrunches.

I sigh. "My life has never been my own. The kind of money I'm talking about means someone picked my clothes, told me where to go and when, prepared all my meals, and a nanny took care of my daughter. I didn't feel comfortable in my own skin, so when Wrecker left me this place, I knew I had to go out on my own. This house feels more like my home than the mansion ever did and these clothes"—I motion to my cut-off shorts and band T-shirt—"feel more comfortable than the couture shit my mom put me in."

"Hold up. You have a kid?" Her eyes dart to the hallway, like Veda will magically appear at the mention of her existence.

"I do. Veda. She's the best." I smile, thinking about my daughter.

"Who's the dad?"

"You're really blunt."

She sits up and reaches for her glass of wine on my nightstand. "I know. I'm sorry. It's a blessing and a curse."

"The dad was a one-night stand when I was seventeen. He took my virginity, gave me the best sex I ever had, and put a baby in me."

"Wow. That was a productive night."

"It was."

"How does your mom feel about you taking her grandbaby and moving five hours away?" she asks.

"She cut me off, same as what her mom did to her when she left. But I think deep down, she gets it. I don't think she likes how her life ended up and probably wishes she would've stayed with Wrecker. That's my theory, anyway. Especially since she hasn't dated anyone since."

"That sucks."

"Eh, it's okay. She's still talking to me, and Wrecker left me some money, so I'm okay for now. Though I should probably start a job search."

She jumps to her feet, wine dribbling from her mouth. Wiping it away with the back of her hand, she says, "You should come work at The Silo with me!"

"What's The Silo?"

"A bar. It's not owned by the Sons, but the manager, Irvin, is a friend of the club, so a lot of them hang out there."

"I don't know," I say. I don't like the idea of getting close to the club when things are so weird between Crash and me.

"I won't take no for an answer." She pulls her cellphone from her back pocket and immediately begins texting. Her thumbs pause, eyes scrolling across the screen. Then she throws a fist in the air and declares. "Done. You're hired."

"Charlotte," I start but am cut off.

"Char. Everyone calls me Char."

"Char, I don't think it's a good idea."

"It's the best idea, Riley."

"I don't have a babysitter," I argue.

She waves a hand at me. "Details, details. We'll find someone."

Not seeing a way out of this, I concede. "I guess I'll give it a try. I've never had a job before."

"I'll train you. It's easy. All you have to do is pour shots, pull beer, and flirt for tips. No biggie."

When she puts it like that, it does sound easy. And it would be nice to get out of the house and not be a mom twenty-four hours a day. I've enjoyed stepping into the role of Veda's only caregiver, but if I'm being honest, I'm bored. A few hours a week won't hurt.

"Okay. Thank you."

"You're welcome." Char grabs a box and the scissors sitting on my nightstand. "Now, let's get you unpacked."

We open box after box of clothes, photo albums, and books, chatting away like old friends. I learn Char was born and raised in Reno. Her dad is a mechanic at the Sons' repair shop, so that's how she met Cyrus. It was a bit of a scandal, and her dad was pissed to learn his baby girl was with a man his age, but he came around when he saw how Cyrus worshipped the ground Char walks on.

Her story gives me hope I might find the same thing one day. Maybe even with Crash if Wrecker's prediction is correct.

"Last box!" Char cheers, downing the rest of her second glass of wine.

Seeing the box she pulled up on the bed, I freeze. That one needs to be opened when I'm alone and preferably drunk. Very drunk.

"I'll do that one later." I reach for the box, but she's too fast and rips it open before I can get it away.

"Ooo," she croons. "Is this your dildo box?"

My cheeks heat. "No, I unpacked that one already."

"Ha! I knew you had some freak in you." She pulls out the one thing packed in the box—Coyote's leather cut.

This time, I'm fast enough to yank it from her grip before she has too long to inspect it. I've told her a lot of my secrets tonight, but this one is better left kept in the dark corners of my mind.

"Sorry," I say, hiding the folded leather behind my back. "This one is private."

"You just told me you like to diddle your bean with vibrating dongs, and you can't show me whatever that is?"

"No, I'm sorry. It's something I'd like to keep to myself."

"Yeah, I get that." She glances at her phone. "I better go anyway. I told Cyrus I'd be home an hour ago."

"Oh no. Is that who's been blowing up your phone?" I couldn't help but notice the insane number of phone calls she received in the last hour. I didn't say anything because she muted the call after one look at the caller ID and went back to unpacking.

"Yeah." She grins devilishly. "But sometimes you have to be bad to give your daddy a reason to punish you, you know?"

I absolutely don't know but nod anyway.

She must know I'm full of shit because her brows raise, and she drags her lower lip through her teeth. "I'll get home, and he'll be all pissed, howling about how he pays for a cellphone I never answer and how he was worried sick about me, blah, blah, blah. Then I'll say something like, 'you're too overprotective. You're not my dad'. And then he'll give me *the look*."

"The look?" I ask, so absorbed in her words I wouldn't notice a car plowing right through my bedroom.

"You know, the *fuck around and find out* look. Then he'll toss me over his shoulder, throw me on the bed, paddle my ass until he's sure I won't be able to sit right for a week, fuck me until my legs shake and I scream his name, and then we'll end the night snuggled up naked together while he tells me how much he loves me."

My mouth hangs open, and I don't even know what to say.

"Girl, you need yourself a man. That look on your face tells me you have no idea what I'm talking about, and every woman should know exactly what I'm talking about." She grips me by the shoulders and yanks me in for a hug. I'm so much shorter than she is that my face goes right into her cleavage. "I'll call you tomorrow to let you know where Irvin put you on the schedule."

"Sounds good," I say, only my voice is so muffled by her tits, I don't know if she hears me.

Then, as fast as she came in, she's gone. The second the door shuts, I pull the cut from behind my back and collapse onto my bed, exhausted from Char's over-the-top energy.

Running my hands over the leather, I trace each patch. Even though I have them all memorized, I take them in again. I run my fingers along his name and along the skull and motorcycle logo of the Royal Bastards. I bring it to my face and inhale the musky, leathery scent.

It brings me back to that night. The best night of my life. I always dreaded losing my virginity, assuming it would be awkward and painful. Boy, was I wrong.

Coyote knew what he was doing, and although he wasn't soft and gentle, he made my body come alive in a way I haven't experienced since. Not that I've had much sex since then.

There was Matthew Striver, a college student Mom set me up with. We had three boring dates before I climbed in the back of his Escalade with him. I should've known the sex would be just as bad as the dates, but I was desperate to feel at least half of what Coyote made me feel.

Spoiler alert, I didn't.

Then there was Christopher Gardner. Another setup from Mom. He was funny and cute, and I had high hopes for us. After a month of dating, he took me to a fancy dinner and rented a hotel suite. I thought he'd be a gentle lover, but he was rough with me and not in a good way.

After giving me friction burn from shoving his fingers inside me before I was ready, tugging on my nipples so hard they bruised because I wasn't turned on, and slapping me across the face as he was coming, I gathered my clothes and ran from the hotel, vowing to never see him again.

Needless to say, I'm still chasing the high Coyote gave me. But even more than that, the connection we had. My soul recognized his. It felt like fate. Like a rekindling of a fire that started long ago, before either of us was born.

Or it could be you romanticizing the entire situation because he was the man who took your virginity.

I push that thought away, choosing to believe I really experienced something special.

Folding the cut back up, I return it to the box and push it to the back of my closet.

I don't know why I took it. Had I known he'd provide me with a living, breathing reminder of that night, I probably wouldn't have. I needed something tangible to remember him by in the moment, and this was the first thing I saw.

I know how important the cuts are to the guys. Wrecker taught me all about club life when I was a little girl, so it was a dick move for me to take it, but I couldn't help myself. I can only hope he wasn't too pissed when he woke up.

It has crossed my mind there's a chance I'll run into Coyote now that I'm living in Reno. It's a bigger city, though, and from what he told me, he's a nomad and doesn't stay in one place for very long. Plus, the Royal Bastards have their part of the city, and the Sons have theirs; they don't cross paths often.

But what if I did? Would I tell him about Veda? Would he want to be a father?

I know it was shitty of me not to seek him out after I found out about the pregnancy. But from everything Mom told me about bikers, they aren't equipped to be dads, and Veda comes first. Always.

So, if I have to live the rest of my life knowing I'll never meet someone who makes me feel the way Coyote did to save my daughter from a dad who would never be there for her, then that's my cross to bear.

I flip off my bedroom light and climb into bed. I can't think about all that. If I ever run into him, I'll deal with it. But until then, I'm focusing on my new life and, thanks to Char, my new job.

Chapter
FOUR

Coyote

I pull up to The Silo and park my bike in the back lot. According to Sly, a bartender here named Irvin was blabbing about a girl named Riley he just hired from the Bay Area. The guy he spoke to is a friend of Sly's, who knew the club was looking for a girl by the same description.

I don't know if it's a coincidence or really her, but I plan to find Irvin and get to the bottom of it.

The place is a dive, but most biker bars are. Lucky for me, it's mostly empty. I take a seat at the bar and make eye contact with the one and only bartender. He's in his early fifties and balding with a healthy beer gut.

He eyes my cut warily before approaching.

"What's up, man? What can I get you?" he asks.

"Looking for a man named Irvin. You know him?"

"That's me. What can I do for you?" He reaches under the bar and pulls out a shotgun, resting it on the wooden bar.

So this is how he's going to play it.

"Heard you have a new bartender by the name of Riley. That true?"

"What's it to you?" His bushy brows narrow.

I can tell this won't be a friendly chat, but I'm not the kind of man to back down. My own gun is loaded and tucked into the back of my jeans.

"She's got something of mine, and I'd like it back."

"Well, you heard wrong. Don't know anyone by that name, and even if I did, I wouldn't tell some asshole how to find her." He places his hands on the bar and leans in.

Since I'm not looking for a gunfight, I stand and hold my hands up placatingly. "No worries. You know where to find me if you think of something."

"Don't reckon I will, but yeah, I know where to find you."

Back in the parking lot, I decide to wait him out and catch him when he leaves. Maybe he'll be more forthcoming without that shotgun sitting in front of him.

I walk the perimeter of the building and make sure there aren't security cameras, which there aren't. It doesn't surprise me. The men who frequent a bar like this wouldn't want any kind of evidence if a fight breaks out or they need to do some business in the parking lot.

Leaning against the brick exterior, I pull out my phone and shoot Sly a text, updating him and letting him know my plan. Then I scroll through my apps until I find Solitaire. I'd never admit it to anyone, but it's my favorite way to kill time.

Even bikers need to decompress.

After an hour, I hear tires crunching over rocks and look up to see a car pulling in. I duck around the corner before the woman in the driver's seat can see me.

Peering from where I'm hiding, I watch as the woman, dressed in a skimpy outfit, struts inside. There's no way she's coming for a drink, so she must be a bartender. Hopefully taking over for Irvin.

I'm proven right when minutes later, the man walks into the lot, twirling a set of keys around his finger. When he spots my bike parked next to what I'm assuming is his car, he freezes and looks around. I step into his line of sight.

He scrambles to unlock his car, but I reach him before he can open the door.

"I just want to talk, man." I place a hand on the driver's side window, making sure he can't open the door and slip inside.

"Got nothing to say to you, *man*," he spits out.

"I think you do."

He pulls something from his jacket, and before I know what's happening, I feel a pinch in my side. I look down and see the leather-wrapped handle of a knife sticking out of my side. Bright red blood oozes from the wound, staining my shirt.

"That was a mistake, Irvin." I rip the knife from my flesh and tuck it in the inside pocket of my jean cut. I never replaced my leather one. A biker is given one cut, and I intend on getting mine back.

I rear back and throw a fist into Irvin's gut. All the air expels from his lungs in a *whoosh,* and he doubles over. The parking lot is empty for now, but it's quitting time for the blue-collar types, and any minute they'll be pouring in to grab a beer before going home to their families.

I need to get the fuck out of here.

Opening the backseat of his car, I whip him over the head with the butt of my gun before shoving his unconscious body inside. He dropped his keys in the struggle, but I find them in the gravel and hop in the driver's seat.

I pull out of the parking lot while dialing Sly's number.

"S'up?"

"Need someone to grab my bike. It's at The Silo. Keys are in the saddlebag."

Muffled voices sound over the line before he puts the phone back to his ear. "Done. Anything else, brother?"

"Gonna need Khan and the use of your basement."

Khan is their VP, and the big motherfucker is intimidating

as hell. He might get more information out of Irvin than I can. I'm asking for access to the basement because that's where their kill room is. Completely soundproof, the newly remodeled room has stainless steel lining the walls and floor, with a drain in the center of the room leading to a tank that's regularly cleaned out and sanitized.

"Not a problem." His tone is cool and collected. This isn't the first or last time he's handled this type of situation.

"Be there in five."

"So it's gonna be the hard way, huh?" Khan says before inhaling deeply.

Irvin hocks a loogie in Khan's direction, the blood-tinged saliva landing on his chest. It fuels Khan's rage, and he slices his knife across Irvin's torso. The fucker lets out a blood-curdling scream that echoes through the room.

A sound from behind me steals my attention, and I spin around, my hand instinctively moving to my hip where my gun is. I relax when I see it's Bexley, the club's lawyer.

"You okay?" I ask, pushing off my perch in the doorway and stepping closer to her.

It was a wrong move because without my body blocking her view of the room, she sees Irvin hanging from his wrists to chains attached to the ceiling. The asshole is in bad shape; his body is covered in blood, first from my attempt to extract information from him and now from Khan's.

Bexley doubles over, coughing and sputtering. Guess she isn't privy to this part of the club she represents.

"Time for you to go, sister." I lift her up by her armpits and set her on her feet.

"Don't touch me," she spits out, and I back off, holding my hands up.

She takes a few steps closer to the Bastards' kill room on wobbly legs. I make a move to stop her, but she pins me with a fierce look that has me backing off. We both watch as Khan circles around the room, flipping his bloody knife into the air and expertly catching it by the handle. I should clue him into Bexley's presence, but something tells me she needs to see this.

"Just tell us where she is, and this will all be over," Khan says, toying with his prey.

"She inherited a couple acres in the Saddlehorn neighborhood." The man's voice is tired, and his words are slurred.

Khan grabs the man by his hair and jerks his head back. "That wasn't so hard, now was it? Loki, hold him."

Loki steps in front of Irvin, gripping the chains above his hands. Then Khan raises the long blade above his head and, with all his might, thrusts it into the man's forehead. All of Irvin's blubbering dies along with his worthless body, and Loki lets go of his hold on the corpse, sending him swinging through the air.

Bexley falls to the ground, shaking and screaming more than Irvin was. I made the wrong call letting her witness that. But I'm not a member of the Reno chapter, and I haven't been around them enough to know their inner workings.

Khan's face crumples when he realizes she witnessed the whole scene. It hits me that this chick isn't just the Bastard's lawyer. He feels something wholly unprofessional for her. He crouches down next to her, trying to comfort her, but Loki steps in.

"You're covered in blood, brother," he says gently.

Khan looks down at himself, seeing that his clothes are drenched in Irvin's blood. As if the offending fabric is the only thing freaking Bexley out, he stands and rips them off his body, leaving him buck ass naked. I shift my gaze away and take a seat next to the freaked-out woman.

"Shh, doll. That man deserved this. Maybe someday I'll tell you about it but just know, I tried asking nicely before it came to this," I whisper close to her ear, hoping she'll stop all her screaming to listen. It doesn't work.

Khan rushes over to a sink in the corner and scrubs his hands clean before ripping off a paper towel to dry them. Then he's kneeling in front of us, pulling Bexley off the floor and lifting her into his arms. He says nothing as he takes the stairs two at a time, disappearing from sight.

"Well, shit," I say, standing.

Loki scratches the back of his neck. "Yep, not the best way to initiate her into our darker dealings."

"That gonna be a problem?"

"Nah. Khan'll handle her." Loki turns to take in Irvin. "And the prospects will handle your friend."

"Appreciate it, brother." I slap him on the shoulder.

"Don't mention it. Anything we need to know?" His question is loaded, and I understand his concern. This kill wasn't club business.

"It won't come back on the club. Swear on it."

"Didn't think it would."

"Fill you in over a beer?" I scrub a hand down my face, and he nods. Once upstairs, we take a seat at the bar.

"Duncan, grab us a couple of cold ones and then take Ford downstairs with you. There's a present waiting to be delivered." Loki smirks.

"I don't like your presents," Duncan, a prospect, grumbles, making Loki laugh. "Where do you want this one?"

"Great Basin. Unmarked. And take the car to the junkyard. Tell Borst it needs to move quick."

Duncan sets a bottle of beer in front of each of us. "Will do."

After he's out of earshot, Loki turns to me and asks, "So, what's the story with the dead guy?"

"You probably don't remember, but five years ago, I was passing through and stopped here for the night. Went outside to go to sleep, and there was a girl by the fence."

Loki lights a cig, offering me one—which I decline—before tucking the pack back in his cut. "Think I can see where this is going."

"Yeah, it went there. But the next morning, I wake up with my cut gone." My blood boils remembering the moment I realized the bitch stole it.

"Shit." Loki curses on an inhale and motions to my denim jacket. "That why you've been wearing this bullshit the last couple years?"

One of the worst things a 1%er can do is lose their cut. If I belonged to a chapter, there would've been serious punishment for that shit, but luckily for me, nomads are more or less self-governed. Since I couldn't replace my cut, I stitched an RBMC patch to a denim jacket to wear until I get mine back.

And I fuckin' *will* get it back.

I nod. "Been trying to find her ever since. She said she was there for the night and lived in the Bay Area. But all I had was her first name—Riley."

"Not a whole lot to go off of."

"Nothing at all. I told Sly about her, and you know how he loves a challenge."

Loki chuckles. "Like a dog with a bone."

"Yup." I take a swig of my cold beer. "Couple days ago, he got wind of the manager over at The Silo talkin' about how he hired some girl named Riley."

The Silo is a dive bar where the Sons of Erebus, a local and less powerful MC, hang out. The Sons had beef with the Bastards back in the day, but that was squashed. Loki maintains an amicable relationship with the rival club.

"So, the asshole downstairs is the manager? Please tell me he's not a Son."

I shake my head. "Nah, just a friend of the club. I only went into The Silo to talk to the man. I could tell he knew something, but he wouldn't spill, so I waited until his shift was over.

Thought he might be more willing to talk without the shotgun he keeps behind the bar handy, but the fucker stabbed me, so I beat him unconscious and brought him here."

Loki glances down at the red stain on my shirt. "You whole?"

Now that the adrenaline has died down in my system, my side stings like a motherfucker. I lift the hem of my tee and see the laceration. It's worse than I thought it was.

Loki tilts his head to get a better look. "Might need a couple stitches."

Letting go of the hem, the shirt falls back down. "I'm good."

"Stabbing you seems like an overreaction to a few questions."

"My thoughts exactly. Still tryin' to figure that shit out."

Things went sideways fast in that parking lot, and I can't figure out why. Either he was being protective of the girl, or he was under threat of someone he perceived as more dangerous than the Bastards. No matter which one, he made the wrong choice.

"Anyone see you leave with him?"

"No," I say with confidence. The parking lot is in the back of the building, and it was empty.

"What're you going to do when you find her?"

"Get my cut back." I laugh. People often think my yoga and meditation are a sign that I'm weak, but Loki knows better. I do those things to keep my dark demon at bay. "I don't even know for sure if it's her."

"You're welcome to camp out as long as you need. If you feel like moving indoors, there's a room open too." Loki peers at me through his periphery.

I blow out a breath and lean back, stretching my arms. "I don't know. Let's see where this lead takes me."

Loki stands and chugs the last of his beer before saying, "If you need any help, bro, you let me know."

"Thanks, and thanks for that." I nod to the door leading down to the basement.

"Maybe if we do enough favors for you, you'll agree to patch in." He walks away, not giving me another chance to decline his offer.

Pulling my wallet out of my back pocket, I fish out a blunt and step outside for my evening wind down. A pack of pit bulls run over to greet me. I tuck the joint behind my ear and squat down to give them a pat. I've always wanted a dog but never could bring myself to settle down in one spot.

I could patch in, make Reno my home. But the winters are too brutal for my pup tent, so I'd have to live in the clubhouse, at least until I found a place of my own. A shiver runs down my spine, and my chest constricts thinking about living inside four walls and a roof.

The nonexistent scent of smoke fills my nostrils, and Mom's screams fill my ears. Before I can stop it, panic takes hold. Even though I'm outside, I feel the narrowed walls of the closet close in on me. I couldn't get out. I couldn't save her.

Squeezing my eyes closed, I shake my head, clearing my mind.

I stand up and pinch the joint between my lips. Flicking my Zippo, I light it up and take a long drag, letting the smoke settle in my lungs for as long as I can before exhaling in a thick cloud. The dogs sniff the air and trot away from me, not liking what they pick up.

The drug-induced fog weighs my limbs down while making my head feel light. My worries fade away, and I meander over to where I've set up camp. Spreading out my mat, I sit cross-legged, facing the hills surrounding the property. Wild horses graze in the field on the other side of the fence, and peace settles over me as I watch them. They're scraggly looking things without humans to care for them, but there's beauty in the wild.

I smoke the blunt until my fingers burn, and I stamp it out before starting my evening yoga routine. I easily move through the poses, twisting and stretching my body.

I close my eyes to block out the world, only to have Riley's damn owl eyes appear. Jesus fuck, this girl.

She doesn't even know how big of a mistake she made by stealing my cut. She probably thought it was a petty token to commemorate losing her virginity to a biker. But my entire identity is tied to the colors sewn onto that leather.

When I patched in, it changed my life. I went from being some punk-ass kid living on the streets to belonging. Even though I ultimately took the path of a nomad, it didn't stop me from feeling like I was part of something much bigger than myself.

Every single minute of the last five years, I haven't been whole.

And if I'm honest, it's not only the cut that has me feeling this way. It's her. It's always been her.

Chapter
FIVE

Riley

"How's it going, twerp?" Charlotte asks with a smile from where she's perched on the bar top.

This is my third shift at The Silo. My schedule is set so Char and I work two shifts together every week on Monday and Wednesday. But after a confirming glance at my phone, I see today is Thursday.

"Where's Irvin?" I remove the jacket covering my crop top and booty shorts, wrap it around my purse, and tuck the bundle under the cash register.

"Fucker didn't show up for work yesterday, so I picked up his shift. Benji is losing his mind." Charlotte slides off the bar.

"Who's Benji?" I ask.

"The owner. He doesn't get involved often. He pretty much lets Irvin do whatever the hell he wants."

"Does Irvin disappear often?" I ask.

"Never. Kind of weird, if you ask me." She moves over to the bin of silverware and begins the arduous process of making more silverware rollups. "I'm not complaining. I could use the extra cash."

"I don't know how much cash you'll make today." I motion to the empty bar.

As if on cue, the front door opens, and three Sons of Erebus members walk in—including Crash. When I took this job, I had a feeling he'd take advantage of knowing where I was, and as predicted, he comes by during nearly all my shifts.

Yet he rarely talks to me—just watches me.

"Ry," he says, sliding onto a barstool. Today, his long hair is pulled out of his face thanks to a beanie on his head. It shows off his sparkling hazel eyes and sharp jawline.

"What can I get you?" I ask.

"Not here for drinks and burgers, babe," Rigger, the new Vice President of the Sons, says. Of all the members, he's my favorite. He doesn't leer at me like the others do, and he has a more level head.

"Then why are you here?" I rest my forearms on the bar, leaning over to take some weight off my already aching feet from wearing these damn heels.

I'd rather be in a pair of Chucks, but according to Char, the higher the heel and the more skin I show, the better the tips. So, I'm wearing a bustier top that props my almost nonexistent boobs up and shorts so short they could double as panties.

Crash's eyes drift down to my cleavage and stay there for a long moment before returning to my face.

He's so confusing. One minute he ignores me like we've never met, and the next, he's staring hungrily at my tits.

He moistens his lips before saying, "Heard Irvin didn't make it in the last coupla days. Came to ask around."

"We were just wondering where the asshole fucked off to." Charlotte takes over the conversation.

Crash's jaw works as his attention shifts from me to Char. "When was the last time you saw him?"

"I relieved him after his shift the day before yesterday," she says.

Vin, the Sons' treasurer, drums his fingers on the bar. "Did he say what he was doing when he left here?"

"Nope. Just reminded me to make the deposit after shift." Char taps a finger on her chin. "I did see a bike in the lot when I got here. The saddlebag had RBMC stitched on it."

RBMC is the Royal Bastards. Why were they here?

The three men share a murderous look that doesn't sit well with me.

"Why do you guys care?" I ask.

Finally, Crash pipes up, his tone vague, "Irvin's been doing some work for us."

"What kind of work?" I press.

Wrecker was careful to keep me blind to the Sons' criminal activity, so I honestly have no idea how they earn a living outside the repair shop. But judging by the amount of money Wrecker left me, it's not from rebuilding engines.

"Nothin' for you to worry about." Crash stands. "If you hear from him, tell him to check in with us, yeah?"

"Okay. Are you worried something happened?" I ask.

"Not sure," Rigger says carefully. "There's a dried-up pool of blood in the parking lot. Either of you know anything about that?"

"Blood?" The hairs on the back of my neck stand on end.

"That's probably from a bar fight. You idiots beat the shit out of each other out there all the time," Char says.

"Could be." Vin shrugs. "You have a good night, ladies."

"Ry." Crash jerks his head to the other end of the bar. "Can I have a minute?"

"Sure." I meet him by the side entrance that leads to a small courtyard the smokers use. "What's up?"

"Irvin was keeping an eye on you for me. Now that he's not around, I want to make sure you're being safe." His hand reaches out and grazes mine.

I think that's the first time he's ever touched me. There's no instant spark like the one I had with Coyote, but his touch is warm and comforting.

"Who do I need to be safe from?"

His head lulls back on his shoulders, and he lets out a breath. "No one. Everyone."

"What does that mean?"

"Just keep your eyes open. Make sure someone walks you to your car."

I give him a tight smile, and he takes his leave.

I want to brush his concern off, but something about it doesn't sit right with me. Maybe it's because of the Royal Bastard's bike in the lot, maybe it's Mom's warnings about bikers playing through my head, or maybe it's memories of club lockdowns from when I was a little girl. I don't know.

So where did the blood come from? And why are they so concerned with Irvin disappearing?

I've been paranoid ever since my chat with Crash. So much so that now I'm pissed off he said anything to me at all.

The quaint home up on the hill that filled me with reminiscent feelings of my childhood no longer feels safe. Instead, I'm left to wonder what the hell I was thinking as a young, single mom moving into a house where the nearest neighbor is an entire football field of pine trees away.

I stare into the surrounding forest and wonder if anything's lurking out there. Every time I hear a car coming down the road, I assume it's some unknown intruder coming to kill me.

If that sounds overly dramatic, it is. But I spent the first eight years of my life with a badass biker for a dad, and over ten years after that behind a steel gate that only opened if a guard approved it. I don't know how to protect myself or my family, and Crash won't even tell me what I'm supposed to be looking out for.

Which is why I called him up earlier and asked him to come over after I put Veda down for the night. After their last inter-action, I'm uneasy about having him around her.

I grab two bottles of beer from the fridge, text Crash to come around back when he gets here, and make myself com-fortable on the patio furniture.

Even my nightly routine of relaxing in front of the most amazing view I've ever seen is tainted by unknown threats that may or may not pop out from behind the sagebrush and kill me.

Branches snapping in half from behind me grab my atten-tion. I turn to see it's just Crash. He's wearing jeans that hug tight around his thighs, a black T-shirt that clings to his pec-torals, and his hair is pulled back in a man bun.

Most women would agree with me that this man is fine. But his lack of a smile and stiff posture makes him appear un-attainable. Like he's not worth the effort it would take to break through the force field he has around himself.

To me, he's like driving down the road and seeing the sign for your favorite restaurant. Your stomach growls, your mouth waters, and you can practically taste your meal. Then you pull into the parking lot and find the restaurant closed.

That's the kind of letdown I feel with Crash. From a dis-tance, he's gorgeous, masculine, commands attention, and has a body like a fitness model. He's everything I could ever want. But up close, you see the vacancy in his eyes and can sense how closed off to any kind of emotion he is.

"Riley," he says, not sitting next to me but across from me on the other side of the fire pit.

"Crash." I lean over and hand him the other beer.

He takes it, wrapping his lips around the bottle and tip-ping it back for a long drink. I try to look away, but I can't. I wonder what his lips would feel like wrapped around other things. Like my nipples.

Check your libido, Riley. That isn't going to happen.

"What's up?" he asks, leaning back in the chair and resting his ankle on his knee.

"I need you to tell me what you meant by me needing to watch my back and be careful." He opens his mouth to speak, but I hold a hand up, stopping him. "And don't give me some vague, bullshit answer. I need details."

His lips twitch, *actually twitch*. There's no way he's humored by me. Maybe a gnat landed on his nose or something.

"There's nothing specific to worry about. But Wrecker told me I should watch out for you if anything happened to him. That's what I'm doing."

My stomach sinks. That's what all this protective shit is about? Wrecker told him to be my babysitter?

"Oh. Okay. Well, that's all I needed to ask, so you're free to leave."

He stares at me with an unreadable expression for a minute or two before he finally says, "Listen. Wrecker was like a second dad to me. I knew him all my life. He took me under his wing, sponsored me into the club when I was eighteen, and taught me everything I know about bikes, the club, and how to be a good Prez. So when he told me you were the most precious thing in his world, you became the most precious thing in my world too."

My mouth drops open. Surely he doesn't mean it in the way I'm taking it. He means it in a brotherly way. Or maybe not. I'm too stunned to ask.

"Like I said, he asked me to look out for you, but I knew I couldn't be there every second of the day. So when I heard Char got you a job at The Silo, I kicked Irvin some money to look out for you. Right after that, there's blood in the parking lot, and Irvin's missing. Maybe it's a coincidence. Maybe not. I don't know yet. But until I know, I want you to watch your back when I'm not around." He chugs the rest of his beer, his Adam's apple bobbing furiously. Then he slams the bottle on the fire pit and stands. "Is that enough detail for you?"

My mouth snaps closed, and my brows knit together. I can't tell if he's being sweet or pissed off that he has to babysit Wrecker's daughter. Goddamn, this man is so confusing.

Unable to speak, I nod.

His hands go to his hips, and he growls in irritation. "Let me break it down. You hear a weird sound, there's a car behind you that you don't like, you have a funny feeling in your belly, or someone looks at you weird? All those things are reasons to call me and tell me you need me. But wanting more of an explanation to something I said, that's not a reason. I got shit to do, so if you're okay, I'm gonna go now."

Well, that clarifies things a bit. Whatever Wrecker said he saw in Crash was wrong. This guy hates me.

"Fine. Okay," I say, stupid tears welling in my eyes.

"I'll talk to you later."

With liquid mortification running down my cheeks, I draw my knees to my chest, hugging them tightly. I'm not so scared of the world anymore. Matter of fact, I wish it would swallow me and my embarrassment whole right about now.

Chapter SIX

Coyote

"Is this her?" Sly points to a surveillance photo he took.

The girl in question is walking into The Silo. She's wearing skintight leather pants and one of those corset tops laced together in the front, pushing her tits up to her neck, which is a feat because her breasts are small.

She's mid-stride, so her long, dark hair obscures her face. Without seeing her head-on, it could be anyone.

It's not until he flips to the next picture that I'm certain.

Cobalt owl eyes stare back at the camera. On anyone else, those big orbs would look comical, but not on Riley. Instead, they give her a sweet and innocent quality that turns me right the fuck on.

She's grown up since I saw her last. Her high cheekbones are more pronounced, her jawline is more defined, and her body has filled out. She's fuckin' gorgeous.

Holy shit. We found her.

As I listen to Sly tell me everything he dug up, I absent-mindedly run my finger across a carving on the wooden table we're sitting at.

Their clubhouse used to be a whorehouse, so the bar, dining room, and lounge are one open room. The men would gather here, pick their woman for the night, and then be taken down the hallway to one of the many bedrooms.

Now, they use the open space to party and the rooms for patched members.

All the rounded tables in the dining area are decades old, and since bikers never miss a chance to use their knives, there are carvings all over each one. The particular carving I'm tracing is of a massive dick with hairy balls. We might be grown men, but we still have the maturity of a thirteen-year-old boy when we get together.

"Go over it again," I say. He gave me too much information to process all at once.

"Either your boy Irvin was lying about who Riley inherited the property from, or he wasn't close enough to the situation to know any better. But seeing as he tried to stab you, I'm going with he was lying." Sly points at the property records. "That land was owned by Wrecker."

"The president of the Sons of Erebus?" I ask.

"Yup. He left it to her because she's his daughter. He wasn't listed on her birth certificate, but from what I found, she lived with Wrecker and her mom on that same property until she was eight."

"What happened when she was eight?" I know the answer; he told me as much only ten minutes ago. But I'm on information overload. There's too much here to sort out.

Sly shrugs. "Maybe Wrecker stepped out on his ol' lady. Maybe she decided she didn't want to raise Riley around a bunch of bikers. I have no clue, but her mom moved them back to California to live with Riley's grandma, who owns a vineyard in the Bay Area." He pulls out a picture of a fancy house with rolling hills of grapevines behind it. "She stayed there until Wrecker died. He left her his property, a car, his fucking bike, and whatever he had in his bank account. Instead of selling it, she moved in."

Riley was more connected to the MC life than I originally thought.

The big question is, why was she at the Royal Bastards clubhouse the night we met? Was she spying on us for her dad? Was she rebelling by seeking out a hookup from another club?

"And there's a kid?" I ask, looking at the birth certificate for a four-year-old girl named Veda.

"That's where it gets interesting. She got knocked up five years ago."

Loki overhears this in passing and stops dead in his tracks. "Didn't you say you slept with that girl five years ago?"

I scowl. There's no way this kid is mine.

Sly pulls out a picture and hands it to me. Riley is holding hands with a girl who looks a hell of a lot like me. From her nose, lips, hair texture, and the way her ears curl in at the top, these are the same features I see when I look in a mirror. Except for her eyes. She has the same owl eyes her mom does.

Loki snags the picture, studying it. I shift in my seat, hoping he doesn't see what I saw. But Loki's an observant motherfucker. He didn't get to where he is by letting things go unnoticed.

He holds the picture up next to me, a brow arched high. "Kinda looks like you."

Sly chuckles. "No shit. She really does." His laughter dies, and his mouth drops open when he realizes it's not some weird coincidence.

"Damn," Loki draws out, clapping me on the shoulder. "Congratulations, Papa."

I cringe and shift out of his reach. "We don't know that."

"Bro, she's your fucking mini-me," Sly says.

"Why? Just because she's not white like Riley?" I toss that out to divert attention away from the actual issue. It's a low blow because the Bastards have never had a problem with race like some other clubs. It's one of the reasons I patched in with having a white dad and a Black mom.

"Fuck that. It's the ears and the nose. Even the lips." Sly darts his gaze from the picture to my face and back again.

I rip the picture from his hands and tuck it into the file. "Until there's a DNA test, I'm not convinced."

It's a fuckin' lie. I'd be more surprised if she wasn't mine.

"All right, Daddy Coyote," Sly says, humor lacing his tone.

"Thanks for the information, Sly. Appreciate it." I stand, tucking the file under my arm. "I'm heading out."

"Will you be back later? Birdie's bringing over a shit ton of food," Loki says.

His ol' lady, Birdie, is in culinary school and likes to bring over whatever dishes she tries out. Turns out she's damn good at it, and I always make myself available when she offers to feed us. But not tonight.

I have other plans.

When I left the clubhouse twenty minutes ago, I intended to bang on Riley's door and demand answers. But now that I'm here, I can't do it. Once I do, everything will change. If that kid is mine, I have even more reasons to be pissed off.

My head is fucked up, and I need to sort it all out before I approach her. My brain is warring with itself, and I don't know how to feel. She lied about her age, omitted she was connected to the Sons, stole my cut, and possibly kept my kid from me for four years.

Maybe I was delusional about what we shared that night, and she's like every other chick I've known since joining the club, lying to get what they want.

Now that I know her dad was the Sons' Prez and that she was only seventeen, it'd make sense she'd rebel against him and find a rival club member to sleep with. It'd also make sense that her dad wouldn't want the kid's paternity to get out. No club president wants their daughter tied to another club.

So for now, I think I'll just watch her. Maybe if I get a better idea of who she is, I'll know what to expect when I approach her.

I leave my bike at the end of her drive so she can't hear me coming. While all the other houses on the street have paved drives, Riley's is a dirt road.

Making my own path to her house through the forest of pines on the property, I notice there isn't a car in the driveway. Taking a chance that she's not home, I approach the front door and listen for any kind of activity. When I hear nothing but silence, I turn the doorknob.

It's locked.

My hand skims over the top of the door frame. I check underneath the rug, flip over a couple of big rocks sitting near the porch, and try to open all the windows on the front of the house. I'm locked out.

Rounding the property, I find the backdoor locked as well. Three windows line the back of the house, and after checking the first two, my mind is already changing plans. I'm thinking about what tools I have to jimmy a lock, but I get lucky with window number three. It lifts with ease, and I hoist myself inside, feet first.

I land inside a kitchen with old cabinets and counters but newer black appliances. Floral curtains hang from each window. A small dining table has a flowerpot full of succulents in the center and four sage green placemats at each chair.

The original hardwood floors creak as I turn down a hallway. The first door I come to is a bathroom. It's been remodeled in the last few years, so the two-sink vanity and oversized tub are modern.

On the lip of the tub, I pick up the white and black shampoo bottle and pop the top. Patchouli and mint, exactly like

I remember. Without thinking, I tuck the bottle in my back pocket and move to the next door. Riley's bedroom. I'll come back after finding the room I'm really looking for, so I continue to the room at the end of the hallway.

While the rest of the house lacks any sort of personality, this room is decorated from ceiling to floor—with owls. Her bedspread is pink and has cartoon owls all over it. Her bookcase, full of books, also has stuffed owls, ceramic owls, and plastic owls. Every kind of owl you can imagine.

Owl eyes.

If I needed confirmation of this kid being mine, here it is. This can't be a coincidence.

Circling the room slowly, I take in each detail, trying to learn something about this little human who is half me. It's surreal. Colorful wooden letters hang on her wall, spelling out her name, Veda. I say the name out loud for the first time, testing it on my tongue. I like it. It's cute and uncommon.

The girl is a reader, that's for sure. But she's also into puzzles and Barbies and—*vintage toys*. Opening the toy box, I see a pink talking diary, one of those creepy furry creatures that repeats your words back to you, and a Mr. Potato Head. All toys I remember being advertised years and years ago.

I pick up the furry owl-looking thing and flip the switch on the bottom. When it comes to life, I set it down and say, "Fuck you." I chuckle when it repeats the curse back to me in a robotic voice. I knew kids who had one of these things. Not me, though, because my family was poor. I was lucky to get toys from the dollar store.

Flipping the switch to "off," I toss it back in the box and leave the room. As interesting as it is to learn more about my potential daughter, I have other priorities right now. I venture over to Riley's room and methodically work my way around the perimeter.

There's nothing on the top of the vintage dresser, so I open the top drawer and find her panties and bras. My cock thickens in my jeans. He's pleased with this find. I pull out a bright pink silky thong. Holding it to my nose, I'm disappointed when I smell nothing but laundry soap, but I still tuck it in my pocket next to the shampoo.

I run my fingers over the lacy cups of a black bra. From the pictures Sly showed me, I noticed her tits are bigger, and her hips are wider than the last time I saw her. I wonder if she has silvery stripes where my baby stretched her. The urge to find out is strong.

I scrub a hand down my face. *Shit.* I need to get control of myself. I don't care what my dick says. Riley's my enemy, and I don't fuck my enemies. I destroy them.

The lower drawers reveal nothing but clothes, so I move to her nightstand and bed. Her comforter isn't anything special, just a white blanket with a crocheted afghan over the top. I check under her pillows and find a kitchen knife. Could she be any more cliché?

I set the knife on top of the afghan, intending to take it. I still haven't figured out what I'll do to her, but I don't want her to have weapons when I decide.

I find more interesting contraband in the top drawer of her black nightstand. Dildos and vibrators in all colors and textures greet me, as well as glow-in-the-dark lube. What the hell?

A long, smooth purple vibrator catches my eye, and before I can stop myself, I'm running my nose down the shaft. When I reach the end, I get the faintest smell of her.

My cock grows hard thinking about this toy teasing her clit, about it being inside her, making her come.

This is coming with me too.

I set it next to the knife and continue searching for what I came for. It takes nearly an hour to go through her room before I find a box in her closet housing my folded leather vest. I know it's mine before I even pull it out. I recognize each worn spot and the dirt-stained Royal Bastards patch.

It's as though a piece of me has returned as I shrug off the stiff denim cut and slide my arms into the leather. It's unreal the amount of relief that fills me. I feel like myself again.

I close the box, make sure everything is put back just how she left it, and grab my tokens. I open drawer after drawer in the kitchen until I find the one she uses for miscellaneous shit. I find a spare house key there and swipe that too before leaving out the backdoor, locking up behind me.

It's time to pack up all my shit from where I've been staying in the clubhouse backyard and find somewhere on her property to set up camp. It won't be hard since the land is untouched and thick with trees. I'll hide out right under her nose until I know more about her.

Then, when I'm ready, I'll knock on her door and deliver the surprise of her life.

Daddy's home.

Chapter
SEVEN

Riley

I stare out my kitchen window while I wash the dinner dishes. Veda splashing in the tub is my background noise. All is right in my world, so why do I feel like something is off? My eyes drift outside to the backyard, and the hairs on the back of my neck stand on end.

Is someone watching me?

My eyes search through the trees but see nothing.

"Mommy, where's the shampoo?" Veda calls out.

"Where it always is," I shout.

"No, it's not," she singsongs.

Drying my hands on a kitchen towel, I pop my head into the bathroom, expecting the white bottle of shampoo to be right in front of her face. But it's not.

That's weird.

"You didn't borrow it to make slime again, did you?" I push the shower curtain all the way to the end of the tub, still not finding it.

It seems like every day, she has a new slime recipe she's

discovered on YouTube. Nothing is off-limits: dish soap, hand soap, and laundry detergent. She's used it all to make the messy stuff.

"Nope."

"Weird." I grab my backup bottle in the hall closet and bring it to her. "Here you go."

"Thanks." She squirts a generous amount into her palm and smacks her hand onto the crown of her head. Not the most effective way to get things done, but I'm just glad she's old enough to do it herself, so I don't nitpick.

After her bath, we pick out pajamas, and I read her two books before I convince her it's time to sleep.

I'm exhausted after a long shift at the bar, then having to come home for all my mommy duties. Of course, I knew there would be more work without chefs and nannies around, but I don't think you can fully grasp just how helpful those are until they're gone.

Doing it all on my own is much harder than I expected, though I'd never admit that to anyone but myself.

"Love you, peanut," I say, flipping off the bedroom light.

"Love you too." Her voice is sleepy, and I know she'll be out in minutes. Which is good because this mommy needs a glass of wine and the view from the backyard.

Glass in hand, I take a seat on the cushioned chaise and look at my phone for the first time all evening. Two missed calls from Mom. Not the way I wanted to spend my night, but we haven't spoken much since I moved, so I figure I should call her back.

She answers on the second ring. "Hello?"

"Hey, Mom. How are you?"

"Better now that I know my daughter and granddaughter aren't lying dead in a ditch somewhere." Her tone is teasing, but the guilt is intentional.

"Sorry. Things have been kind of crazy."

"What do you mean by crazy?"

I take of sip wine. "Getting a job, finding childcare, and unpacking. It's been hectic."

"You did this to yourself. You could've stayed here and—"

"Mom," I interrupt. "I didn't call to get a lecture. I might be busier than I'm used to, but I'm happy. More importantly, Veda's happy."

"That's good. I'm glad."

Since I can remember, every conversation with Mom has gone this exact way. It's as though she battles between her reactive heart and her rational mind.

"Me too."

"So, where are you working, and who takes care of Veda?"

"I got a job at a restaurant." I can't tell her it's a bar; she'll only worry more. Plus, they sell food, so it's not technically a lie.

"And Veda?"

"I found a nice girl looking for a little extra cash. She's in college to be a kindergarten teacher." Partial truth. The nice girl is a hangaround at the Sons' clubhouse. But Char said she's super sweet and *is* in school to be a kindergarten teacher. She just likes to have a good time on the weekends with the guys.

"Did you do a background check?" she asks, knowing full well that's not something I would think to do.

I close my eyes and rub my forehead. "Yeah, Mom. She's squeaky clean."

It's quiet for a second before she says, "How's the *house?*"

If there's one subject that's been off-limits growing up, it's the first eight years of my life. When I was seventeen, I cornered her and begged for answers. That's when she told me about the affair and how she led Wrecker to believe I was his.

The one thing she wouldn't tell me, though, was who my real dad is.

It wasn't a lot to go off of, but it's what brought me to Reno the night Veda was conceived.

I had to find out for myself if he still wanted a relationship with me, so I booked a ticket and flew out here alone. But after I got here, I checked out my own theories on my bio dad first. That went sour real quick. But it was okay because I met Coyote and got screwed seven ways to Sunday.

It was after I left Coyote's tent that I finally called Wrecker. Of course, he came and got me because that's the kind of guy he was. We hadn't seen each other in nine years, but it was as if no time had passed. He welcomed me back into his life, and nine months later, he welcomed Veda too.

"It probably hasn't changed a bit since you lived here." I'm pushing it since she pretends her walk on the wild side doesn't exist, but I'm tired of walking on eggshells. "Could use a little updating, but it'll be fine for now."

"Did he. . . leave anything behind?"

"Why do you ask?" I wonder what she's getting at, but then it hits me. She's worried I'll find something to tell me who my biological father is.

"I was just wondering if you had to waste time getting rid of all his stuff."

"The club emptied his closets and stuff, but they left behind anything they thought might be sentimental to me." There's a whole bookcase of stuff I've yet to go through. "How come?"

I wish she was a straightforward person. All this dancing around is exhausting.

"I don't know, Riley. I'm making conversation, that's all," she says with a scoff.

"They left his cut, some pictures, and all the legal documents I need to get the house transferred into my name. Stuff like that."

"Have you been conversing with anyone from the club?"

For as much as she refused to talk about my childhood, she never had a problem warning me of the dangers of getting mixed up with a biker. She spewed cautionary tale after cautionary tale about how all bikers are cheaters, criminals, and murderers.

As a little girl, it was hard to reconcile that image with my memories. Wrecker was an amazing dad. He took me on what he called adventures but was really hikes through the desert. He brought me home gifts, and I remember he was always sweet with Mom—always touching her and kissing her. And the guys from the club spoiled me rotten.

"Not really. I've seen the guy who's the president now a few times."

"Riley, I really wish—"

"I know, Mom. Bikers bad, bankers good. Got it."

She sighs. "I'm worried. That's all."

"I know, and I'm sorry about that, but I'm all good here."

"You're finding your way around and stuff?"

"Yep. If you remember, I've been bringing Veda around once a month since I was eighteen so she could spend time with her granddaddy. I know my way around."

My trips out here were another bone of contention. Once a month, she'd pretend I was going on a weekend getaway and not to Reno to spend time with Wrecker. I let her live in her fantasy world, but more than once, I wanted to shake her and make her admit that time in her life existed.

"He's not her grandfather. Her real grandfather lives here."

I roll my eyes. "That's her great grandfather, and Wrecker was as close to a paternal grandfather as she'll ever get. Unless you want to tell me who my real dad is."

"Riley," she scolds.

"That's what I thought. Drop it, okay?"

"I don't understand why you insist on reliving my mistakes. I don't know what I did wrong with you." Her voice cracks, and she sniffles.

Here come the guilty tears. I need to get off this call before she progresses to rage tears.

"Oh, Mom. I have to go. Veda's calling for me."

"Okay. FaceTime me tomorrow so I can talk to her. And

plan a trip home soon. I need to see you with my own eyes before I'll believe everything is going as good as you make it out to be."

"I will," I say, even though I have no plans to return to St. Helena anytime soon. I need some distance from that judgmental, soul-sucking place.

"I love you. Give Veda kisses for me."

"Okay. Bye, Mom."

"Goodbye."

The line goes dead, and I chuck my phone to the other end of the lounge seat. Sipping my wine, I take one more glance at the city's sparkling lights and head inside. It's time for bed.

I make quick work of brushing my teeth and washing my face, then walk across the hall to my bedroom.

Stripping down to underwear and a tank, I climb between the sheets and flip off the lamp on my nightstand. My mind wanders back to the weird feeling I had earlier, followed by the missing shampoo. I can't shake the eerie sensation that someone has been inside the house.

I reach under my pillow to make sure the knife I stashed is still there. Wrecker has a gun safe full of rifles and handguns, but I don't want Veda to accidentally come across one in my room, so I keep them where they are. Which reminds me, I need to have Crash get them out of here. If Mom is right about the things Wrecker's done in his life, I can't be sure the guns are clean.

I search some more, expecting to feel the plastic handle of the butcher knife, but come up empty-handed.

Flipping back on the light, I lift the pillow up to see nothing but my sheet. *It's gone.* What the hell is going on? First the shampoo and now this. What else is missing? I scan my room, but everything else seems to be in its place. Until I open my nightstand and see the space where my battery-operated boyfriends live. One of my vibrating dildos is missing. The purple one.

"You've got to be kidding me," I whisper, digging around in the drawer in case I just missed it. I didn't. It's not there.

Who would take a dildo? Who would go through my house?

After putting my clothes back on, I run through the kitchen and out the back door, grabbing one of Wrecker's Carhartt coats along the way. I flip on the floodlights and scour the vast expanse of Wrecker's property.

Are they out there? Are they watching me right now?

I get the same sensation as earlier, like someone is watching me. It sends a shiver down my spine that I feel all the way to my bones. Someone's out there; there's no doubt in my mind.

What do they want from me? *Oh God. Veda.*

I rush back inside, locking the door behind me. My bare feet slap against the hardwoods until I'm inside her room. Thankfully she's still asleep, covers pulled up over her head so only the tips of her curls peak out. When she was a toddler, it used to terrify me that she slept this way, but for whatever reason, she's always liked to be completely buried in her covers.

It's why I only give her a sheet and her muslin comforter that's covered in owls. The fabrics are breathable, so I worry less.

I uncover her face and run a finger down her squishy cheek before bending down and kissing her pouty lips. God, I love her.

I might not have been happy when the pregnancy test came up positive, but the second I felt her kick for the first time, it was over for me. That love only deepened after I gave birth.

I'll protect her at all costs. Even if that means calling Crash for protection.

Chapter
EIGHT

Coyote

She knows I was inside her house. I can see it all over her face as she stands on the back porch in an oversized coat, searching for any sign of me. She won't find it. I've been living outdoors for too long. I know how to disguise myself.

It makes me an asshole, but the frightened kitten look on her face has my dick throbbing. My lips turn up in the corners, knowing I put it there. Right now, the dark side of my brain is winning, and I want her to be afraid. I want her to be questioning my every move. She deserves it after all the shit she's pulled.

She darts inside, no doubt locking the door behind her. *Silly girl, locks can't keep me out. Nothing short of death will keep me from you.*

On light feet, I creep up to the house. I still haven't figured out my end game with her, so until then, I plan on learning as much as I can about her and. . . my daughter.

My daughter.

I scrub a hand over my nearly bald head. Jesus fuck. I have a daughter. I can deny it all I want in front of my boys; it's harder to deny it when I've seen the resemblance and been inside the room that is no doubt homage to our night together.

Riley has the blinds drawn on every window, stopping me from seeing in. As I circle around the house, I find her bedroom light on, and possibly the hall light since there's a dim glow coming from the living room window.

It's brazen as fuck, but I take a seat on the porch and wait. She has to go to bed at some point, and when she does, I'll be back inside.

My heart pounds as I wait. This isn't something I've done before. I don't even know why I'm doing it now. I'm not in control. My dark demon is, and I'm just along for the ride.

It's an hour before the lights turn off and another hour before I'm confident she's asleep. As if I have every right to, I unlock the door and step inside. It would terrify her to know I'm here, but she's safer with me around. Still, it's better she doesn't find out. Not yet.

I silently shut the door behind me and, using techniques I've honed throughout the years, slowly make my way to what I know is her bedroom. The door is open, no doubt so she can hear the kid if she were to wake up.

It makes things easier for me.

I pause in the doorway, waiting for any sign of her still being awake. But in the silent house, her slow and steady breaths are the only audible sound, letting me know she's off in dreamland. It takes four steps to reach her bedside, then I see her.

She's facing away from me, her long hair swept up and over the top of her pillow, exposing her long, swanlike neck and prominent collarbone. My dick chubs, and I reach down to adjust myself. What is it about her that has me reacting like this?

She's pretty, gorgeous even, but I've been with a lot of beautiful women. What is it about her I can't shake? I've thought about this moment for so long. It's almost surreal to see her in the flesh again.

Her lips part. She lets out a soft sigh, then turns over so she's facing me. In sleep, she looks more like she did back then. Soft, sweet, and young. I was stupid to believe it when she said she was nineteen. The dark thoughts rage in my head, thinking about how she lied and how she hid from me for so long.

I tamp it down. There'll be time to demand answers.

Leaning over her unconscious body, I get close enough to smell her hair. Even though I have the shampoo and can smell it anytime I want, it's different when the scent is on her, better somehow.

I inhale deeply, and like a junkie getting a fix, euphoria kicks in. This is a risky game I'm playing, but that makes it even more exciting. Just to ramp up the danger, I get close to her ear and whisper, "You'll be mine again someday, Riley."

Having done what I set out to do, I leave her room and travel further down the hall to check on Veda. That's what a good dad does, right? Her door is also open, but all I see is a mop of coiled hair when I approach her bed.

I wish I could see more of her, but I don't want to chance waking her up. The first time we meet shouldn't be with me standing over her bed in the middle of the night. That would be traumatizing. So, I make my way out of the house, locking up behind me, and trek back into the woods for a little shut-eye, leaving my family safe and sound.

At least safe from everyone but me.

"Where you been sleeping?" Goblin, the enforcer of the club, asks. Enforcer by title but not by actions. A voice of reason when things get heated. Which, in my opinion, makes him the best kind of enforcer. He's level-headed and sensible, someone you want making life and death decisions. "Noticed your tent gone last night."

"Found a new place to camp out," I say.

I came back to the club after Riley left for work. Some chick I don't know showed up to watch Veda. I kept an eye on her for a bit, but when I saw my daughter liked her, I decided my time was better spent elsewhere.

Goblin shoots me a look. "You mean Riley's place?"

My brows bunch together. "They told you?"

"Loki might've mentioned your situation at church this morning."

"Christ, you guys are like gossiping teenagers." I give the prospect, Ford, a chin lift and tap my empty coffee cup. He's quick to retrieve the pot and fill it up.

"He's got a feeling this is going to blow back on us."

They're not wrong about being worried. Sly did some digging on Irvin, and it turns out he was more connected to the Sons than I originally thought. I doubt they've figured out we're the ones who took him out, but if they're anything like us, they won't give up until they find out.

"They won't find out we're the ones who dealt with Irvin," I say.

"Maybe. Maybe not. But if they do, shit'll get messy."

Loki walks over and sits at the bar where Goblin and I are. "What are we talking about?"

"Irvin," Goblin grumbles.

"Good. Needed to talk with you about that anyway," Loki says to me. "Sorry I had to spill all your secrets."

"Yeah, thanks for that," I grumble.

I'm a private person. It's another reason I've never patched in anywhere. When you're a member of the club, you have no secrets. Everything is out in the open.

"Someone at The Silo said a Bastard nomad was asking about Riley the same day Irvin went missing." Loki lights the cig he had tucked behind his ear.

"Aren't you supposed to be quitting?" Goblin asks.

"Fuck off. I cut down."

Goblin pulls his phone from his pocket and aims it at Loki. "You won't mind if I send this to Birdie."

"You do that, and I'll have your balls, asshole."

Goblin chuckles and sets the phone down. "Badass Loki is scared of Biker Barbie."

"Must've been the bartender. Maybe she saw my bike," I say, bringing the conversation back to the topic at hand.

"Loki!" Another prospect, Miles, shouts from the front doorway. "Visitors. Told them they could wait in the parking lot."

"Who is it?" Goblin asks.

"Sons."

"Shit." Loki stubs out his cigarette and gives me a pointed look. "You're dealing with this."

He's not my president, but I owe him the respect of following orders. Goblin and I both stand and walk outside, Loki leading the way. The parking lot is dirt and gravel, so when we get outside, there's a cloud of dust still circling the air from the Sons' bikes pulling in.

"Burly one with the dumb bandana on his head is Crash," Loki says in a hushed tone. "Taller one is Vin, and the third one—the one with crazy eyes and bald head—is Rigger."

The three of them walk over to us with dead serious expressions on their faces. I hear boots on the ground behind me and know a few more of my brothers have joined the party. A quick glance over my shoulder, and I see pretty boy Roch, the Sergeant at Arms, and the biggest motherfucker in the club, Khan, the VP.

"Crash," Loki greets him in a tone that says he's not throwing out the welcome mat.

"Loki," he returns. "Need to talk."

"What about?" Khan says in a voice so deep, it can only be described as deadly.

"Not gonna invite us in?" Vin chimes in, a stupid ass grin on his face.

74

Loki flips his Zippo, lighting up another cig. "We're not prepared for company."

Crash's head bobs. "We'll make it quick then. You know a guy named Irvin?"

So far, the Sons haven't so much as glanced my way, but the second Irvin's name crosses Crash's lips, his eyes home in on me.

Bring it, motherfucker. I'll wash the floors in your blood.

"Isn't he the manager over at The Silo?" Goblin asks, sounding mildly interested.

Rigger closes his left hand over his right fist and cracks his knuckles. "He's one of us."

"Never wore colors." I shrug.

"More like a friend of the club," Crash clarifies.

"The answer to your question is yes, we know who he is. Doesn't answer mine. Why are you here?" Loki asks, smoke billowing from his mouth and nose.

"Heard your nomad was at The Silo the day Irvin went missing. Wanted to see if he knows anything about that."

I shake my head. "Don't know shit about that. Stopped in for a beer a few weeks back, though."

"Not the only reason you came by, though, right?" Rigger asks.

"If you have something to say, just say it." I widen my stance and square my shoulders.

"Riley belongs to the Sons. I don't know what you want with her, but she's under our protection." Crash says.

Those words burn through my body, and it takes every ounce of self-control I possess not to pull out the Glock tucked into my waistband and blow this guy's head off. If Riley belongs to anybody, it's me. After all, she had my kid.

"Don't know what you're talking about, man," I say.

"I think you do. And I think you know all about Irvin's disappearance too. Can't prove it right now, so out of respect to Loki, I won't take you out," he starts, then adds. "Yet."

"Not going to find that evidence, Crash." Loki flicks his cigarette, hitting Crash's boot.

"Yeah, we'll see about that." Without a goodbye, the three Sons whirl around and jump back on their bikes. They peel out, spraying us with small rocks and dirt.

Khan charges forward, but Loki stops him. "Let 'em go. It's not the last we'll see of them." He turns to face us. "Church. Now."

I don't move, knowing I have to be invited before I'm allowed in their Chapel.

"Coyote, you too," Loki says, and I follow.

Inside the windowless room is a long wooden table with the RBMC skull carved dead center and chairs circling the perimeter. Along the walls are framed pictures of fallen members, but other than that, it's an empty room.

I wait until everyone else is seated before taking an empty chair next to Goblin.

Once everyone is settled, Loki bangs the gavel. "Coyote, you know you're always welcome here."

"I sense a 'but' coming," I say.

"You're right. We were happy to help you with the Irvin situation, but I should've asked more questions. That's on me. But you bringing this shit to our door? That's on you."

I want to be pissed at being called out in front of everyone, but that's my pride talking, not my logic. Looking at the situation rationally, he's right. And everyone in this room knows it.

"I'm sorry about that, Loki. You know I only set out to ask the man some questions."

"I get that, but it doesn't mean shit anymore. I see only one option." He pushes back from the table and crosses an ankle over a knee, resting his elbows on the arms of the chair and steepling his fingers. "If you want us to back you, we need a commitment."

"Aw, are you proposing, Prez?"

"No, dumbass. I'm telling you it's time to patch in."

Khan bangs his fist on the table, Sly and Moto following

suit. Soon, every man in the room has their eyes on me and their fists pounding on the table.

Jesus fuck. I'm backed into a corner. I can't leave. Things aren't settled with Riley, and now that I have a kid, I need to stick around for who knows how long. Suddenly my chest feels tight, and sweat beads along my forehead. I need to get the fuck out of here and into some fresh air.

But I can't. Not yet.

"Fine," I shout. "I'll do it."

Loki bangs the gavel, and the room quiets. "Time for a vote. All in favor of Coyote patching in, raise your hand."

Hands shoot into the air. Goblin pounds me on the back while panic chokes me around the neck, and I fight to breathe. These attacks are embarrassing, and I've taught myself to mask the beginning stages. But I'm quickly veering into a full-on uncontrollable storm.

"Vote's unanimous. We're proud to have you, brother." Loki grins my way.

It takes every drop of energy to mutter, "Thanks."

"This calls for a celebration. Let's get rowdy," Khan shouts, banging his fists on his chest like a wild animal.

The gavel comes down one more time, signaling the end of the meeting. I jump to my feet and stumble out the door. My chest heaves, and my vision blurs. I use the wall to hold myself up as I work my way toward the back door. The smell of gas and smoke fills my nostrils.

I've been through this enough to know it's not really there. It's just a trick my broken mind is playing on me.

Someone lifts my right arm and ducks under it, supporting me. I glance over and see Roch.

"C'mon," he says in his clipped tone.

I lean on him, and together we get out the back door and into the fresh air. I suck in lungfuls of air as Roch deposits me in a chair. Eyes burn into my back, and there's no doubt everyone witnessed my episode. I'm fuckin' humiliated.

It takes a few minutes for my heart to slow and the tightness in my chest to ease. It's been a long time since things have gotten this bad.

"Sorry. Not feeling so great," I say to Roch, hoping to play it off like I'm sick.

"PTSD?" he asks. I don't know Roch well, considering the man rarely speaks a word to anyone. But the knowing look he's throwing my way tells me he knows all too well what I'm going through.

"Yeah."

"S'okay."

It's one word—a made-up word at that—but knowing he gets it calms me further. He claps me on the shoulder before leaving me and walking across the yard to the tiny house he shares with his woman, Truly.

The tightness in my chest eases, and I'm finally able to breathe without feeling like my lungs are on fire. This is nothing new; I've had these attacks since I was eight years old, and a fire made me an orphan. I thought I'd grow out of it; I mean, how can you hold on to shit from that long ago?

With the show over, someone turns on the jukebox inside, blasting rock and roll. Bottles clink, and the guys chatter. The celebration has begun, but I don't feel much like joining.

The back door slides open, and Loki sits down next to me. "You good?"

"Yeah. Sorry about that."

"Don't apologize, brother. We all got our demons."

I peer over at him and see nothing but concern and understanding. He tosses a Royal Bastards patch with the Reno chapter embroidered on it. "You're one of us now. Your shit is our shit."

I hope that's true because I have a feeling there's about to be a lot of shit coming my way.

Chapter
NINE

Riley

"Can I talk to you about something?" I ask Char, plopping down on my sofa with a bottle of beer in hand.

Earlier today, Char had called to invite me to a clubhouse party later that night. But I feel guilty enough leaving Veda with a sitter every time I work, so I declined her offer. Other girls would've pressured me or gone off to the party without me. Not Char. Instead, she asked if she could come over and have a girls' night with me and Veda.

It's strange to have a friend with no ulterior motives. There's no social gain to be had by being my friend, and I don't have money or status to benefit her, yet she still chooses to be my friend.

After that phone call, I decided we're besties now, whether or not she likes it.

Char, who's sitting on the living room floor with Veda, sets down the Barbie that she was dressing per Veda's instructions. "Of course."

"These shoes, Char," Veda whines.

"Let me talk to your mom for a minute, then I'll get the

shoes on, okay? Why don't you go find a matching purse in your room?"

"Okay!" Veda jumps to her feet and runs to her room.

"Are you and Cyrus planning on kids? Because you'd be an amazing mom," I say.

"I don't know. Cy is inching toward fifty, and I'm not quite ready for kids. I guess we'll talk about it in a few years. After we've mastered the Kama Sutra." She waggles her brows.

"You are such a horn dog."

"I know. So, what's up with you?"

"I've had this strange feeling all week. Like someone is watching me. And what's even weirder is that I think someone's been in my house."

All week I tried to convince myself it's all in my head, but I can't shake it. I feel like I'm losing my mind.

She rests her elbows on her knees, and flutters her lashes, ready to hear some gossip. "Why do you think that?"

My face pinches, unsure if she'll believe me. "Things have gone missing."

"Like what?"

"My shampoo, a knife I kept under my pillow, um. . . a sex toy, and my favorite pair of undies." That last one I didn't discover until today.

Her eyes widen. "You have a stalker."

"I think I do."

"Can you think of anyone who would want to stalk you?"

"No. There's no one." I wring my hands together. "But Crash told me he was paying Irvin to keep an eye on me while I was at work. One day later, he goes missing. And now someone has been in my house, and I feel eyes on me all the time. I don't know if it's connected or if it's all random, but I don't know what to do. Do I call the police?"

"No," she's quick to say. "Never call the cops. Are you sure you can't think of anyone? According to my true crime podcast, three out of four victims know who their stalker is."

"What about the guy whose leather cut is in your room?" she asks, eyeing me suspiciously.

I wasn't sure she got a good enough look at what was in that box to know it was a cut, but I guess they're easy to recognize when you grow up with bikers. Even if you only get a quick glance.

Should I tell her? Would she run and tell Cyrus?

"Can I trust you with a secret?" I ask.

She gives me the universal sign for "my lips are sealed." "I'm like a vault. Information goes in but never comes out."

I chug the rest of my beer before continuing. No one knows about that night, and I mean no one. I told everyone who asked that Veda's dad was a guy I dated, but the second he found out I was pregnant, he wanted nothing to do with me. In my mind, I thought it'd make me sound less slutty to my judgmental mom and my circle of friends.

Of course, they were skeptical since I never spoke about dating someone. But I explained that off by saying he was a server at a restaurant, and I was too embarrassed to tell people we were dating. I kind of hated myself for that one. But how fucked up was my life that I'd rather admit to being a pompous asshole than tell people I met someone who touched my soul more in one night than anyone has my entire life?

I'm so glad I left that place and can just be me now. No worrying what others will think, no biting my tongue when someone says something offensive, and no longer delivering practiced answers from the scripts Mom fed me. That weight is off my shoulders, and I finally feel free.

"I told you Veda is the product of a one-night stand, but what I didn't tell you is that the guy was a Royal Bastard." I cringe, expecting a huge reaction. But Char's face is impassive. "Why are you not freaking out?"

"I recognized the rocker and put two and two together. Being married to a member of the Sons, I learned to recognize the colors of all the other clubs in the area. Even when I don't get a good look."

"And?" Even if she knew, why isn't she saying anything?

"And nothing."

This is not how I thought this conversation would go. Juicy gossip like this is right up Char's alley.

"Why?" I ask.

"Because it means trouble. Crash and the Sons have claimed you as one of theirs. Even if nothing happens between you and Crash, you belong to the club. And if whatever Bastard knocked you up finds out about Veda, there'll be problems. Big problems. Clubs don't mix like that," she says. I deflate, staring at her deadpan expression. I didn't think about the ramifications in that way. Then her lips curl up on the ends. "Tell me everything."

"Charlotte!" I complain.

"I'm sorry. I had to give you the talk to limit my culpability. Now that I have, gimme the deets." She motions for me to continue.

My eyes widen. "Give me a second. I'm experiencing whiplash."

"Hurry up and get over it before Veda realizes all her Barbie purses are right here." She holds up a plastic bag full of tiny plastic and cloth handbags.

"You're evil."

"I know."

"Veda's dad's name is Coyote. Do you know him?" I ask.

She thinks for a second. "I don't think Cy has ever mentioned him."

"He's a nomad, so that makes sense."

"You slept with a nomad? Jesus, Ry. If you're going to the dark side, at least make sure he has a title," she chides.

"It wasn't like that. I didn't sleep with him for his rank or even because he was a biker. The second our eyes met, it was like bolts of lightning shot through my body. It felt like I knew him. Not his favorite color or where he was born, like our souls recognized each other. I know it sounds stupid, but—"

"It doesn't sound stupid. That's how it was with me and Cy. Even as a little girl, I remember thinking I knew his mind. Like we were kindred spirits in a way."

I shift in my seat excitedly. "Exactly. That's what it felt like."

"I'll bet the sex was amazing."

"I didn't have anything to compare it to at the time—"

"Wait. You were a virgin?"

I grin. "I was. He almost didn't go through with it after I told him, but I made it. . . difficult for him to say no."

"You vixen."

"It was so unlike me. I grew up being taught to always let the man lead in whatever exchange you were having. I was so used to watching for the queues of men, it was instinctive for me. But I couldn't let him turn me down. I needed him, and, in the end, he couldn't say no."

"So it was good?"

I melt inside and out. "So good. He was rough but attentive, demanding but also giving. I've been with a couple of guys since, and there is no comparison."

"Well, if you're going to hell, might as well have an orgasm on your way down," Char says.

"Or two," I add.

"Hell yeah."

Veda chooses this moment to walk in. I know our talk is over, though now that I've told her this secret, I have the urge to tell her all my secrets. I guess it'll have to wait for another time.

It's dark when I'm startled awake with a parched mouth and the world spinning around me. After Veda went to sleep, Char and I had one or two beers too many. She was going to stay the night, but Cy didn't like that idea, so he drove out and picked her up.

I glance at my nightstand, hoping I had the foresight to pour myself a glass of water. I didn't.

Peeling my tongue from the roof of my mouth, I get out of bed. The room tilts, and I have to steady myself with a hand to the mattress. My stomach turns. I haven't been wasted in forever, and now I remember why. Tomorrow morning with Veda is going to suck.

I use the walls for stability and pad my way to the kitchen on wobbly legs. It's a miracle I can get a glass from the cabinet and not drop it as I fill it with tap water.

I gulp the entire glass before going back for a refill with plans to stop by the bathroom for aspirin on my way back to bed. Suddenly, my skin prickles with awareness, and that same feeling I've had for a week crawls over me. Only this time, whether from my intoxication or reality, I don't just feel like I'm being watched. I feel like someone is in the room with me.

The glass falls from my hand, crashing to the floor as I whirl around and scour through the darkness.

Are they in my house? Looking through a window? Right in front of my face?

Without my contacts, seeing anything is a challenge, let alone when the room is pitch black. Bile burns in my stomach and spews up my throat. I swallow it down, taking a cautious step forward. Only I forgot about the broken glass, and my heel catches a shard.

"Shit," I curse, lifting my foot and plucking the glass from my flesh with a shaky hand.

Tears, not from the pain but because I'm terrified, blur my vision, and I don't know what to do. I'm stuck in place, and I'm certain someone is creeping around inside my house.

Damn it. Veda. I need to get to her and make sure she's alright.

Chancing hurting myself further, I take the biggest leap I can muster while also drunk. Thankfully, it's far enough to avoid further injury. Running as if someone is chasing me—because that's what it feels like—I reach Veda's room and shut the door. The knob has a lock that I turn before slipping into bed next to my still sleeping daughter.

Once I've made sure she's all in one piece and okay, I relax. Until I realize I don't have my cellphone. I can't call anyone to check things out. I'm almost certain this was one of the things Crash said I could get ahold of him over.

I listen, trying to hear anything or anyone on the other side of the door, but it's silent. Maybe it was all in my head. My imagination has been in overdrive since stuff went missing from my house. It's no wonder I'm overreacting.

Even so, I can't talk myself into going to my room for my phone. At least in here, there's a locked door between us and the possibility of an unknown intruder. Snaking my arm under Veda's head, I turn her so she's curled around my body. She'd be no help if something bad happened, but just having her here with me is comforting.

She's okay. I'm okay. For now.

I lie awake for what feels like hours, waiting for the sun to come up so I can feel safe enough to leave. Whether from the alcohol or exhaustion, I fall asleep before that happens and don't wake up again until morning.

"Mommy." Veda pinches my cheeks and shakes my head. "Wake up."

I stretch and moan. My head is pounding, and there's a sharp pain coming from my foot. I startle, sitting up straight and popping my eyes open.

"Mommy, you're bleeding." Veda points and I look down at my foot, where dried blood has stained her comforter.

"I guess I have an owie. It's okay. It doesn't hurt." I bop her on the nose and get out of bed. "Can you get your blankets and sheets off your mattress while I go get a bandage?"

"Okay."

I can always count on her being helpful. Keeping her busy for a minute will give me time to inspect the house. I stop in the bathroom first to put on my glasses, then go room to room, looking in closets, cabinets, and behind the doors. There's no sign of anyone being in here last night. Until I get to the kitchen.

I expect to see shattered glass on the floor, but there's nothing. Not even a drop of blood from my foot.

What the hell?

I look in the trash, thinking maybe I forgot I cleaned it up. Highly unlikely, but so is having a stalker who cleans up messes. There's no glass in there either. I check the bottom of my broom closet too. I don't know what I expect to find, maybe tiny glass fragments? But it's as clean as it was the last time I used it.

I'd think I was hallucinating about the whole thing, except my foot is bloody. How else would that've happened?

There's no other explanation.

And that scares me more than anything.

Chapter
TEN

Coyote

I toss the bag of glass in the dumpster back at the clubhouse before going inside.

The adrenaline from almost being caught last night is still bubbling underneath my skin. After getting hammered with her friend, I thought she'd be passed out all night. I was wrong, which almost got me caught.

The glass of water she was drinking crashed to the floor the second she felt me in the room. The urge to rescue her was almost unbearable, but I fought it off. It's not the right time. I'm not ready.

I refuse to step into their life until I know I'm not a shit dad like mine was.

Then it hits me. That's the crux of the problem, isn't it?

If this deep desire to take care of the two of them is instinctive, then it makes no fuckin' sense how my dad could turn on me and Mom.

What if the demon that lived inside him is also the one in me? I don't want to fuck up Riley and Veda's life the way Dad fucked up mine. There's no doubt I have darkness in my soul, but Riley lit a match that still burns bright five years later. It's something I've never felt before. I don't understand it, and I'm worried it'll extinguish, and the demons will win.

Despite the turmoil swarming in my head, the instinct to protect them both grows by the day. It's why I cleaned up the glass; I couldn't stand the thought of Riley hurting herself by cleaning it up, or worse, Veda waking up and not realizing it was there.

Did Dad ever feel that same protective drive? Or was he so lost to the demons he didn't experience it? Is that why he tried to kill both me and Mom?

There are too many questions, and until I have answers, I'll keep doing what I'm doing. Keeping them safe from my place in the shadows.

"Hey, bro. What's up?" Sly asks from behind the bar. He's pouring coffee into three mugs and placing them on a tray with muffins and donuts.

It doesn't surprise me he's gathering enough for three. He and Moto have been circling around this mousy girl the club adopted after they killed her asshole husband. She's skittish as fuck and rarely comes out of her room, but that doesn't stop them from trying.

"Not much. Loki around?"

"Nah. Should be back in an hour. Went on a run with Goblin and Miles to Oregon yesterday. They had a drop in Bend but were too tired to make it all the way back, so they stayed the night in Susanville."

My Reno brothers have had their hands in a lot of different things the last few years, but recently Loki got them back into gun-running. Their contact, Miguel, is one of the top gun smugglers on the West Coast. He works directly with drug cartels and gangs, buying and selling a wide variety of firearms. He then uses the club to distribute the weapons.

"I'll wait for him."

He lifts the tray and moves to the other side of the bar. "You good?"

"All good, brother."

He nods and disappears down the hallway. One of these days, I'll make him tell me what the hell is going on with the three of them. But I have enough shit going on without adding someone else's shit to my pile.

I pour a cup of coffee and take a seat on the worn leather sofa. This section of the room has a pool table, darts, and the biggest TV known to man in front of me. The ultimate fuckin' man cave.

But I'm not in the mood to watch a show, so I get out my phone and open my pictures. My thumb flips through the endless photos I've taken of Riley and Veda over the last week. I realize it's sick and twisted for me to stalk them the way I am. Especially since Riley knows someone is watching her.

It'd be so easy for her to find out it's me. All she has to do is look in her closet and find the empty box my cut was in. It's the biggest clue I've left her but one she hasn't discovered.

"What the fuck happened?" Loki's shouting startles me awake.

My eyes pop open, and I'm on my feet in seconds. I must've dozed off waiting for them to return.

"I have no fuckin' clue. Get Roch in here and have him call Aiyana." Goblin's being held up by Miles, holding a rag soaked in blood to his head.

Aiyana is Roch's old lady's mom. She's a vet, and as much as she hates getting involved in club business, she never says no when a Bastard has a minor wound she can take care of. Hospitals ask questions and are required to report gun injuries, which would not go over well for us.

"On it." Miles drops Goblin's arm to run through the clubhouse and out the back door.

"Sit the fuck down before you pass out," Loki says.

Goblin lurches over to the couches and collapses on the one in front of.

"Jesus fuck. What happened?" I ask.

"Don't know. We were on the freeway, and some dickhead appeared out of nowhere, popping off rounds at us." He leans back, wincing. The rag is nearly soaked through, so I grab another one from behind the bar and hand it to him. "Thanks."

"You got shot?" I ask.

He lifts the bloody rag and exposes a huge gash on his temple. "Just grazed me, but Loki thinks I need stitches."

"He's right, brother. That looks gnarly." My lip curls up in disgust. The gash is so deep, I think I see his skull.

"Did you get a good look at him?" Loki asks, his phone out and his thumbs sliding across the screen.

"It was Crash," Goblin snarls.

"How do you know? All I saw was a guy in black." Loki tucks his phone into the pocket inside his cut and sits down next to him.

"I recognized his neon green fuckin' rims from when they stopped by the other day. Stupid motherfucker, making himself identifiable like that."

Shit. That means this is my fault. That asshole is determined to figure out my connection to Irvin and, more importantly, Riley. He's dumber than I thought if he thinks he can take on our club. It didn't work out that well for the Sons the last time they tried this bullshit, and it won't work out well this time either.

I pull out my gun and make sure it's loaded. "I'll kill him for this."

"No, you won't," Loki says, lighting up a smoke. "We need to be smart about this. Crash could've killed all of us right then and there. I don't think he got to his position by being a shit shot. He's goading us, which means we need to keep our heads on straight."

He's right. I know he is. But fuck if I don't want to do it anyway.

"I'll get Sly on this, and if any of you have any contacts that are friendly with the Sons, reach out to them. Let's get some intel before we squash the assholes." Loki whips his phone back out and starts tapping out messages.

Three hours later, Goblin's head is stitched up, and we're gathered in the chapel for church.

"Sly, you're up first," Loki says.

"My buddy who works at their shop is opening his ears. He'll call if he hears anything. But the motive is obvious. He thinks Coyote is going after his woman."

"Fuck that. His woman?" I scoff. "They aren't together. I've been at her house every day and night for a week, and he hasn't been around once."

"So you finally confronted Riley?" Loki asks.

"No," I say sheepishly. "I can't yet."

"This could all be over if you cleared shit up with her," Goblin says under his breath. The comment pisses me off. He doesn't know why I'm being cautious. None of them do.

"It's not your business." My tone is harsh and clipped.

"Goblin's head begs to differ," Khan returns.

"Fuck off."

Loki pounds the gavel. "That's enough. Goblin, I don't think I need to mention the last time we had issues with the Sons, it was because of your ass."

"I was seventeen and a prospect."

I haven't heard this story before. The only mention of that squabble with the Sons was that it happened, and they worked shit out before anyone had to spill blood.

"You were a legacy and knew better." Loki's dark brow lifts.

Goblin backs down, lifting his hands up in surrender. "Fine. But let's figure this out before they start a war. We have enough shit going on with Khan's trial. We don't need drama."

"Okay. For now, we keep our heads down. I want to double down on guys doing runs. Keep your eyes open." Loki pounds the gavel down, and we all stand. Before I can get out the door, though, Loki speaks again. "Coyote, need to talk."

I scratch my brow and turn to sit. It's like getting called into the principal's office.

"I need you to be straight with me. What's your plan for this girl?" he asks.

"Not sure yet."

"Not good enough, bro. If you're claiming her, we'll do what it takes. I've had someone try to take away my old lady before, and we burned down heaven and earth to get her back. We'll do the same for you, but if you're not claiming her, then you need to fuckin' let it go. Yeah?"

My head is so fucked up. I don't like my arm being twisted because I don't know the right answer.

"Let me ask you a question," he starts. "What's your hold up?"

"Not sure I'm the right guy for her." I clasp my hands together on top of the table, squeezing until my joints scream at me. "And I'm not sure I'm cut out to be a dad."

"I can't help you with the dad part. Birdie and I aren't there yet. But the other part, I might be able to." He pulls the black beanie off his head. "When I met Birdie, she was young, younger than Riley is now. She grew up with the kind of money men like you and me can only dream of. I wasn't the right guy for her, not even close, but the second I thought about her being with anyone else, I lost my fuckin' mind. Right or wrong, she was mine. Thank fuck she felt the same." He lets that set in for a minute before adding, "You feel like that about Riley?"

"To my fuckin' bones," I say without hesitation.

"Then it's time to grow up. A woman you connect with like that, one who will stand by you no matter what, who'll look past all your hard edges, lay down with you at night, and make you feel like a king? You wife that chick up, bro. No hesitation. We live hard lives. We need someone soft to come home to."

"Birdie ain't soft," I say. That bitch is snarky as hell and hard-headed too.

Loki chuckles. "No, she's not. But the second her clothes come off—"

"All right. Don't need to picture her fuckin' you the next time I see her."

"Better not. I'll kick your ass." Loki pulls his beanie back on his head, covering his messy, dark hair.

"You could try." I smirk but turn serious when I realize I have something else I need to ask. "You asked me a question, now can I ask you one?"

"Hit me."

"You had a pretty good dad growing up, yeah?"

"Trucker was great until he wasn't. After my mom was killed, he kind of went off the deep end. Went from being my best friend to my enemy. Fuckin' sucked, to be honest. Why do you ask?"

"My dad, he was never my best friend. He was always a piece of shit. Tried to kill me and my mom. Succeeded with my mom, but I made it out. And that was after he tormented me for the first eight years of my life," I admit. I patched in. Might as well be honest about my life.

"Goddamn. Need a smoke for this." He pats his chest, feeling for the right pocket, then takes a pack of cigarettes out. "You want one?"

"Tobacco ain't my thing. But this is." I reach behind my ear and place the hand-rolled blunt between my lips. Loki lights his cig with his Zippo, then leans over and gives me a light. "Thanks."

"How did you live after that?" he asks.

"Foster care for a while, then when that didn't work out, I lived on the streets until I found the club."

"And now you're worried you'll turn out like your old man with your kid?" He hits the nail on the head.

"Yeah," I say, holding in a lungful of smoke.

"I don't know about any of that, but I do know there's a kid out there who doesn't know her father because he's over here being a chickenshit."

He's right, though it's painful to admit.

With the blunt dangling from my lips, I wrap my hands around each side of my head, lean forward, and squeeze, cursing, "Damn it."

Loki lets me have my meltdown for about ten seconds. "Do you want to be your dad?"

"Fuck no."

"Then prove you're not."

Chapter
ELEVEN

Riley

I watch the clock in irritation. Chaplain, the club chick who's been watching Veda, is late. Ten minutes late. I texted her twenty minutes ago, and she left me on *Read*. Should've known this wouldn't work out.

"Where's Chap, Mommy?" Veda asks. She planned their entire afternoon, pulling out games and art supplies for them to work on together.

"I don't think she's coming, baby." I dial up The Silo, and Char answers on the first ring.

"The Silo, what do you want?"

"Are you always so pleasant when you answer the phone?" I ask.

"Only when I'm here during the lunch rush by myself," she snaps.

"I'm so sorry. Chaplain never showed up, and I don't have a sitter for Veda."

"Crash been to see you yet?" Her tone tells me she knows why my babysitter ghosted me.

"No. Why would he?"

"I'm sorry, Riley. I really am. But Cy would've whooped my ass if I kept the whole Coyote thing to myself."

What. The. Fuck.

"Tell me you're joking." I quickly stand and look out my front window to see Crash pulling into my driveway.

"Wish I was, honey. Trust me, it's better they know the truth so they can protect you. Cy said something about the Bastards being responsible for Irvin. If that's true, they might be after you next."

Crash gets off his bike and hangs his helmet on the handlebars. His face is stone, giving me no sign of his mood. I can guess, though.

This goes beyond me having a kid with a member of another club, and I know it. His biceps flex, and his eyes narrow to slits as he makes his way onto my porch.

This is bad.

"You there, Ry?" Char asks, reminding me I'm still on the phone.

"Sorry, babe. I gotta go."

"Oh, God. Is he there?"

"Yeah. And he doesn't look happy." As though I'm walking the plank, each step toward the door is slow and dreadful.

"I'm so sorry. So, so sor—"

"It's fine, Char. I'll talk to you later." I can't even be mad. I know the code old ladies follow. If anything, she should be mad at me for asking her to keep a secret from Cyrus.

I hang up and tuck my phone into the back pocket of the black pleather shorts I'm wearing, then steel my spine and square my shoulders before opening the door.

"Crash, what are you doing here?" I beam at him like I don't have a care in the world.

Veda chooses that moment to run down the hall, excitedly yelling, "Is Chaplain here?"

"No, it's not Chap. She can't make it today, but we can play games instead, okay? First, I need you to go read a book in your room for a minute or two, okay?"

"Awww." She all but stamps her foot while side-eyeing our unwelcome visitor.

"Veda," I say in my best Mom Voice.

"Fine." She disappears down the hall, and I turn back to Crash.

"So, what's up?" I ask.

"Need to talk." His tone is low and abrasive. Not surprising coming from him.

I lead him through the house to the back porch, where I at least have an epic view to look at while I listen to the lecture I know is coming my way.

"Heard some shit," he says, not sitting down, unlike me.

"Oh yeah? What kind of shit?"

"Don't play games, Riley." His hazel eyes burn into me like I'm staring at the sun. Beautiful but dangerous.

I throw my hands up. "I'm not. If you want to know something, then ask. Simple as that."

"Did you fuck a Bastard and get yourself knocked up?"

"Did I have a one-night stand with a member of the Royal Bastards that ultimately resulted in a pregnancy? Yes. I did."

"Did Wrecker know?" He crosses his arms over his chest.

"No. No one did. Until I told Charlotte. Now the entire world knows, apparently." I throw my hands up. "But I wasn't in Wrecker's life at the time. It was before we reconnected, and I hadn't seen him in years at that point."

None of this is his business. He might think he has some chivalrous claim over me because he feels like he owes Wrecker, but that's all in his head.

"You fucked up, you know that?"

I tuck my knees to my chest and curl around myself. "No. It's not like that."

He can try to make my night with Coyote feel wrong, but

it won't work. I'll never look back at that night as anything be-sides perfect.

"It *is* like that." He storms over to the back door, pulling it open with too much force. "Make room for my toothbrush. I'm moving in."

My mouth goes dry, and my head spins. What is he talking about? "Excuse me?"

"Coyote's back in town. He killed Irvin to get information, and now he's coming for you. Stay inside and lock the doors while I pack up a few things. I'll be back later." He holds the door open, but my ass is still glued to the chaise, trying to pro-cess everything he said.

"Riley!"

I jolt at his sharp tone and get up, running inside where it's safe.

Safe?

The missing shampoo, knife, and dildo. Feeling like someone is watching me. The shattered glass that was mysteriously cleaned up.

"Coyote's back?" I ask dumbly as Crash's heavy boots clomp to the front door.

"Are you stupid or something?" he spits, and I flinch. "Stay inside."

The back door slams shut, and my back hits the kitchen wall. I sink to the floor, everything becoming clearer in my mind.

If he was that pissed just learning who Veda's dad is, he'd be homicidal if he knew Coyote had been in my house and watch-ing me for over a week now.

"Can we play now, Mommy?" Veda asks, peeking her head around the corner.

I stare at my beautiful child—made that way because she's half him. The most gorgeous man I've ever seen in my life. One I never thought I would see again.

"How about ice cream in the bath instead?" I ask, feigning

excitement. Ice cream in the bath is something I reserve for bad days because it's her favorite thing in the world.

She jumps up and down, kicking her shoes off and tugging on her pants. "Yes!"

I laugh. "I'll scoop ice cream; you put your clothes in the hamper."

"Okay. I will."

After she's settled in the tub with two enormous scoops of chunky chocolate chip, I go right back to the kitchen and pour a shot of tequila. It burns on the way down, but the second it hits my stomach, the world around me softens.

I take one more shot for good measure and sink down onto the couch where I can hear Veda singing to herself between bites of ice cream. I might be doing shots at two in the afternoon, but I'm not a totally a shit mom.

So the person watching me is Coyote. Equal measures of excitement and worry pour through me.

Is he out there right now? I jump up and look out the window. It's stupid. He's not going to suddenly show himself after hiding for so long.

Why is he hiding, anyway? And why did he kill Irvin? Irvin didn't even know me. It makes no sense.

Oh God, he killed Irvin? Does he want to kill me? Is the father of my child a psychopath?

But no, that doesn't make sense either. He had a thousand chances by now, and all he's done is steal and clean up messes. I'd be dead ten times over by now if that was his goal.

If he's been watching me, then he knows about Veda. Does he know she's his?

My mind won't calm, reeling from all the information and possibilities.

Then I remember Crash telling me he's moving in, and I run back to the kitchen for another shot. I can't live with him. He's rude, arrogant, and he hates me. Or at least it feels that way.

True to his word, Crash shows up later that night with a tan canvas backpack slung over his shoulder.

"Where do you want me?" he asks.

"Back at the clubhouse or wherever it is you sleep." I lead him into the living room, where I've piled spare blankets and pillows. This is a two-bedroom house, and I'm not giving up my bed or making Veda sleep with me for his comfort.

"I'm only doing this to keep you safe." He tosses his backpack on the floor in front of the sofa.

"Coyote won't kill the mother of his child," I say in a hushed voice so Veda doesn't hear. She's asleep in bed, but I don't want to risk her waking up.

"You don't know that. And after what happened yesterday—"

My brows pinch as I interrupt him. "Wait. What happened yesterday?"

"Thought Char would tell you that too."

"She didn't. Do I have to call her to find out?"

He sits down and leans forward, resting his forearms on his thighs and tipping his head up so he can meet my eyes. "They fucked with us, so I fucked with them."

My teeth grind together, every muscle in my body tensing. "How did you fuck with them?"

He smirks. "Fired a warning shot. They got the message."

"Are you fucking insane?" I whisper shout. "Did you hit someone?"

"Calm down. It was that fucker's own fault for not wearing a helmet." He casually leans back and rests his ankle on his knee, throwing an arm on the back of the couch.

"Was it Coyote?" I immediately regret the question when Crash's face turns an unnatural shade of red, and I backtrack. "Not that I care. I don't even know the guy."

"No, it wasn't him. I'm sure the Bastard's fine." Thankfully he lets it go. His eyes leave me to travel around the room. "Looks like you're settling in."

I shake my head, trying to keep up with the topic change. "I am."

"That's good. Wrecker would be proud of you, you know that?"

"I hope so."

"Come here. We have something else to talk about." He pats the space next to him.

Arms folded, I plop down. "Did you shoot anyone else I should know about?"

His lips quirk, and I see it this time. I wish it didn't please me that I amused him with my snark.

"No. Nothing like that." He takes me in with his vacant hazel eyes. I wonder what he sees. I'm wearing one of Wrecker's Sons of Erebus T-shirts that hangs to my knees, a pair of shorts that you can't see because the shirt is so long, and my hair is down and straight, the way it always is. There's not much to see. "I think it's time I start bringing you around the club. Getting the guys used to seeing you."

"Why?" My face scrunches in confusion.

"It's time I do right by Wrecker and make you mine."

"Crash, that's not going to happen. You don't even like me. Most of the time, you can't even stand to be around me."

In one swift movement, he has me pinned on my back, something hard grinding into my core. His face is inches from mine, so close I can taste his minty breath. "That feel like I don't like you?"

Oh God. That steel rod is his dick? My clit swells and tingles. Obviously, she has a mind of her own because my brain is not turned on. My brain is confused as hell.

"What are you—"

He cuts me off. "I'm not an emotional guy, Riley. And I don't do romance. Wrecker left me in charge of your well-being, and I take that very seriously."

I shove at his chest, pushing him off me, much to my pussy's dismay, and get to my feet. "Wow. Nothing is sexier than bringing up my dead father while you're trying to get laid."

"You and me make sense, Ry. I don't know why you're fighting it."

"I'm my own person with my own wants and desires. I won't be with you just because my dad had some fairytale notion about you and me. That's stupid."

"You say that now, but just wait. I'll break you down," he says with determination.

Unable to continue with this discussion, I storm away to the safety of my bedroom and leave him to fend for himself. Locking the door behind me, I do something I've wanted to do since I heard Coyote was back. I was too busy with Veda earlier, but I have all the time in the world now.

I push back the clothes in my closet until I see the brown cardboard box I'm looking for. It doesn't surprise me when I find it's too light to still be hiding Coyote's cut, but I'm disappointed. Peeling back the flaps, I look inside, hoping to find a message from him or some sign he was the one who took it. But I'm let down again because it's empty.

I toss the box into the corner of my room, frustrated. He's out there right now; I know it.

I need figure out how to get Coyote to step out of the shadows and talk to me. And I have to do it with Crash watching my every move.

Chapter
TWELVE

Coyote

It's late, and the fucker is still inside. Was he serious when he said she was his? Did I miss something?

I creep around the house to her bedroom. Her curtains are always pulled tight, so I don't expect to see anything. I do it anyway because I need to know if he's in that bedroom with her.

My heart rate picks up, and my dark demon jumps around in my chest. I don't know what I'll do if she's taken him to bed. Lose my goddamn mind, that's for sure.

I'm surprised to find her blackout curtains aren't pulled shut—only the gauzy ones she leaves closed during the day to filter out some of the sun. With the light on inside and pitch black outside, I get a pretty view of her room.

The pounding in my ears lessens to a dull roar in the background of my mind when I find Crash isn't in there. It's just her. . . and she's damn near naked.

Lying in only a lacy bra and panties, she reaches to her nightstand and pulls out one of her toys. This one is blue and girthy with a white knob on the end that she uses to turn it on.

Jesus fuck.

She arches her back and digs her heels into the mattress as she skims the vibrating toy across her lace-covered nipples. Fuck me, she's so sexy. My cock digs painfully into my zipper, so I lower my fly and pop the button to give it some room.

Setting the toy down for a second, she sits up and reaches around her back, unhooking her bra. Her hair hangs over her shoulder, covering the breasts I'd give anything to see. Then it happens. She pulls her hair into a ponytail long enough for her to lie down then splays it across the pillow. Her dark pink buds are drawn in tight and pointing to the sky. They look delicious. Exactly as I remember.

She picks her toy back up and teases her nipples, squeezing her legs together as she does. If I were there with her, I'd spread those thighs and eat her cunt out, all while she plays with her tits. My mouth waters. I remember the way her little clit hides under the hood, and I had to spread her open to get to it. I remember the way she tastes and smells. The best pussy I ever had.

Her head falls to the side, and her eyes flutter closed as she slowly moves the toy between her breasts and down her flat belly, stopping at her pussy. Her legs spread wide, and she rubs the length of the dildo up and down her panty-covered seam.

My dick throbs in time with my pulse, my balls drawing up and begging for release. I figure I might as well get some pleasure out of this too, so I pull it free and spit a line of saliva down my shaft. I pump up and down in slow, measured strokes while watching the scene before me. My own little pornstar.

She lets the dildo rest on her abdomen while she slides her panties down her legs. I wish I could see her pussy better. I want to see her slit glisten with arousal and know if she's still bare or if she leaves hair down there now.

I groan when she teases the tip of the toy along her slit a few times before slowly working it inside. I curse Wrecker for updating the windows to double pane, making it impossible to hear if she's making any sounds while she works herself up.

Sliding a hand over my tip, I collect the precum and use it for more lube. My strokes come harder and faster, coordinating with the thrusts of the dildo. The hand that's not moving the vibrator lowers from her tit, where she's been massaging herself, to rub at her clit.

It must be exactly what she needs because her back bows off the mattress, her lips part, and she squirms with her release. My release happens too, hard and pulsing in a way that makes it difficult to stand, and my cum sprays onto the side of the house, painting it white.

My first thought is, I'll need to clean it up later. But my second wins out. I'll leave it there, marking my territory outside her window.

It's animalistic and juvenile, but I don't give a shit.

My eyes go back to the window as I tuck myself into my pants and zip up. Riley is sitting up on the bed now, facing me, but with her eyes cast down, focusing on straightening out her underwear to put them back on. She draws them up her legs and stands to get them over her hips.

As she turns to search for her bra, her eyes skim past the window, and I quickly duck down. Jerking off while watching her through a window isn't how I want to reintroduce myself.

She thinks about putting the bra back on but gives a slight shake of her head and tosses it into the corner. When I have her back in my life, I'll burn every single bra she has and force her to go without so I can have access to her tits whenever I want. My dick twitches at the thought.

But first, I need to get her back.

After pulling a T-shirt over her head, she jiggles her door handle, testing to make sure it's locked, and gets into bed, pulling her covers up to her neck.

Was she checking to make sure it was locked? Why? Is she worried about Crash getting in?

She doesn't need to. I'll kill the fucker if he even thinks about trying anything with her.

Right before she turns out the bedside light, she bites her lower lip with a smile and gazes back over to the window. This time I don't duck. For a second, I think she can see me. But maybe she doesn't because she turns the light out with no recognition on her face, dousing the room in darkness.

It was a close call, too close, actually. I'm getting reckless and a little too brave. But after my talk with Loki, the thought of her knowing I'm here is a lot less scary. The thought of meeting Veda doesn't terrify me anymore, either.

Maybe I can be the guy they need me to be.

I walk into the clubhouse a week later, pissed that fuckwad, Crash, won't leave. He takes Riley to work while a prospect sits at the house with the babysitter. Then he brings her home, eats the food she prepares, and hangs out with my kid. He's taking my place in my family before I had a chance to ease my way in.

I hate that motherfucker.

The one thing he doesn't have, though, are her nights. Those belong to me and her, even if she doesn't realize I'm watching her while she makes herself come. Each night she has on different lingerie and uses a different toy.

Last night, it was an oval-shaped device with what looked like puckered lips protruding from the top. She came five seconds after holding that thing up to her clit. I'll have to remember that.

"You ready to raise some hell?" Khan asks and slaps me on the back before taking a seat next to me at the bar.

"That fuckin' hurt," I gripe.

I'm not a little man. I'm tall and strong from years of yoga and riding, but instead of having bulky muscles like Khan, mine are long, lean, and tight.

"Pansy." He pounds on the bar. "Duncan, need a beer."

"On it," Duncan says, and is quick to get one in front of him.

"And no, I'm not ready. I'm heading out in just a minute." I look at the time on my phone, noting Riley's nearly done with work. Sometimes, I'll stick around her place and watch my kid play while she's at work, and others, like today, I'll hang out at the clubhouse and catch up with the guys.

"You patched in over a week ago, and you have yet to party with us as a full-fledged member. That's some bullshit, right there." He fists the pint glass, making it look like a coffee mug in his oversized hand.

"Can't leave Riley alone with that asshole. I don't trust him."

Khan turns from me to the bar. "Duncan, you're on Riley duty tonight. Make sure that fuckin' creep doesn't make his way into her bed, yeah?"

But it's not just Crash I'm worried about. Duncan watching my girl play with her pussy through her window has blood roaring in my ears, and I growl out, "Not fuckin' happening."

Sly comes over, having heard our argument. "Come on, bro. It's one night."

"Would you let someone else watch over Bexley?" I ask Khan.

It's then Bexley appears, flinging her arm around Khan's shoulders. "Bexley doesn't need anyone to look after her because Bexley is a grown-ass woman who can take care of herself. Right, babe?" she asks, and because it's her, she doesn't kiss the ogre on the cheek. She bites the flesh just above his beard hard enough to leave teeth marks.

"Damn straight," he says, wrapping an arm around her waist and bringing her in close. "Stay for a few hours, Coyote; Duncan can handle it."

I debate his suggestion, knowing Riley won't be going to bed for a while and I could get back before my nightly show begins.

"Fine." I eye Duncan down, pinning him with a murderous look. "Anything happens to her, and it's your ass. Park your bike at the end of the drive and hike through the trees to her house. Stay out of sight."

"No problem. I can handle this," the eager prospect reassures me.

"You better," Khan says, letting him know it's not just me who will beat his ass.

Two hours later, the clubhouse is full of bikers—members and hangarounds alike—and women. Not as many as I'm used to seeing at a party, but enough to keep the men busy.

The two house mice who cook and clean up after the guys, Tabitha and Sissy, set out trays of food that are devoured the second they hit the bar. The beer is flowing, shots are being passed around, and everyone is looking to party. Even Khan's uptight lawyer.

"I got something I want to talk to you about," Loki says to me.

We're playing a game of pool, or at least I am. He's too busy showing Birdie how the game is played, which he's doing by sliding up behind her and grinding into her ass as she leans over to make a shot.

"Oh, yeah?"

"Let's talk about this outside, yeah?" He kisses Birdie's neck. "Gotta take care of some club business, babe."

Watching the easy way Birdie fits into Loki's life makes me jealous. For a long time, I believed that having a woman made you weak, took away your focus and your freedom. Spending so much time with Loki, Khan, and Roch has changed my mind.

Having women at their sides has given them an unstoppable drive to protect everything we stand for.

"I would argue with you since this is a party, but I'm dying to show them pictures of my dress." Birdie claps her hands excitedly and dashes away.

"Wedding's coming up. Can't believe you're getting hitched." I give his shoulder a shove as we walk outside.

"If it were up to me, we would've driven to Vegas by now. Can't wait to make this shit legal." He thumps the end of a pack of cigarettes before pulling the plastic off. "Don't say shit. I'm drinking, and I can't not smoke when I drink."

I shake my head, grinning. "Wasn't going to."

We sit down on two sturdy Adirondack chairs Khan made. Now that he doesn't have a court date looming over his head, he's had a lot of time on his hands. On top of being the general contractor for Roch's house and his own, he's making furniture built for big men like him. Guess the fucker was tired of breaking chairs every time he sat down.

Seeing me and Loki talking, he joins us by the fire pit.

"We've been earning more than we can wash," he starts. "So I've been looking into businesses that might be a good investment for the club. I came across a strip club downtown. Owner wants to offload, and I told him we might be interested."

"Oh, yeah?" I scratch my chin through my beard.

"I like it. It'd be easy to cook the books and free up our cash a lot quicker than construction and the shop," Khan says. "Plus, it'll piss Bexley off, and I fuckin' love making that woman mad."

"Now we just need someone to run it. Sly, Moto, Bullet, Roch, and Goblin are busy with the guns, Khan is running construction, and I need to be free to go wherever I'm needed," Loki says, and both men turn to me.

"I don't know anything about strip clubs."

The thought of a confined space with no windows and a smoke machine makes my skin itch, and the demons claw at my insides. Not even a room full of naked chicks could make me want to spend time there.

"You don't need to. You'll have a manager for day-to-day

shit. Just need you to hire good people, make sure those good people don't fuck with business, and keep an eye on the customers coming and going. Sly will take care of the books," Loki says, smoke leaving his nostrils and mouth as he speaks.

"Sounds like something I could do." I wondered when he was going to tell me how I could contribute to the club. The situation isn't ideal, but I'll figure out a way to make it work.

"Cool. I'll get in touch with them." Loki tosses the butt of his cig into the fire. "Now, what are we going to do about the Sons?"

"Fuckin' kill 'em all." Goblin touches the bandage on his head. Aiyana ended up putting in thirteen stitches.

"It'd be hard to find somewhere to bury that many bodies, don't you think?" I ask, humor in my tone even though I want nothing else.

"He sent us a warning shot. Let's return fire," Loki says cryptically.

An hour later, we have a plan in place, and it's time for me to head back to Riley's. As I move to leave, I laugh at Khan, who currently has a TENS unit attached to his abdomen at max level. He drops to his knees, screaming like a baby. I had no idea such a big man could reach such a high pitch.

"That's what I have to go through when this baby's ready to come out," Truly says to Roch, the control box in her hand.

Roch yanks it from her grip and turns it off, shaking his head.

"Thank you, brother," Khan breathes, panting like he ran a marathon.

I chuckle and slip around the side of the house. I have a big night ahead of me. With things in motion for the Sons, it's time to make a move. I need her by my side to protect her from the aftermath when the Sons no doubt retaliate.

Chapter
THIRTEEN

Riley

I have done everything in my power to goad Coyote into stepping out of the shadows. I wear my best lingerie, get myself off in the most provocative ways I can think of, and each night, I make eye contact through the window.

What the hell is he waiting for?

Having an almost stranger stalking me should be terrifying; even after only knowing Coyote for a few hours, I know he wouldn't hurt me. And to be honest, I get off on the fact that he watches. It's wrong, but it makes me feel powerful and desired.

God, I'm so fucked in the head.

Last night, I even suction-cupped a dildo to my full-length mirror and fucked myself on it. The man must have some serious resolve not to burst through my window and show me how it's done.

Which is why I woke up this morning in a mood. I'm tired, I'm PMSing, and I'm cranky, so instead of getting ready for work, I decide to call in sick and spend the day at home with Veda.

"The prospect is outside if you need him," Crash says as he pushes his feet into his shitkickers.

I wave him off. "I'm fine."

He pauses in front of where I'm curled up on the couch with a heating pad. "Need anything?"

"Nope." I've resorted to only supplying him with one-word answers, making it perfectly clear that I don't want him here.

It's been a week of him sleeping on my couch, and I'm over it. I know who the threat is, and I welcome whatever he wants from me.

Bending over, he sweeps a piece of hair off my cheek and tucks it back into my ponytail. It's a move that would've had me obsessing about its meaning before knowing Coyote was around. But not now.

I give him a tight smile my grammar school teachers would've scoffed at. Pleasantries are woven into the fabric of my being, but as I work to deconstruct everything about the way I was raised, I'm discovering who the real Riley is. I don't think she's someone who is kind to a man who won't leave her house.

"See ya."

"'Kay," I say, keeping my eyes on my phone.

He leaves, and I go check on Veda. Finding her camped out on the bench in her bay window with a stack of books next to her, reading out loud, I kneel and look at what she's reading.

"Who are you reading to?" I ask.

"The man," she says, calm as can be.

"What man?" I look out the window and only see the trees and the view of downtown Reno.

"The nice man who looks like me." Her eyes don't leave the page.

Shit. She's seen Coyote, and not only that, but she recognized the resemblance. Has he shown himself to her? Or has she just caught a glimpse? It's one thing to spy on me, but spying on Veda has my mama bear instincts kicking in. While I don't think he has bad intentions, I don't know that for sure.

This changes things.

"I see. When did you see him?"

"Yesterday in the trees. He smiled at me."

Standing up, I decide it's time for the stalker to get stalked. "I need to do some stuff outside. Can you stay inside for me?"

"Okay, Mommy."

I push my feet into a pair of boots and set off into the forest. If I were him, I'd camp out on the west side of the property because my neighbors are further away on that side.

There's no question in my mind that he's sleeping here. He's pretty adamant about sticking close and keeping an eye on things.

I know for sure he doesn't follow me to work since Crash would've noticed another biker tailing me. But I don't know if he stays at the house all day and watches Veda or if he leaves.

I walk for what feels like forever while keeping an ear open for Veda and making sure I stay clear of the front of the house, where the prospect is standing guard. I've almost given up when I come across a small pup tent I recognize. Holy hell, I found him.

Well, not him because the mesh tent is unoccupied. I unzip it and slip inside, feeling all kinds of excited at being in his space. The blue and yellow sleeping bag I remember is gone, replaced by a plain black one, but the backpack looks the same.

I open the front pocket and find a multi-tool, a lighter, a fat stack of cash, a bag of weed, and wrapping papers. *Boring.* I put it all back and move to the main pocket, finding mostly wadded-up clothes and socks. But then my hand touches a book. I pull it out and realize it's not a book but a photo album. The edges are stained black, and the corner looks like it's been burned.

I move outside, where I'll be able to hear Veda's shouts if she comes looking for me, and take a seat on a tree stump. The first page is full of baby pictures. I do a double-take, thinking they're pictures of Veda, but no. These are of a little boy.

I run my finger down the chubby cheeks of a baby Coyote, wondering what his real name is. The resemblance is uncanny. God really said copy and paste with these two. Everything except her eyes, I think.

On the next page, there's a family photo. A white man stands with his arms crossed, not looking all that happy to be posing for the picture. A Black woman, who's holding a six-month-old baby Coyote, beams at the camera, unaware of the miserable man behind her.

I get a feeling of satisfaction seeing who Coyote comes from. These are Veda's grandparents. I wonder where they live and if someday we'll get to meet them.

Slowly, I study page after page, watching Coyote grow up. Then, around age eight or nine, the pictures abruptly stop. I flip through a few more blank pages until I come across a stack of papers and pictures that aren't neatly pressed behind plastic like the others.

I unfold a newspaper first, careful not to tear it because I can tell it's old. *The Reno Gazette* is big across the top with teasing pictures from stories inside.

Skimming lower, I read the headline, *Reno Man Charged with Arson and Homicide.*

My heart jumps in my chest, and my stomach sinks. I know what this is before I read it, but the desire to know the details has my eyes taking in each word like it's the most important thing I've ever read. I don't realize I'm crying until a drop falls from my cheek onto the paper.

"Shit." I pull it off my lap and wave it back and forth to dry it off. After my tear has evaporated, I fold it back up and set it in the album, ready to look at the rest of the papers. One is his birth certificate. I smile. "Apollo Hawkins."

It's such a cool name.

I put that back in a pile and flip through more pictures of Coyote from when he was older, and though I don't know what the story is behind them, he doesn't look happy. In fact, he looks miserable. The pictures stop before I see what he looked like as a teenager.

Carefully, I put everything back in the album the way I found it. The excitement of learning more about him is gone, and now I just feel like I'm violating his privacy. It was wrong for me to snoop this way. I may not care that he's been going through my things, but something tells me he would care a lot.

Putting it back in his backpack, I return his belongings to their rightful place, brush my hands down his sleeping bag so he doesn't see hand and knee prints, and zip the tent up.

"Mommy, I'm hungry," Veda's voice calls out.

Perfect timing. My feet move double-time back to the house. I scoop Veda up into my arms, something I rarely do anymore because she's so big. She definitely got her height from her daddy. I hug her to my chest, burying my face in her neck.

Coyote lived such a hard life. My heart hurts for a child who lived through such a nightmare. No wonder he's a nomad and doesn't like to be indoors. Trauma like that is enough to last a lifetime.

"I want lunch." Veda's words are labored since I'm holding her so tight.

"Sure. Let's do it."

"Where were you?" A voice sounds behind me, making me jump. Turning around, I see the prospect, Tigger. Like the fictional character, he's tall, lanky, and bright orange. His hair, his eyebrows, and his freckles, all orange. I'm assuming the carpet matches the drapes, but we aren't that close.

"A walk. Is that okay with you?" I ask.

"Sorry, it's just that Crash doesn't want you out of my sight."

"I know, and I appreciate it, but it wasn't a big deal." I go inside to make my daughter lunch.

The day goes on slowly. My body goes through the motions, but my head isn't here. It's off somewhere else, unable to think about anything other than a boy, only a few years older than Veda, losing his dad to prison and his mom to smoke inhalation.

I don't bother making dinner, claiming to still not feeling well, even though a little ibuprofen and caffeine sent my headache and cramps packing. But Veda was excited to have cereal for dinner, something I rarely allow. And Crash? Well, I don't know how Crash felt about it because I'm still ignoring him.

Bath and bedtime go easily, and I excuse myself from Crash's presence, telling him I'm tired. Once my bedroom door is locked behind me, I take a seat on my bed. It's still a while before my stalker will show up, and I need to figure out a way to get over this mental doom cloud I'm under.

His nightly visits are all we have, and I don't want to waste it by not being at my best. But as the minutes tick by and my mood doesn't improve, I know it's not going to happen. So instead, I close the curtains and get under the sheets.

My stalker won't get a show tonight.

I startle awake and sit up. I don't know what woke me up, but it has me on guard.

"You think a locked window and drawn curtains will keep me away?" a gruff voice says.

My heart picks up its pace, and I blink rapidly to see through the dark. A shadowed figure steps toward me, and I scream. Seconds later, the person is flying across my bed, wrapping a hand around my mouth, and pressing their nose to my temple.

"Shh." Their warm breath hits my skin.

If I wasn't still in the place between sleep and awake, I'd

realize right away who it was. But my brain can't get past the fact that an intruder is in my room.

"Stop screaming, Little Owl. I'm not here to hurt you."

Little Owl.

I turn to face him, but it's still too dark to get a good look. His hand lowers, and I ask, "Coyote?"

Before he can answer, Crash is knocking at my door. "You okay? Thought I heard something."

"Tell him you're okay," Coyote instructs in a low voice.

"Am I okay?" I need to know if Coyote is the man I've built him up to be for all these years or if I was entirely wrong.

"What do you think?"

The question feels weighted, like he's testing me.

Everything in me says that I should trust him, so I shout, "I'm fine. Nightmare."

Coyote's chest deflates audibly, and I know I said the right thing. As much as I was questioning his intentions, I think he was questioning mine too. And with good reason, because what I've kept from him is enough to make a man like him go to the extreme.

"Need anything?"

"No, thank you."

"Okay."

Coyote relaxes, taking his hands off me and reaching to the nightstand to flip on a lamp. I rub my eyes, trying to adjust to the sudden light, and do it quickly because I want to see the man next to me on my bed.

I hold my breath as he slowly comes into focus. His light brown complexion is flawless except for an unruly short beard. He has new piercings now: his nose, septum, lip, and both ears. He's the epitome of a bad boy. But one look into his soulful brown eyes, and I know every assumption I've made about this man is true. He's pure and kind.

117

Don't get me wrong, I see the darkness. It's there in spades, but it's not for me.

My heart stutters in my chest as flashbacks of the last time we were this close play at a warp speed in my mind.

"Coyote," I breathe out.

"You've got some explaining to do, Little Owl." His voice is hushed, and his tone is teasing, but there's an intensity there that tells me he means it.

My eyes drift lower, stopping on the black leather vest he's wearing. The same one I spent so many hours memorizing while it was in my custody. "You found your cut."

"Not what I meant."

"You've seen our daughter." It's not a question. Veda told me as much.

"I have." His eyes bounce back and forth between mine, searching for what? Deception? He won't find it. I'm ready to tell him everything.

"She's beautiful, huh?" My voice cracks, and my eyes well with tears thinking about how he must've felt finding out I kept his kid from him for all these years. But I had my reasons.

"Just like her mama." Guilt makes me tear up, and fat tears run down my face.

"You're going to love her," I offer.

"You saying that because you got caught or because you want me in her life?"

"I want you in her life. I always did, but I was scared." I reach over and move to rest a hand on his in support, but he jerks it away before my touch lands. I freeze in midair and bring my hand back to my lap.

"Scared of what?"

"We weren't in a relationship, and I didn't know you at all. I was worried you'd reject me, or worse, Veda, and I couldn't risk it. Every time I visited Wrecker, I thought about going back to the clubhouse and seeing if you were there. But I chickened out over and over until Veda was old enough. I knew you'd be pissed I waited so long. If you even wanted her at all." It's true. I didn't set out to keep her away; it just happened.

"So you kept her from me because you were nervous?"

"When you put it like that—"

"You mean the truth?" His lips thin into a line.

"I'm not explaining it well."

"I don't know how you'd ever explain it in a way that'd make fuckin' sense to me." The muscles in his neck are so tense I can see his carotid pounding just below the skin.

"You're right. I'm sorry. There's no excuse good enough."

"To make matters worse, you took my cut. Might as well have taken the blood from my veins or the air from my lungs." He pounds a fist to his chest. "This means everything in the world to me, and you took it."

"I don't have an excuse for that either. It was dumb and childish," I say.

If he doesn't let me get away with keeping Veda from him after explaining the intense inner turmoil I was experiencing, I don't think he'll let me get away with stealing the cut just because I fell in love the night we met. That would make me sound even more pathetic than I already do.

"Damn right it was."

Chapter

FOURTEEN

Coyote

I didn't think I'd have this much rage when I finally came face to face with Riley, but here we are. I've thought about this moment more times than I'd like to admit, and in none of those fantasies was I this damn pissed.

"I can't take it back. I don't have a time machine. But I can try to make it up to you," she says. She's looking up at me with eyes so wide I can see the whites all around her bright blue irises. So innocent, I'd swear they belong to a newborn baby.

"How will you do that?" I skim down her body suggestively, taking in the pebbled nipples that poke through the thin fabric of her tank top. With one leg dangling over the edge of the bed and the other spread wide, bent at the knee, I can see her cotton panties and the outline of her cunt. It's a dick move, but I'm not feeling very nice right now.

She pulls her long, dark hair over her shoulders and draws her old lady afghan over her bottom half, effectively keeping me from ogling her.

"I don't know, but I will. We can start by introducing you to her."

I arch a brow. "With your guard dog in the other room?"

Her expression sours. "He's only there because he thinks you're after me. He said you killed Irvin. Is that true?"

It's not a question I was expecting, but I should've known Crash would say whatever he needed to and scare Riley off. "Yes."

Her sculpted brows pull together. "Are you after me?"

"If you only believe one thing I ever tell you, believe that I'd never do anything to hurt you or Veda." It's the God's honest truth. The second I saw them, both she and Veda became my family.

"Then why did you kill Irvin?"

I push back my cut and lift my shirt to reveal the wound. "Fucker stabbed me."

"Oh." Her gaze latches onto the bandage. Or at least that's what I think until I notice her tongue peeking out to lick her lower lip and her fingers tickling up and down her other forearm.

My dick begs to skip to the part where I can sink into the tightest, most perfect pussy I've ever known. But my head won't get on board. Not yet, anyway. I still have more questions.

"You want to explain why you were at the Bastards' clubhouse the night we met?" I ask, dropping my shirt.

My ego is stroked when she blinks as though coming out of a dream. I've been lusted after by women before, but it was always more for my title or my image, not for who I really am. There's no doubt in my mind that Riley is attracted to me, with no ulterior motive. She's in this world already; she has a biker on the other side of that door who would make her his old lady in a heartbeat. Yet it's me she's giving hungry eyes to.

"I don't even know why I was there. Not really." Her finger weaves through the small holes in the crochet on her lap.

"Not good enough." I stand up and move to the other side of the room, putting space between us. Being this close to her, I'm likely to let her off easily by allowing vague answers. "I'm not interested in lies and games, Little Owl. Be real with me."

"I am being real. It's just a long story."

"Got nothin' but time," I say.

She bites her lip as she gathers her thoughts. "I spent eight years of my life thinking Wrecker was my dad. Then, out of nowhere, my mom moved us away. She told me he wasn't really my dad and then refused to say anything more about it. I accepted it because I was a child and trusted my only remaining parent. But by seventeen, I had questions, so I began digging. That's when I found a picture of my mom and a man with a Royal Bastard cut."

Wait, her dad was a Bastard. Who? I run through the list of potential members, but I haven't been a member long enough to know who was around back then. I was in my early teens and living on the streets when all this happened.

"Your dad was a Bastard?"

"That's what I wanted to find out. At the time, I was battling with who I was and thought it might give me some answers."

"What kind of answers?" I ask.

"I never fit in with my mom's side of the family. The important things to them—money, image, and clout—weren't important to me. So I booked a ticket to Reno. I figured I could kill two birds with one stone. I'd go find the man who was supposedly my bio dad and then go see Wrecker."

"How did you know Wrecker would even want to see you?"

"At that point, it had been nine years since I'd seen him, but I remembered everything about him. He loved me, and I couldn't imagine that love had disappeared when he found out I wasn't his. So I got on a plane—without my mom knowing—and went to the Royal Bastards' clubhouse. I walked in the door with this dumb, naïve notion that it'd be like the movies. I'd find that my dad had spent his whole life feeling like a part of him was missing, and the second he saw me, he'd know."

"But that's not what happened," I guess.

"No. What I saw made me sick, so I turned tail and ran."

"What did you see?" I try to remember that night, but nothing stands out as being anything other than the usual clubhouse shenanigans.

"Naked chicks dancing, porn on the TV, bikers having sex out in the open." The look of disdain on her face rubs me the wrong way.

"You think Wrecker's clubhouse looked any different? Because darlin'—"

"I know that now, but you have to remember I was a very sheltered seventeen-year-old. I wasn't even allowed to watch rated R movies." She stares at the wall, transported back to that night. "I was scandalized in the worst way possible, and I thought, if any of those men in there really were my dad, I didn't want anything to do with them."

"So you went outside and cried, which is where I found you," I fill in for her.

Her lips turn up, and her eyes meet mine. "Exactly. You weren't anything like the men I just saw."

"I'm more like them than not."

"Maybe, but not in the ways that count." She gets a dreamy look in her eyes. "You were wild in the way waves crash into rocks and lightning storms light up the sky. Unpredictable and beautiful. Nothing like the men I saw that night who were wild in a 'fuck everything that moves and drink until your liver gives up' kind of way."

I like that. I like it a lot. The heart of a biker resonates with me like nothing else ever has, but all the other bullshit doesn't speak to me at all. It's shocking and fills me with some unfamiliar emotion that she knew all of that after only an hour of knowing me.

"You lied about your age," I remind her.

She blushes. "I was hoping you didn't pick up on that."

"Feels like shit knowing I slept with an underage girl."

123

"The age of consent in Nevada is sixteen. I looked it up." She has the gall to look proud of herself.

"Doesn't fuckin' matter. You weren't a legal adult. That was a rule I made for myself a long ass time ago, and you made me break it without even knowing."

"Would you have slept with me had you known?"

"Hell no." I tug at the neckline of my shirt, the suffocating feeling of unease clawing at my throat.

I know I'm destined for Hades, but I want to have a clean conscience when I go. I want to know all the shit I did in my life was for a reason I believed in. I never wanted to be a man who took whatever he wanted, regardless of consequence, and I don't mean legally. My morals are important to me, and she made me violate my code by lying.

"Then I don't regret it." Her soft tone goes even quieter as she plays with a loose piece of yarn on her afghan.

She doesn't get it, proving that she's still that naïve girl.

I scoff but choose to move on with my questioning. "Where did you go after I fell asleep?"

"Our time together was so perfect. I didn't want to risk things being weird in the morning, so I called Wrecker."

I push off the wall and move to sit on the corner of the bed. "After you stole my cut."

Her chin tucks, and she straightens her spine. "Yes."

"Wrecker didn't wonder what you were doing at the Bastards' clubhouse?"

"If he did, he didn't say anything to me about it. He made a pot of coffee, and we talked for hours. I even missed my flight the next morning because we had so much to say to each other. I think he was just genuinely excited to have me back in his life." The soft smile on her face tells me she really loved the man. It must've hurt to lose him. "Anyway, I started visiting him once a month after that, and I realized I didn't need a relationship with my bio dad because I had him."

"When did you find out you were pregnant?"

"It took me a while. Sex education was non-existent where I went to school, and my mom's idea of "the talk" was telling me only whores open their legs before there's a diamond on their finger. It didn't even cross my mind until a friend told me I was getting fat."

I fuckin' hate that she grew up in an environment like that with so much judgment and negativity. A girl as sweet as she is should've had nothing but love and acceptance.

"How did your mom take the news?" I ask, praying she doesn't give me a reason to make that woman's life hell.

"She wasn't happy. She tried to marry me off to whoever she could find willing to make an honest woman out of me. I refused, which embarrassed her and royally pissed her off. But then Veda was born, and she fell in love the way everyone falls in love with Veda. After that, she dropped it." Her gaze drifts over to the framed picture of our daughter on her nightstand. "Do I get to ask questions too, or is this one-sided?"

"What do you want to know?" The words feel like acid coming out of my mouth. This isn't something I do, but Riley has a way of bringing things out in me no one else ever has.

Too quickly, her gaze shifts down, and she goes back to fiddling with her blanket. Whatever she wants to talk about is making her uncomfortable, which has me feeling uncomfortable.

"I guess I'll start with easy questions. What's your real name?"

If that's easy, I don't want to get to the hard stuff. One Google search of my name will tell her all my dark secrets.

"Why does it matter?" I fire back a little too harshly.

"Veda's birth certificate, for one," she says softly. "I wanted your name on there, but they wouldn't allow it unless I had your legal name."

"Why do you want me on it?"

"You're her dad, aren't you?"

"I haven't even met her."

"I guess that's my next question because it doesn't matter what I want anymore. It's all about that little girl in the other room. Do you want to be her dad?"

I think about it for longer than I should, but Riley gives me the mental space I need to walk myself through it. I never pictured myself becoming a dad. Not once. Thinking about it now, I can come up with a hundred reasons it doesn't make sense. Despite that, I say, "Apollo Hawkins. Add it to her certificate."

Her eyes shine with happiness, and a beautiful smile blooms across her lips. "Okay. I will."

"What's your next question?"

She clears her throat, and her cheeks turn an embarrassing shade of red, but the smile stays fixed in place. "Have you been *watching* me?"

The question is rhetorical, but I answer anyway.

"We both know I have." I place my hand at her side, leaning my body toward her. "You put on quite a show for me."

"I thought it was the best way to grab your attention." She tries to brush it off with a giggle, keeping her eyes trained on where her fingers are tangled in the blanket. "I don't know what I was doing."

I tip her chin up. "Looked like you knew exactly what you were doing, Little Owl."

"I really wanted to bring you out of the shadows."

"It worked. Night after night, watching you make yourself come. Drove me fuckin' crazy." I brush my thumb over her heated cheeks.

"I'm glad you're here. Feels like a dream with how many nights I wished you were with me." She cups a hand over mine, holding it against her soft face.

"You didn't have someone else to warm your bed?" It's a question that I've been obsessing over. The last time we were together, she was so innocent. I don't think she even knew what a dildo was back then. Now she's a connoisseur, and I don't think she got that way on her own.

She loops her hands around my neck and lays down, pulling me down with her. I part her legs with my knees and settle myself between them, holding my upper half up on my elbows.

"I've spent five years chasing the high you gave me that night. When I couldn't find it with another man, I turned to toys, buying every different style I could find," she whispers.

I'm close enough to taste her breath now. "And did they work?"

She shakes her head, her lips nearly brushing mine with the movement. "Not even a little."

"Your poor, neglected pussy." I grind my rock-hard erection against her, earning myself a whimper. "Guess I'll have to do something about that."

"Please," she begs.

"We have a lot more to talk about."

"I know, but can't it wait? I need to be close to you again."

I take her mouth with mine, fusing our lips together and swallowing her surprised gasp. Fuck, she tastes like sin, and I know without a doubt I'll never walk away from this woman. I've never had an addiction before, but I do now, and it's Riley's soft lips moving with mine while her body writhes underneath me, begging for more.

My tongue sweeps through her mouth, inviting her own to tangle with mine, which it does in the most seductive way with little flicks of the tip followed by slow, deep strokes.

It makes me think of where else I can put that talented mouth to good use.

"I'm going to fuck you, Little Owl, but you have to promise you'll be quiet. We don't want to wake your best friend in the other room. Can you do that for me?"

She nods, giving me all the permission I need.

Chapter
FIFTEEN

Riley

Before I know what's happening, he's sitting up and yanking the covers off me. Had I been expecting this, I would've worn my sexiest lingerie, but I wore cotton briefs and a tank top to bed since I'm expecting my period any day now. I can't bring myself to care, though, not when he gazes down at my body and mouths a silent, "Fuck."

He snakes his hands under my tank and pushes up, his thumbs brushing over my nipples as he goes until the fabric is bunched under my arms. I quickly pull it the rest of the way off while he watches intently.

"They're bigger," he mutters, cupping my breasts at the side and pushing them together. After giving birth, I went from an AA to an A. It's a small but noticeable difference. "Sexy as fuck."

He leans down and sucks a nipple into his mouth, flicking his tongue along the tip before moving to the other and giving it the same attention. Spikes of pleasure zing down to my clit, making my hips undulate, searching for any kind of friction they can find.

Sitting back up, he grips the side of my plain white panties and rips the hem, then moves to the other side and does the same.

"I could've taken them off," I say as he tosses them over his shoulder.

"Easier this way." His hand moves to my belly, and a finger traces along the skin right above my pussy. Glancing down, I see he found the silvery lines from when my body was stretched beyond its capacity. I'm a small girl with a short torso, so Veda had nowhere to go but out.

"Stretch marks," I say, my cheeks heating. "They're ugly."

"Don't ever fuckin' say that again. They're beautiful." He skims over each one with something akin to worship. "I staked a claim on you five years ago. These scars belong to me, and it turns me on knowing any man you were with saw proof you were mine first."

Oh God. Somehow, he turned my biggest insecurity into something sexy. Arousal floods my core, dripping down my crack and most likely soaking the sheets under me.

He jumps up and crouches down at the side of the bed to untie his boots. Once those and his socks are off, he slides his arms out of his cut and reverently lays it on the other side of the bed before stripping out of his shirt.

My mouth goes dry at the sight of his bare torso. With clothes on, he could pass as thin, but seeing him like this? He's anything but. His abs are chiseled, his pecs are defined with just a smattering of hair between them, and his shoulders and arms are built with muscles stacked on muscles.

With his eyes glued to my naked body, he undoes the silver Royal Bastards belt buckle and pops the top button of his jeans. The last time we were together, it was dark and there was no time to look at him like this, so I eagerly take in every detail of the V leading down below his boxer briefs, his slight outie belly button, and the trail of hair below.

"Like what you see, Little Owl?" he smirks.

"Please," I beg for the second time, unable to come up with any other words.

"Part those thighs for me. I've been hungry for your juicy pussy for a long fuckin' time."

I let my knees drop to the side, biting on a fingernail to ease the anxious energy his dirty words gives me. He moves back onto the bed, resting his palms on my upper thighs. His long, calloused thumbs rub soothing circles onto my overheated skin while he makes himself comfortable on his belly.

He's now eye level with my most private of areas, but I'm so desperate to have his mouth on me again, I can't bring myself to care.

"Look at this cunt. Goddamn magical pussy," he murmurs before licking a path straight up my slit.

I gasp at the contact and grip the sheets at my side. It won't take much to get me to come, not the way it does with my arsenal of toys. He spreads my lower lips open wide with his thumbs and latches onto my clit, sucking with just the right amount of pressure to make my eyes cross and my toes curl.

"Coyote. Oh God. Yes," I say, entirely too loud and making his mouth pull away.

"Quiet, Little Owl. Don't want this to be over before I've had my fill."

I cover my face with a throw pillow to muffle my screams. It's the only way I'll get through this without alerting Crash about what's going on.

"Good girl," he says and gets back to business.

A finger enters me, hooking upward until it finds the spot I'm never patient enough to find on my own. All the while, he sucks and licks my clit, devouring me like the starved man he said he was.

I curl an arm over the pillow the second I feel the orgasm coming. My hips leave the mattress, and my thighs come together, squeezing around his head. It can't be comfortable for him, but my body is moving of its own volition at this point. I have no control.

A second finger enters me, and I bear down, intensifying the already mind-blowing orgasm. It lasts and lasts until I'm a quivering mess.

This! This is what I've been missing, what I've been searching for. It's Coyote. Only he can play my body like a fiddle, bringing me to life while also killing me in the best way.

I tear the pillow from my face, gasping from the self-inflicted lack of oxygen. Gazing between my legs, I see Coyote smirking from behind his beard that's glistening from my liquid arousal. He reaches for his shirt and rubs it down his face before crawling on top of me.

"Poor pussy was wound so tight, can't wait to feel it strangling my cock." He kisses me hard, thrusting his tongue in my mouth and forcing me to taste myself. It's dirty and wrong but turns me on all over again. "Is that what you want, Little Owl? You want my big dick inside you?"

I nod but then remember he likes it when I use my words. "Yes. Right now."

He palms my breast while he sucks and nips at my neck and earlobe. I wrap my legs around him and, with the insides of my feet, push his boxers down until his cock springs free.

"Such a greedy girl," he whispers next to my ear, then bites my lobe so hard it's bound to leave a mark.

Reaching between our bodies, he guides himself to my entrance. I remember the overwhelming fullness of our first time. It's something I haven't felt since but am desperate to again. He inches his way in, little by little, with a teasing slowness that drives me insane.

"God, you're so wet for me. Were you this soaked for the others, Little Owl?"

"No. Only for you," I admit.

"I hope you enjoyed your time with them because that shit

131

won't happen again. These are my scars, my tits, my pussy. No one else will ever get any of it from you. Do you understand me?" His eyes burn into mine with such seriousness that I know this isn't his usual dirty talk.

"Yes. I understand," I whisper.

"I'll fuckin' kill anyone who tries. Including that lonely motherfucker on your couch in the other room. You feel me?"

I scrap my nails down the sides of his shaved head, his soft neck, and further until I land on his shoulders to pull him closer. "I feel you, sweetheart."

"Good." With that settled, he thrusts all the way in, holding himself deep inside.

My back bows, and he bites down on my nipple, tugging it with his teeth.

I moan at the overwhelming mixture of pleasure and pain. This is all I want for the rest of my life. Nothing but his mouth on me, his cock inside me, and his body on top of mine. There's nothing better.

He lifts back onto his knees, tossing one of my legs over his shoulder. Both hands squeeze my thigh, and he rolls his hips as he pumps his cock in and out, taking his time to feel every inch of me. His head turns, and he drags his tongue up my inner calf before placing a kiss near my ankle, spots I never considered erogenous until this moment.

Without warning, he pulls out and picks my leg up to set it down over the other, my torso now twisted, before slapping my ass.

"On your knees." His words are hushed but demanding.

I raise to my knees, facing away from him and peering over my shoulder to watch his next move. His hand goes to the center of my back, and he pushes me forward. I catch myself on my hands, but he keeps pushing until my chest is on the mattress and my ass is in the air.

"Jesus fuck, this ass." He palms my cheeks, massaging them

and pulling them apart. If I weren't so aroused, I might be embarrassed by his view. But Coyote doesn't do anything unintentionally, so I know he's seeing exactly what he wants to. "Any of those other boys fuck you here?"

"No," I say, somewhat scandalized.

"Good. Then I'll be first." He rubs a finger through my sex and brings the moisture up to my puckered entrance, where he rubs small circles. "You'd like that, Little Owl, wouldn't you?"

A zing of pleasure tears through me. I've never once thought about anal sex before, but now that I am, I'm not sure how to feel about it.

"Will it hurt?"

"For a minute. But then it'll feel so fuckin' good." He presses the tip of his finger inside. I clench around the intrusion. "Gonna have to work on getting you to relax before we can go there, though."

His finger leaves me, and his cock is at my pussy, rubbing up and down before pushing inside. He grips my hips and pounds into me so hard a loud *slap* echoes in the room.

"Gonna be so hard keeping this quiet. Next time I fuck you, better make sure he's not around." His next thrust is gentler but feels no less powerful. He stretches me in the most delicious way from this position, and I'm back to gripping the sheets.

His fingertips dig into my hips as he controls his movements. He rolls his hips so that every time he pushes in, the base of his cock brushes up against my swollen clit. Holy shit, I really, really like this position.

"My pussy," he says in a raspy moan, bending over me long enough to fist the hair at the base of my skull. He uses his grip as leverage to fuck harder into me.

The sting grounds me while his dick sends me flying in pleasure. I press my face into the mattress as another release hits me hard and without warning.

If the last orgasm was rolling waves of ecstasy, this one is a tidal wave, swallowing me whole.

"That's it. Milk my cock, Little Owl," he says through gritted teeth. "Just like that."

He's talking as if I have any control over what my body is doing right now, which I absolutely don't. My pussy continues to spasm around him as he releases my hair and wraps an arm around my middle. The other presses into the mattress, holding both of us up. With his sweat-slick body curled around mine, he buries his cock as deep as it's ever been, right before warmth gushes inside me.

I should panic at the lack of condom, but it feels good having his seed inside me. I'm not on any sort of contraception since the pill throws my hormones off, and I've heard too many horror stories about IUDs. But since my period is so close to starting, I'm not worried about another unplanned pregnancy.

He brushes my hair to one side and bites into my shoulder. "Next time, I'll be there when you take the test, I'll be there to run to the store at three a.m. to get you pickles and ice cream, and I'll sure as shit be there when you push out more of my babies."

I freeze, completely shocked at his statement. Was he trying to get me pregnant this time?

"Don't look so surprised, Little Owl," he says with amusement.

"I'm not on the pill," I say.

"I know."

"How could you possibly know that?"

"I've searched through every inch of this house. No contraception of any kind."

We both know he's been in this house multiple times, but I assumed it was something we'd ignore because I mean it when I say out loud, "That's really creepy."

He pulls out, and his cum drips down my thighs. "Don't give a fuck."

I shake my head at how easily he dismisses his behavior, but if I'm honest, I don't give a fuck either. Nothing about us has been conventional or traditional, two things I've had in spades throughout my life. Neither one has gotten me anywhere, so I think it's time to change things up.

"I'd go get a towel, but I think seeing my big dick might give your boy a complex." He gives my ass two quick pats.

I roll my eyes and fall to my stomach, squeezing my thighs together to stop any more of the mess from getting all over my bed. "Grab a T-shirt from the hamper?"

He doesn't have to find where the hamper is because, as he said, he's searched through every inch of the house. He opens the closet and reaches in, pulling out an oversized band tee. Glancing over, he raises a brow in question, and I nod.

"Spread," he orders, and I obey.

He's gentle as he cleans me up the best he can. Once he's done, I get under the covers and prop myself up with a pillow, watching as he gets dressed.

"So what now?" I ask.

"What do you mean?"

"What happens now? Do we date? Do I introduce you as my friend to Veda, or should we just tell her the truth right away?"

He zips his jeans but leaves the belt swinging and the button undone as he leans over to place a bruising kiss on my lips. "The first thing you do is get that fucker out of your house."

"He's just a friend, a worried friend. He thought you were going to kill me."

"He's not your friend." He returns to dressing himself. The second his cut is on, I realize he's leaving.

"Where are you going?"

"My tent is pitched on the west side of the house."

"You can stay," I offer.

"Don't think that's a good idea yet." Disappointment has me frowning. I don't want to be without him so soon after I just got him back. He sits on the edge of the bed. "Don't worry your pretty little head. I'll be back."

"When?"

"When I can." He leans over and kisses my frown. "Good night, Little Owl."

Then he opens the window, climbs out, and closes it in near silence.

I flip out the light and turn on my side. My mind churns with how the hell I'm going to get Crash out of my house. Even more, how the hell am I going to make him understand I want to be with Coyote, a member of a rival club?

Something tells me it won't be as easy as "getting the fucker out of my house."

Chapter
SIXTEEN

Coyote

"**T**his is it," Loki says, unlocking the door of the strip club. Looking up, I see a neon outline of a woman with huge tits and a big ass sitting on top of the words *Boom Boom Room*. Below that, an LED sign scrolls through phrases like *Live Nude* and *Full Exposure*.

"Are we keeping the name?" Goblin asks.

"Unless you can come up with something better." Loki leads us inside to a small lobby with a black tile floor, black painted walls, and a black velvet curtain stopping anyone who comes in from seeing inside. Next to the split in the curtain is a pedestal with a built-in tablet.

"How about Bastard Chicks?" Khan suggests.

"Or Royal Treatment," I say.

"Royal Treatment," Loki repeats, pulling open the curtain and flipping on the lights inside. "I like it."

"Might help class the joint up a bit." I take my last breath of fresh air from the propped open door and step inside. I'm surprised to find it's not so bad with the lights on, and unlike what I thought, there are windows lining the right-hand side of the room. They're just blacked out so no one can see in or out. That knowledge helps ease my demon.

"Brother, it'll take more than a name change to make this place classy." Loki's lip curls in disgust.

He's right. It's tacky as fuck in here. Lining the perimeter are black vinyl booths with neon triangles, squares, and circles that must glow under a black light. But with the fluorescent overhead lights on, it looks straight up out of the 80s.

A runway in the middle of the room leads to the main stage, complete, of course, with a pole. The stage is framed by a counter and bar stools for those who want to be up close and personal. Four smaller stages, also fitted with poles, are in each corner but surrounded by tables and chairs. To the left is a fully stocked bar lined with bar stools.

"Are we doing any renovations?" I lean over the bar to see what kind of setup they have.

"That's up to Khan." Loki steps onto one of the small stages.

"Hell yeah. Let's get this place fit for Royal Bastards."

"How long would a renovation take?" I ask.

"I think we could get it done in three months. Can we stay closed that long?"

"The girls might find other work, but there's never a shortage of pussy." Loki grips the pole and spins like a child.

"Probably better I vet anyone we hire on anyway," I say.

"It's a tough job, but someone's got to do it, am I right?" Khan chuckles.

"Let's go check out the office and backstage." Loki types in a code to unlock the door. "There are only two ways to get back here. Through the stage and through this door. The office is to the right."

"It's bigger than I thought it would be." I poke my head into the room, noticing a large desk, a velvet sofa, a fireproof safe, and an attached bathroom.

"I recognize this place," Goblin says. "Didn't we—"

"Yeah, this was one of Zach's clubs." Loki circles the desk.

"Who's Zach?" I ask.

"Some slimy bastard we were hired to take care of." Goblin chuckles. "Loki was on his game that day."

Before getting their gun business back, the Bastards were murder for hire. Whenever I needed some quick cash, I'd stop in and help them with a job. It was lucrative as fuck but messy and risky. Gun-running is a much cleaner business.

"Didn't you pop that guy's eyes out and stuff them in his mouth?" Khan's eyes light up with excitement.

"That's right!" Loki bends over laughing.

"Is this what you call a full circle moment?" Goblin jokes.

"I'm going to check out the rest." I lead the way to the changing room set up for the girls. One wall is lined with lockers, while the other has a row of vanities. The white counters are stained with makeup and leftover hair products. "I hope a cleaning crew is in the budget."

"I think your first order of business should be making a list, figuring out what we need to change and what we can keep. Coordinate with Khan on the renovations, and a month before we're due to open, you can start hiring." Loki grabs a knife from his belt and uses it to pick up a blue thong left behind. "Birdie isn't going to be happy about our new business venture."

"You haven't told her?" I ask.

"Not yet. I was waiting until after we're married so she can't call off the wedding."

Khan hooks an arm around the back of Loki's neck. "We can tell our women together. There's safety in numbers."

"Let's get out of here," Goblin says. "We need to prepare for tonight's festivities."

"Fuck yeah!" Khan hollers. "Time to fuck up some Sons."

Years ago, the Sons of Erebus were known for their grow operation. They supplied much of Northern Nevada and NoCal with grade-A weed. Once the drug was legalized, they had to adapt. Now they own a chain of weed shops and have a side hustle distributing PCP-laced marijuana.

They've mostly been left alone by the Royal Bastards since our lanes don't cross. But that was before their Prez shot Goblin. That kind of disrespect isn't tolerated, and now they'll pay.

"This warehouse is where they grow their own weed and dip it," Sly says, pointing to a building on a map. "There are windows on the east and west sides of the building. Coyote and Moto, you'll have to break the glass and toss the bottle bombs."

"Then run," Loki says.

"That's a given," I mutter.

"It's nothing but desert out there, so there'll be nowhere to hide until you get back to your bikes where we'll be waiting in case there's trouble. Hopefully they'll be too busy getting away to worry about looking for you." Sly pushes back from the table we're gathered around at the clubhouse. "Easy peasy."

"You guys good?" Loki pins us with a serious look that shows his worry.

I'm so used to doing whatever the fuck I want, whenever the fuck I want, and any blowback from it falling directly on me. I always thought that was the best way for me, but I can't deny that it feels fuckin' good to have someone else watching my back.

I glance over at Moto, who's cracking his knuckles and nodding. Excited energy radiates from my Japanese brother. We're both dressed in black and are without our cuts. If something goes wrong, and we get caught, wearing our cuts makes it a gang-related crime and carries more charges, so we leave them in our saddlebags.

"Fuckin' right, we're ready," I say.

It's dark out when we hop on our bikes and take off for Carson City. I haven't spoken to Riley since last night, and I briefly wonder if I should've warned her I wouldn't be around. Is that something she'd want to know?

I sent Duncan to watch over her and make sure Crash didn't lose his head, but I suspect he won't be sticking around after he gets the call that his warehouse went down in flames.

That thought has me grinning.

After this job is done, I'll go back to her house and fuck her all over again. I can already feel her warm and wet pussy gripping me tight.

I thought I'd hyped my first time with her up too much in my head, and I'd be disappointed after the second time, but the opposite is true. I'm fuckin' addicted, and I'll never get enough. Which is why I made sure she understood she was mine, not just for right now. This shit is for fuckin' ever.

Her body is so responsive. One touch has her squirming, wanting more. And when she's about to come, Jesus fuck, it's like watching the sunrise. Every minute that passes, colors get more vibrant and intense. Then when she finally lets go, her beauty is fuckin' blinding.

I spent so much of my life living for today because I never knew what tomorrow would bring. Now that I have a family, I have so much to look forward to. I haven't even officially met Veda, something I hope to resolve tomorrow. It's time she knows who her daddy is.

With all my thoughts consumed by Riley, I don't have a chance to get my head right when Loki slows and parks next to an old farmhouse, long since been abandoned, where we take cover. We line our bikes up and work to prepare without a word spoken. I double-check that we have everything we need in our backpacks before Moto and I take off toward the warehouse.

It's a half-mile away, but the sagebrush and tumbleweeds make it difficult to navigate in the dark. Both Moto and I nearly eat shit several times but make it without spraining an ankle.

It's quiet outside, but I can hear conversation and music blaring inside. We anticipated at least one guard, so it's not a shocker when we see a member of the Sons standing outside, his eyes sweeping back and forth. We could shoot him, but the gunshot would alert those inside, and that would be bad.

"Rock, paper, scissors?" Moto whispers.

"No need. I'll take him." I pull the backpack off. "Be right back."

"Cocky bastard," he mumbles as I creep toward the building.

I walk up behind him on light feet. He doesn't hear me until the last minute when I lock him in a rear naked chokehold. He tries to call out and struggles to get me off him, but it's impossible. Nine seconds, that's all it takes before he goes limp in my arms. I release him, and he falls to the ground, out like a light. Since I don't know for how long, I run my ass back to Moto.

"Lean into it," he calls out as we split up.

Those three words sum up my entire life. As a stupid teenager, I fought against any turns I came across. I thought I deserved better and riding that straight line—having a singular focus—would get me there. It wasn't until I joined the MC and heard the term *lean into it* that it finally clicked. The measure of a man is in how he handles the bad shit that comes his way. If you spend all your time fighting the bad, you'll miss all the good.

I place myself just under a high window and get out my supplies. I pour the petrol and motor oil mixture inside the bottle, shove a torn cloth in until it reaches the liquid, and then shoot a text to Moto. We need to be in sync with our attack for this to go smoothly.

He sends me a countdown of ten seconds, giving me just enough time to grab the rock in one hand and the bottle bomb in the other. When I see my phone flash, I throw the rock through the window first, then launch the bottle inside. I don't stick around to find out if it worked, but if the frantic shouting from inside is any sign, we're golden.

Moto and I meet at the back of the building and run, doing our best to avoid nature's tripping hazards. PCP is highly flammable, so we're expecting the big boom that comes when we're a mere twenty yards away. That doesn't stop the blast from knocking both of us off our feet and sending us fly-ing forward.

Cockleburs and other spiky desert plants embed them-selves in my arms and face, but I don't have time to pick them out. I jump back to my feet and help Moto up, then hightail it out of there.

Loki slow claps as we approach. "That was a thing of fuckin' beauty, brothers."

Moto and I turn around to see what we accomplished. The building is completely engulfed in flames. Only time will tell how many made it out of the building and how many died. But an explosion like that will no doubt attract law enforce-ment, and we need to be far away when that happens.

"Let's go," Khan shouts as he straddles his bike.

I feel the scrapes and bruises all over the front of my body, but pain is a liar. It tricks your body into thinking you should slow down. That shit's for the weak. Pain is temporary, but prison isn't, so I ignore it and start my bike.

The cool night air numbs my skin on the forty-five-min-ute ride to Riley's house. I should go back to the clubhouse so we can reconvene and talk about how it went, but fuck that. I need my girl, and with Crash no doubt busy for the rest of the night, I won't have to worry about him finding me sneaking into her room.

I park in my usual spot, seeing Duncan's bike there too. The kid has done right by me, and since his goal is to patch in, I vow to help get him there. I'd be damn proud to make him my brother.

Once off my bike, I do my best to brush off the worst of the cockleburs and fuckin' cactus spines from my skin, but I'm too excited to get to Riley to do too much. However, I'm not too excited to skip pulling my cut out of my saddlebag. The pride I felt being a nomad for the Royal Bastards is nothing compared to how I feel now being a patched-in brother of the Reno chapter.

I make a mental note to call Dunk and Mac to let them know I won't be going up the coast with them. I doubt they'll be surprised. They know how long I've been looking for Riley, and they're not dumb. It was never about the stolen cut. It was about losing *her* with no explanation or way to contact her. I wasn't fooling anyone but myself.

"Duncan," I call out when I see him leaning against a tree next to the house.

He turns around, grinning. "Must've gone well. Crash took off spittin' mad about thirty minutes ago."

"He's probably watching close to a million dollars in illegal weed and PCP going up in flames."

He holds out a fist, and I bump it with my own. "Guess I'm no longer needed here."

"Thanks for keeping watch, brother."

"Anytime."

We go in separate directions, him to his bike and me to my woman. *My woman.* I'll never get over how quickly things have changed.

Not needing to climb through a window this time, I get

out my key and unlock the front door. It's late, nearing midnight now, so it's not surprising that the house is calm and quiet. I lock up after myself and head straight to Riley's room. Her door is open, but I close it and flip the lock. I don't want Veda to meet me while Riley's riding my dick. Might be a little traumatic.

Riley wakes as I stumble to take off my boots while standing. She sits up abruptly and flips on the light.

"Coyote?" Her voice is raspy from sleep and sexy as fuck.

"Hey, Little Owl," I say.

I must look like I got dragged through the desert because her eyes widen in the way I love. She jumps out of bed and rushes over to me wearing flannel pants and a sports bra. "What happened?"

"Rough day at work."

Chapter
SEVENTEEN

Riley

"**O**h my God." I turn his face side to side, seeing tiny rocks and spiky things protruding from his skin. "Are those cactus spines?"

Add this to the list of reasons tonight has been weird. I spent all day waiting for the sun to go down and Coyote to climb through my window. But it never happened. Right when I decided he wasn't coming, I heard Crash in the living room shouting into his phone.

He left without telling me why or what had happened. But seeing Coyote show up like this, only a half-hour after Crash left, has me wondering if he's the reason.

"Probably." He grips my hips and tugs me close. "Nothing a kiss can't cure."

I lift on my tippy toes and press my lips to his chastely because my mind is still focused on his injuries.

"Not the kind of kiss I was after," he mumbles.

"I'll do more than kiss you, but we need to get you cleaned up first." I take his hand and quietly pull him across the hall to the bathroom. Veda usually sleeps like the dead, but I don't want to risk it, so I close the bathroom door and hold a finger up to my lips, showing that we need to keep quiet.

I find my tweezers in the medicine cabinet and force Coyote to sit down on the toilet. Only now do I see it's not just his face that's torn up. It's his arms too. Thank God for his jeans because even though they're dirty and worn thin at the knees, they held up through whatever accident caused this.

Tipping his chin up, I carefully pull out coarse weeds and barbed needles from his forehead and cheeks. He doesn't so much as wince. He just stares at me with an unidentifiable look on his face. Something close to awe, I think.

"Are you going to tell me how this happened?"

"Nope." He places his hands at my lower back, precariously close to my ass. It's not an inherently sexual touch, but my body doesn't understand. Especially since I started my period this morning, and though it's the worst time to have sex, it's also the time when I'm most horny. It's not fair.

"Why not?" I ask, plucking the final spine from between his eyes.

"Club business."

"Does it have anything to do with why Crash isn't here right now?" I detach one arm from around me and turn it over to clean his forearm up.

"Maybe." He flashes me a roguish smile.

"Fine. Don't tell me." I place that hand back at its rightful spot on my back and pull the other off. There's a gnarly scrape on the underside of his forearm that's crusted over with blood, but there are pebbles in the wound, so I won't risk reopening it. I wet a washcloth with warm water and gently rub the dirt off. "Does that hurt?"

"Not really."

"You don't have to be macho in front of me." I grin down at him. "You can cry and complain if you want."

"Little Owl, you want someone to cry and complain to you,

go wake up our daughter. I'm letting you fret over me because I know it's what you need it. But this shit is superficial. Doesn't hurt. Even if it did, I'm a man, and men don't cry over a couple scratches."

I roll my eyes and purse my lips. "Okay, tough guy."

"Feel that, baby?" He palms my ass and tugs me close enough to feel the hardness between his legs. "All man."

"Perv," I tease.

"Only a perv for you." They aren't flowery words, but they move me all the same. "Are we done here? Because I'd really like to fuck my woman now."

My woman. I like the way that sounds. I almost agree before I remember I'm surfing the crimson wave.

I smack a kiss to his lips. "Sorry, Casanova. It's not a good time."

His brows bunch. "What do you mean?"

"I started my period this morning," I say without meeting his eyes.

Besides not discussing sex with me, normal bodily functions were also not discussed in my home. Whenever I'd mention to Mom that I needed tampons or was cramping, she'd shun me and tell me those things were supposed to be kept private. I still feel a lot of shame around things that shouldn't be shameful. Just something else on the long list for me to deconstruct.

"I don't fuckin' care about a little blood." His bold words cause a blush to creep over my cheeks and chest.

"I think it's too soon for that level of closeness," I whisper.

Next thing I know, he's on his feet, cupping my face and forcing me to look into his eyes. "You don't want to have sex because you're uncomfortable, you're tired, or you flatly aren't feeling it are reasons I will respect. But being embarrassed isn't. So which is it?"

This man turns me on with his words even more than his hot as hell body. But I'm not comfortable.

"I'm sorry. I can't. Not yet. Let me keep the charade up for a little while longer that I don't do things like poop or fart or have a period."

He smiles. "Okay, Little Owl."

Then an idea sparks. "I think I know a way we can both get what we want."

I grab his hand and drag him back to the room, nervous about doing something I've never done before but excited too. If Coyote has proven anything to me, it's that he doesn't care about much. As long as I'm into what we're doing, he's down with it.

I close the door and push him to sit on the bed. His deep brown eyes twinkle at my sudden burst of energy. While pulling my hair back into a ponytail, I sink to my knees in front of him.

"Not what I thought was going to happen, but I gotta tell ya. I'm not complaining." He runs a hand down the back of my head.

"I hope you're not expecting much because this is another thing I haven't ever done." I unclasp his heavy buckle, pop the button of his jeans, and unzip him.

He groans, biting his lower lip. "Jesus fuck, you can't say things like that to me, or I'll blow the second your lips touch my cock."

"That might be better for the both of us," I joke.

Taking a steadying breath, I pull him out. His big cock is already rock hard, the fat head weeping with pre-cum. I lick the tip, curious if I'll mind the taste. Much to my surprise, it's not that bad. The tangy, salty flavor is more than tolerable, and knowing that it's his flavor makes it even better.

I stroke him up and down, eyes downcast for fear I might see him cringing with displeasure as I get comfortable with my movements.

"Good girl," he says in a rough tone that's only used when he's aroused.

A shiver runs down my spine. His praise feels like a blanket of happiness that boosts my confidence and gives me the courage to continue. Tentatively, I wrap my lips around his tip and suck like it's my favorite flavor lollipop. His flavor bursts on my tongue, and now I'm the one moaning.

"I fuckin' love that, baby. Your mouth on me. Ain't nothing better," he continues to praise.

I take him in deeper, though admittedly, still not very far. I have a bad gag reflex, and even brushing my tongue with my toothbrush can set it off. He might be okay with a lot of things, but throwing up around his dick would definitely kill the mood.

"Reach down and roll my balls in your palm. Think you can do that for me?" Uh, yeah. Of course, I can. Especially when he's asking like that. "That's it. Oh God, feels so fuckin' good."

They feel a lot different from what I thought they would. They're surprisingly heavy and soft. With my other hand, I stroke him up and down in time with my mouth. Getting braver, I bring him further and further into my mouth until I go too far and gag. I look up to see if he's concerned, but there's nothing but bliss in his expression.

"Take out your tits, baby. I want to see them while you get me off," he says. The dirty words sound sweet on his lips, and I pull the sports bra off. Coyote lets out a strangled noise when the air hits me, making my nipples pucker.

Taking his hard length in hand, I rub the tip over my nipples. Watching his pre-cum make my skin glisten feels dirty in the best way possible. If I had bigger breasts, I'd fuck him with my cleavage, but I don't, so this will have to do.

I glance up at him before I put him back in my mouth and see his eyes wild with arousal, not at all turned off by my inexperience. "Keep going. I'm close."

Knowing I'm responsible for putting that look on his face, I double my efforts. Saliva runs down his shaft, which feels wrong in a very right way. Sex is messy and wild; I need to let go and let it happen. So that's what I do. I'm surprised when my thighs rub together on their own accord because now that I'm not thinking so much, giving him head is turning me on.

Coyote places a hand on my head, not pushing me down exactly, just applying enough pressure to guide me in the speed he prefers. I like him giving me direction, and I really like his praise.

"You know how lucky I am? My girl wakes up in the middle of the night to patch me up, then she gets on her knees to give me a world-class blowjob. Luckiest fuckin' man ever." Those last words come at grunts, and the hand on my head tells me it's time to speed things up.

I slurp and suck, earning more sounds of pleasure from him. I enjoy it more too. So much so that I slip a hand into my sleep pants and panties to rub my clit.

"That's right, play with that pretty pussy."

Oh my God, nothing is off-limits with this man. It frees me in a way I didn't think was possible. If Mom could see me now, she'd have a lot to say, and honestly, I don't care.

Especially not when Coyote's thighs tremble, and he practically growls out, "Gonna come, Little Owl. You pick where that goes. Either your tits, your face, or your mouth."

That's a big choice to make when I'm put on the spot, but I've made it this far, and I want the full experience.

"Come in my mouth," I say, keeping the tip of his cock on my lips as I do.

"Then show me what a good girl you can be and swallow it all down." Oh boy. I don't know which I like better, when he calls me Little Owl or when he says, "good girl." Both make my insides swirl around.

I suck harder and take him down further, all while rubbing my clit. The second his chest rumbles, and he holds my head down on him, I know he's coming. It's such an erotic feeling that it sparks my own orgasm. I moan around his cock, which only seems to intensify Coyote's orgasm.

I roll my tongue back and forth along the underside of his

tip as I drink down his cum, careful not to let any of it spill so I can make him proud. As both of us come down, my movements slow.

"Come here," he says, lifting me up under my arms and moving me to straddle him. "My perfect girl. You did such a good job."

"Really?" I ask.

"Fuckin' really." He kisses me long, deep, and hard. I know he can taste himself, but it doesn't bother him. It's so strange to see how comfortable he is with everything. No inhibitions, no reluctance, just unabashedly doing whatever feels good to him. He's amazing. "Come get into bed. Let me tuck you in."

I fall to the side and pull back my covers. "You're not going to stay?"

"I'll stay on the property," he says, zipping himself in.

"If Crash isn't here, why don't you sleep with me?"

"There're still things we don't know about each other, Little Owl. My reasons are one of them. I'll tell you all about it one day, but not right now." He bends down and kisses my head. I should tell him I already know, but the moment is so perfect, I don't want to ruin it.

"Okay."

"Can I meet my daughter tomorrow?" he asks.

My smile could light up a room. "Of course."

"Sweet dreams."

"Good night." My eyes are already closing when I hear the front door shut and the lock flip. I don't question how he has a key. Of course he does. Nothing stops Apollo Hawkins.

Chapter
EIGHTEEN

Coyote

I wake up more alert than I am after three cups of coffee. I'm meeting Veda today, and something about that makes me more nervous than I was to approach Riley. There's a chance she won't like me, which would crush me more than anything else in the world.

I move through a series of basic Asanas as the sun rises, followed by a guided meditation. Yoga was something one of my foster parents introduced me to. Her house was the only one I ever felt welcome in. She knew I had a demon inside and taught me yoga to help me focus my energy on something good.

At first, I went along with it because I wanted to stay in her home and the only way I knew how to make sure that'd happen was by being respectful. Not that it mattered. Six months later, she announced she was pregnant.

"You'll be happier with a foster mom who can devote the time and energy you deserve," she said. It sounded nice, but we both knew she was the best foster home I'd had. I eased her guilt by agreeing because what could I say?

I left her home with a love of yoga and a steel cage around my heart so I never got my hopes up again.

Once my mind and spirit are calm, I make my way to the house. Crash's bike isn't here, so I unlock the door and walk in to the smell of pancakes and sausage. My stomach rumbles. I haven't eaten since yesterday at lunch.

I follow my nose to the kitchen, where Veda is up on the kitchen counter pouring pancake batter onto a griddle while Riley stands by, ready to help if needed. There's music playing, some pop song I've heard in the clubhouse.

Veda's adorable in a pair of pajamas that have owls on them. When I saw her room, it was an *a-ha* moment, but now that it's passed, it feels like a bond we share, even if she doesn't know it. Her hair is covered by a silk bonnet, making me smile and think about how Mom wore one very similar while she slept.

Riley's wearing the same thing as last night, her baggy flannel pajama pants that are too long and curl over the tops of her feet and a sports bra. Her long hair is piled high on her head, and her little ass is shaking to the beat.

It hits me that this is my life now. An overnight family, and I'm not even scared. All that fear I'd been clinging to has dissipated to nothing but a memory.

I clear my throat, and both pairs of eyes turn to me.

Veda's head tilts to the side, and her cute button nose scrunches. "Who's that, Mommy?"

Riley motions for me to come closer. I step through the doorway and into the galley kitchen. The sink, dishwasher, some counter space, and the stove are on one side, and on the other are more counter space and the refrigerator.

Riley huffs and steps away from Veda just long enough to grab my hand and bring me even closer. She wraps an arm around my waist, making Veda appear even more curious.

I glance down at Riley, looking for instructions, but she

appears just as perplexed about what to say as I am. Time for me to step up.

"My name's Coyote. I'm... your mom's friend." It feels wrong to drop a bomb on the kid. After we get to know each other, we can tell her the truth.

"Coyote? Like the animal?" she asks in her high-pitched voice that can't be described as anything but adorable, even though I'd never admit to knowing that word.

"Yeah, kid. Like the animal."

"I never even asked how you got that name." Riley lets go of me to flip a pancake.

"It was given to me because I have the instincts of a wolf, but I'm small, like a coyote." I stick my hands in my pockets and wonder if it's okay to say something like that in front of a kid. "My real name's Apollo, but my friends call me Coyote."

"You're the man in the trees," Veda says, still tracking me with her eyes.

I choke on my spit and have to turn away to cough. I thought she saw me once when I watched her read in her bay window, but she didn't freak out or call for Riley, so I assumed I was wrong. Guess not.

"Coyote loves to hike, and it's really pretty here," Riley explains.

I regain my composure and agree. "I prefer to be outside."

"You're right in time for some pancakes and sausage." Riley points to the plates of food, thankfully changing the subject.

"I *love* pamcakes." Veda wiggles excitedly.

Pamcakes. Well, that's fuckin' adorable too.

"Can you take the food to the table while I get her cleaned up?"

"Sure." I pick up the plates, syrup, and butter, balancing them carefully in my arms and taking them to the table that's already set for three.

The girls are seconds behind me and take their seats. I sit

down in the one that's not claimed and rest my hands in my lap, waiting for further instruction. Riley and Veda dig in, stabbing pancakes and sausage links with forks and bringing them to their plates while I watch on, trying to get a read on their dynamic.

"Aren't you going to eat, Coyote?" Veda asks, a mouthful of sausage.

"I am. It just looks so good, I don't know where to start."

Riley takes pity on me and fills my plate with food. "We have manners. We just choose not to use them when we're at home."

"Yep," Veda agrees.

I like that. Dad was big on manners when I was young, especially at mealtime. I never could relax because I was too worried I'd do something wrong, and when that happened, it meant my night would be spent in pain.

Picking up my fork, I dig in. The pancakes are sweet with a hint of vanilla, and the sausage tastes like spicy maple syrup. It's delicious.

"What are you two ladies doing today?" I ask.

"I called in sick to work again today," Riley says. "I thought we could spend the day doing something fun. Do you want to go with us, Coyote?"

"I'd love to, but I have an errand to run." I avoided the clubhouse last night but need to check in.

"That's okay. Want to meet us at Wild Island in a couple of hours?" Riley's lips quirk, knowing a man like me has no business going to a damn water park. But I can't say no. Something tells me she knows that too.

Veda cheers something fierce. "I love Wild Island."

"What do you say?" Riley reaches under the table and sets a hand on my thigh.

"Sure. Sounds. . . fun."

We finish our breakfast while Veda tells me all about the

water slides she likes and the ones she's not tall enough to ride. She talks so fast that I miss every other word but still keep up.

Veda runs to change into her swimsuit while Riley and I clean up. It's strangely domestic, something I haven't had in a long time.

"Sorry about the Wild Island thing. I couldn't help myself," Riley says while running water over the dishes before putting them in the dishwasher.

I step up behind her and crouch to wrap my arms around her middle. I bite her earlobe, happy to have a minute where I can touch her freely. It was hard as hell to keep my hands off her while Veda was around.

"You don't sound sorry now, but you will be later," I whisper into her ear.

She spins and jumps into my arms, wrapping her legs around me.

"You haven't seen me in my bikini yet." She presses a chaste kiss to my lips.

"At least I have that to look forward to." I squeeze the globes of her ass and back us up against the back door.

She bursts out laughing, catching herself with a hand over her mouth. "Do you even own swim trunks?"

"I'm not going in a pool that a million kids have pissed in."

"That's what chlorine is for."

"I'll meet you there and have a good time watching my kid play around and get an eyeful of my girl in a bikini, but I'm not going in," I say adamantly.

"Will you at least leave the boots and cut behind?"

The question, as innocent as she thinks it is, irritates me. "Why? You don't want to be seen with a biker?"

She cups my face and forces me to look at her. "That's not what I meant. I just think you'll feel a little silly dressed in jeans, boots, and leather while it's ninety degrees outside and everyone else has on bathing suits."

"I'll be okay."

"All right. It's up to you." She pecks small kisses around my mouth until I finally cave and give her the kiss she needs. Long, hard, and deep.

We freeze when we hear a motorcycle pull into the driveway. Riley struggles for me to set her down, but I tighten my hold.

"Coyote, this isn't the time or place for a fight like this."

"You and Veda are mine. About time he knew it."

She struggles more, a seriousness on her face like I've never seen. She's scared.

"Please don't do this right now. Not in front of Veda. Do you think she'll like you after she has a front-row seat to you and Crash beating the shit out of each other?" She has a point there, so I set her down.

"I don't like this one fuckin' bit."

"I know. It's temporary, I promise. Can you sneak out the back door?" Her wide eyes blink rapidly.

I know I should go, but my pride has my feet cemented to the floor. Everything in me wants to meet him at the front door and tell him he's not welcome anymore.

"You and Veda, you're my family. Just know, if he tries to get between that, he'll be six feet underground before he knows what hit him. You understand me?"

"Coyote. Go. Please." She's not asking, and that pisses me off. She should be telling him to leave, not me. None of this is sitting right.

The front doorknob jiggles. Asshole doesn't have a key, so a knock follows. Riley pleads with me with her eyes. The demon inside rubs his hands together, ready for a fight, urging me to pummel Crash to the motherfuckin' ground.

"Someone's at the door, Mommy. Can I answer it?" Veda appears, and it's like a cup of cold water gets poured over my head. She's so small and so innocent. My job now is to protect her from the bullshit in this world, not bring it to her fuckin' front door.

"No, baby. I'll get it in just a second." She lifts Veda into her arms, probably worried she'll disobey and answer it anyway. "Coyote," she deadpans.

I glare at my woman, hoping she can see how serious I am. "Last time, Riley."

"Okay." Her tone is annoyed, which pisses me off even more. I'm not the one she should be mad at. I'm not the one who should sneak out the back door.

"See you later, Veda." I pat her on the head as I walk out.

"Bye, Coyote."

Usually, a ride is enough to clear my head, but I'm still grumpy as fuck when I walk into the clubhouse.

"Hey, brother. You disappeared on us last night," Khan says. He's sitting at the bar with blueprints laid out in front of him, making changes with a pencil.

Bexley's sitting next to him, fingers flying over the keys of her laptop. She stops long enough to wave and then gets back to work.

"Sorry about that. Had some other shit to do."

"Like boning Riley?" He waggles his brows.

"God, you're such a man-child," Bexley mutters under her breath.

"Something like that." I look around. "Is Duncan here?"

"Why? You need him to swing up to Saddlehorn?"

"Yeah."

"He's getting some pricing on supplies for me, but Ford is around."

The prospect pokes his head out of the kitchen. "Need me?"

"Can you head up to Saddlehorn? I'll text you the address. Don't let her know you're there," I say.

"Sure. Anything particular I'm looking for?" He pulls his black bandana from his back pocket and ties it around his stringy, shoulder-length hair.

"Crash is in the house with Riley. Just make sure everything stays quiet."

"On it." He jogs out the door.

"So, what happened after I left?" I ask Khan.

"Not in front of the lawyer."

Bexley closes her laptop and stands. "I'm headed to the office anyway."

"Not before you give me some sugar." Khan pulls her into his arms and lands kisses all over her face while she swats at him and grapples to get away. But she's smiling, so she must secretly like it.

Not hearing him walk in, I do a double-take when Loki steps up beside me. "Didn't see you last night. All good?"

"Yeah," I say, watching Bexley land a punch to Khan's gut that loosens his grip, but he catches her at the last minute. It's oddly entertaining to watch.

"As soon as they're done, I'm calling church." He puts his hands on his hips. "Never heard of hand-to-hand combat as foreplay. Might have to try it."

"You haven't even married Birdie and things are getting stale?" I joke.

"Fuck no. You've heard about the cage, right?" He elbows me.

I nod because I've heard how Birdie likes to be locked up in a life-size birdcage. It sounds pretty kinky.

"You bit me, you asshole," Bexley shouts. I look over in time to see her drive a high heel into Khan's boot.

"Goddamn it, woman." Khan hops around as Bex packs away her laptop.

"Now I have to go to court with a bite mark on my neck."

"Good. Gotta keep those fancy lawyer assholes away from my woman."

Loki and I watch them like a tennis match, eyes bouncing back and forth.

"You're fucking infuriating," she growls out, and grabs her briefcase before walking toward the door.

"Love you," Khan singsongs. She flips him off and leaves.

Once everyone is settled in the chapel, we go over the aftermath of the warehouse explosion.

"Four dead. Only two were Sons. The other two were chemists or some shit. Cops are still investigating, but it doesn't look like there was anything to tie the Sons to the lab," Loki says. "But since our goal was to send a message, all that's left to do is make a phone call." He slides a cell phone over to me. "I think you should do the honors."

"I'm the one who got shot," Goblin protests.

"But Coyote's the one Crash has an issue with," Khan says.

I pick up the phone and hit the call button. It rings four times before Crash picks up.

"Yeah?"

"Hey, buddy. It's Coyote. Heard you had some complications last night."

"Fuck you," he spits out.

"I'm pretty sure you're the one who's fucked." This is the most fun I've had that doesn't involve Riley in a long time.

"You think this will make me give you Riley? Newsflash, asshole. She's mine. It's what her dad wanted, and that man meant everything to her. You think she'll go against that?"

"She went against it last night when she was sucking my big dick," I say, earning a chorus of cackles from my brothers.

"You want a war? Well, congratulations." The line goes dead, and I hand the phone back to Loki.

"We're going into lockdown until this is over. I want

everyone under this roof within the hour. Anyone who leaves needs to take a buddy." Loki turns to me. "Crash is at Riley's place?"

"Yeah." I wasn't worried before since he seems to care for her, but she's become a bargaining chip, and Crash is getting desperate.

"Figure out how to get her the fuck out of there."

"On it. Who'll be my buddy?" I ask.

Goblin raises his hand. "I'm in the mood for a little danger."

Chapter
NINETEEN

Riley

Ever since Crash walked in the door, he's been on the phone. Not wanting Veda to hear the cursing that's flowing from his mouth, I take her inside her room to play.

"Let's turn on some music," I suggest.

"Ella Jenkins," Veda cheers.

I connect to her Bluetooth speaker and hit play on her favorite album to drown out Crash's shouting.

This is ridiculous. He can't stay here any longer. So, even though he's clearly having a bad day, it's time to have a talk.

"I need to talk to Crash for a minute. Are you okay to play alone?"

She doesn't even look up from what she's doing. "Uh-huh. Bring snacks when you come back, okay?"

I kiss her head and sneak down the hallway to listen in on his conversation. I know this has something to do with the Royal Bastards, but I want to know exactly what.

"You want a war?" Crash shouts. "Well, congratulations."

I flinch when I hear him hurl his phone across the room. I've never seen him like this, and it's scaring me. I look outside the living room window, wondering if Coyote or one of the other Bastards is out there watching over me.

I hope so.

I roll my shoulders and walk into the kitchen where Crash is.

"Everything okay?" I ask, playing it off like I don't know he's losing his mind.

"No, Riley. Everything is not fuckin' okay."

"Does that mean it's a bad time to sit down for a chat?" I wring my hands in front of me and balance on the outer part of my feet.

He glances over at me, his hazel eyes bloodshot and tired. I'd feel bad for him, except he's kind of ruining my life right now.

"What is it?"

I motion to the kitchen table, and he joins me when I sit down.

"I think it's time for you to leave. I know you feel like you need to protect me from Coyote, but you don't. I spoke to him, and we worked things out. We want to be a family—" I stop short, watching his face turn an ugly shade of red. "You okay?"

He jumps up from his seat and flips the round table over, sending my pot of succulents and placemats crashing to the ground. I push back and jump to my feet.

"What the hell, Crash?"

His hands go to the sides of his head, fingers digging into his hair. Bending over, a guttural sound from deep in his chest reverberates through the room. His breathing is labored and heavy, like a wild animal.

I've never seen anyone react this way, and I don't know if I should be scared or worried. Currently, I'm both.

"No. No. No. No," he chants over and over. He stands to his full height with his hands remaining on his head, his knuckles turning white from how hard he's tugging on his long hair.

He repeats the word, spittle flying out of his mouth and eyes nearly bugging out of his head.

I move to rest a hand on his back, thinking he needs comfort, but the look he gives me is murderous. Taking a few steps back, my thoughts go to Veda. She's alone and unprotected in that room.

His hands drop, and an eerie calm washes over him that frightens me even more than his crazy.

"No. That's not going to happen. Wrecker said you're mine. He said if I stuck by you, got you settled, that you'd realize we're good for each other."

"Crash," I say. I try to use a soothing and calm voice but can't hide the slight quaver. "I'm a human being. Not an object that can be passed down from one person to another. He didn't mean it the way you took it."

"There's only one way to take it. I did everything right. I did exactly what he said." He rocks back and forth on his feet nervously. It's unnerving how undone he's become.

"This conversation isn't going anywhere, so I think it's time for you to go." I fold my arms across my chest.

"No. No. No." Over and over he repeats, pacing the kitchen floor. I have no idea how I'm going to get out of this.

"Listen. Veda and I are going to the water park for the day. While I'm there, I'll think about everything you said. Then we can sit and discuss it when everything has settled down a bit."

His head turns and what I see chills me to the core. "No. You're not going to the water park. It's too dangerous for you to be out in the open. I think you should come to the clubhouse with me."

"That's not going to happen, Crash. You're making me feel very unsafe right now."

He storms over to me and grips me by the arm, tugging me to the back door. "Come on. It's for your own safety."

I panic, trying to pry his fingers off me, but his grip is

bruising, and I have the strength of a slug. My every thought is on Veda. Should I tell him I need to stay for her? I can't. Because right now, he seems to have forgotten about her existence and something in me says that's better than her going with me.

Leaving her alone feels wrong too. *Shit.*

He drags me out the back door. When I grip onto the door handle and stop our progression, he places a hand on the back of my head and slams it into the glass window on the door, shattering the glass and dazing me. Warm blood drips down my forehead, getting in my eyes and blinding me.

But my hands are still glued to the handle, holding on with everything I have in me. If I go with him, there's a good chance I'll never see my daughter again. He's going to kill me; there's no doubt in my mind.

He lets go of my arm, wiping the blood and stroking my face gently. "I'm sorry. I'm so sorry."

"You don't want to do this, Crash. Please. Just let me go."

"I can't. Don't you see? This is what's supposed to happen. Wrecker made a promise." He pleads with his eyes. I take advantage of the moment and lift my knee, aiming for his junk. But I'm dizzy from the blow to my head and miss my mark. His features turn stone cold, all traces of sympathy gone.

"Let go of the door, Riley," he says through gritted teeth.

When I don't, he shoves me forward again, this time cracking my head against the wood frame. My head pounds, and my thoughts get blurry. More blood pours out, gushing down my face and hitting the porch.

Still, I hold on.

"Help." I try to shout, but it comes out as more of a whimper. Still, I'm hoping and praying someone will hear me. Coyote has been stalking me for nearly two weeks, but the minute I need him, he's nowhere to be found.

"No one can stop this from happening. It's fate." With one

hand still glued to my arm, the other wraps around my hands on the doorknob. "I'm sorry. But this is for the best. You'll see."

He singles out the middle finger of my left hand and yanks it back roughly. I hear the snap of the bone before I feel it. But once the pain receptors in my brain register what just happened, I cry out and instinctually let go of the door.

It's the break he needed to get me away from the house. Gripping the hair on the back of my head, he pulls me away from the house and over to my car. Somehow I missed him snagging the keys I hang by the back door because they're in his hand.

"Hey!" someone shouts, and the smallest glimmer of hope sparks.

It's a Royal Bastard but one I don't know. He looks like a young Axl Rose with his long blond hair held back with a rolled bandana, dressed in an AC/DC tank top, leather cut with a Prospect patch, and tattoos up and down his arms.

My hope wanes knowing he's a Prospect. It means he's not experienced and hasn't proven his loyalty.

Crash opens the back door of the car and shoves me in before reaching behind him and pulling out his gun. It's steel gray, big, and scary looking. I recognize it as one that was in Wrecker's gun safe.

"What are you going to do about it? What are you, twelve?" Crash taunts.

Looking through the back window, I see the prospect has a gun out now too. His is small in comparison. I don't know enough about guns to know if size matters because if it does, Crash will win.

"Old enough to fuck your mom," the kid taunts right back. He's ballsy; I'll give him that. "Back away from the girl, and we can pretend this never happened."

Ignoring them for a second, I glance over at the house. I see Veda in her window, staring out at me. Her hands are braced against the glass, and tears are streaming down her face. I smile and mouth the words, "Stay there. I love you," while holding my hands up, palms out, hoping she understands.

She nods in understanding. No matter what happens to me, it's okay. As long as she's safe.

Then a gunshot goes off, the sound mostly absorbed by the trees. I whirl around, praying it's Crash who took the bullet. But it wasn't.

The prospect was hit in his right shoulder—his dominant hand—so the gun falls to the ground. My last hope. Gone. He falls to his knees and clutches the shoulder that's gushing an insane amount of blood.

This was all my fault. He was here because of me. Now he's likely to die because of me.

Crash slides behind the steering wheel and starts the car. He throws it in reverse and hits the gas, making the motor scream from the effort. It's an old car and can be temperamental at times.

The prospect jumps behind the car, holding the gun up with his left hand, blood drenching the entire right side of his body. He fires but clearly hasn't trained to fire with his non-dominate hand, and the shot hits the side-view mirror.

Crash doesn't slow, and before the prospect can move, the car runs right into him, propelling him onto the trunk. The tears I've been holding in break free, and a sob rips from my chest.

I've never seen anything so horrific. I'm terrified, and I have no idea what to do.

Once he's out of the drive, he tears off down the road. The prospect rolls off the car and is left in the dirt, unmoving. He's dead, and now there's no one to help my baby.

She's only four, but I taught her about 911 and what an emergency is. I can only hope she finds my cellphone and calls.

"Those Bastards think they can blow my shit up and take you away from me. Not a chance in hell. You're mine. He said so," Crash mutters to himself. He's lost in his head somewhere I don't think anyone can reach.

I see myself in the rearview mirror and cringe. There's dried blood crusted over my entire face, and my hair is a tangled mess. Hopelessness and fear that I'll never see my daughter again send me over the edge.

"Pull over now!" I shout, smacking Crash's head from where I'm sitting behind him. My broken finger swings limply, sending an insane amount of pain up my arm. It's almost too much to bear. Almost.

I take every ounce of despair and anger out on him, and when he leans forward out of my reach, I throw myself onto the console and reach for the steering wheel.

I refuse to go back to his clubhouse. If I'm not making it out of this alive, I'm going down with a fight.

At least until Crash throws his elbow back into my nose. There's a crack of bone, and blood bursts out, spraying all over the side of Crash's face and the interior of the car. I wobble side to side, unable to gather my wits. Too many hits to the head, too much violence, too much insanity.

The last thing I remember is falling down onto the bench seat, my head taking one final blow when I connect with the hard plastic of Veda's car seat.

That's it. Game over.

Chapter
TWENTY

Coyote

I'm almost at Riley's house when Ford's SOS text comes
through. My stomach sinks, and I curse.

It was stupid to leave her there and let her talk to Crash.
Especially after we blew his warehouse up. That was bound to
unhinge him.

A hundred different possibilities run through my mind.
Everything from Riley and Veda being killed to Crash abduct-
ing one or both of them. Goddamn it.

When I get my hands on that fucker, he's dead. No more
chances to do the right thing. It'll be a special death too. One
that involves pain being delivered over days, weeks, maybe even
months. Depends on what he's done.

I nearly wreck when I take the corner onto her dirt road
too quickly, my handlebars going into a death wobble. But I
gain control and take off again. Goblin was behind me, but I've
left him behind in my haste. Don't give a shit. He'll catch up.

I skid to a halt in the driveway, noticing Riley's car isn't here.
But there are deep tracks in the dirt from her car peeling out.
That's not a good sign.

Tossing my helmet onto the lawn, I run inside, hearing Veda's cries. It's a kind of cry I've never heard in my life. Something panicked and scared. My heart cracks apart at the sound. I just met her, and already she has the power to bring me to my knees.

I follow the sound to her room and try to push in the closed door, but it won't budge. Like something heavy is in front of it. Throwing my shoulder into it, I ram into it over and over, opening it inch by inch. The whole time, Veda wails.

I'm not ready for what I see when I get inside. Riley is nowhere to be found. Veda is standing in the middle of the room, tears streaming down her face. And Ford, pale as a ghost and covered in blood, is collapsed on the ground. His breathing is labored, and his eyes are barely open, but his hand is on his gun, ready to protect my kid.

Jesus fuck.

I dial up Loki, pressing the speaker button while crouching down in front of Veda.

"Need you. Ford's shot. Don't know what else he got put through, but he has an open fracture of his left leg."

"On it."

"Hurry. He doesn't look good." I set a hand on Veda's back, trying to comfort her.

"I want Mommy," she cries.

"We'll see her soon, okay? Can I pick you up?" I give her a smile I hope is reassuring.

My chest warms when she nods. I pick her up, and Jesus fuck, the kid melts into me, her hands clutching around my neck with surprising strength. I've never held anything more precious, and I swear to Christ, this is the last time she'll ever see the darkness in the world. You can bet on that.

"I'll get Ford over to Aiyana. If she thinks he needs a hospital, we'll take him to County," he says reluctantly. "She's going to kick my ass."

"Okay. Make it quick, yeah? Riley's gone, and I need to be out there lookin'. Can you bring Truly too? Need someone sweet to be with my kid while I get my woman back."

"Shit. Okay, yeah. On my way."

I end the call and set Veda down on her bed. "Can you stay right here while I go see if my friend is okay?" She nods, and I hand her a book from her nightstand. "I'll be right back, and we'll get out of here."

There's no way we should be in this house right now. Crash knows exactly where we'll be and how best to hurt us. We need to get to the clubhouse. Now.

"I'm sorry, Coyote. He shot my firing arm, and I'm shit with my left. Then he ran me over. I tried to stop him, man. You gotta believe me." Poor asshole thinks I'm pissed at him. He gets shot and hit by a car, but instead of lying on the ground, waiting for help, he dragged his ass into the house and pushed a dresser in front of the door to protect my kid.

Fucker is a goddamn hero.

"Shut the fuck up, brother. You did good. Only thing you need to worry about now is staying alive. Hear me?"

He nods, and I assess his leg first. I gingerly remove his boot and touch the bottom of his sweaty sock. "Feel that?"

"No. Did you touch me?" His voice pitches high in panic. "Why can't I feel it?"

"The fracture is cutting off blood flow. Gotta set it, and it's gonna hurt like a bitch. But my kid's over there, and she's seen more today than her little brain can handle. So I'm beggin' you to please keep quiet, yeah?"

He lifts the bottom of his cut and places it between his teeth, then nods, sweat beading across his forehead.

"Jesus," Goblin drawls, running a hand through his head. "What happened?"

"Come help me out," I say, grateful to have someone else here to help. "Hold his leg right below his knee."

"Okay." Goblin kneels down and grabs hold.

"When I say 'three,' pull like your life depends on it."

"Shit. Okay, yeah."

I get in position with my hands bracing his leg just below the fracture, then say, "One, two, three."

True to his word, the kid doesn't scream. Thankfully, the bones realign. It's not perfect, and it's not pretty, but that can be fixed later.

"Feel that?" I touch the bottom of his foot again, and I swear to Christ, he tears up.

"Yeah, I feel it."

"That's good. Still need a doc, but this'll hold you over." I lower my voice to a whisper. "Need to get Veda out of here. Too much blood for a little kid. Goblin will sit with you until Loki gets here, yeah?"

"Yeah. Feeling better already."

I shake my head. "No point in being a tough guy. Not when you get this banged up."

I walk back over to Veda and scoop her up in my arms. She goes willingly and once again rests her head on my shoulder. I've never really been around kids. Not since I was one myself. Definitely never held one in my arms.

If it wasn't for the current situation, this would be the best moment of my life. I've felt the urge to protect before. Every time I do a job, I get that familiar pull to keep things straight. But this is different. Veda is fragile and small. She *needs* me, and knowing that places a weight on my chest that I'll carry with me like a badge of fuckin' honor.

"I'm going to take you to my house," I tell her.

"No. I want Mommy," she whines.

I don't know what to tell her. The truth would traumatize her, and she might not understand. I need a lie. And a good one.

"Your mom had to go visit your grandma for a day or two.

But she asked me if I could take care of you because they were going to do boring grown-up stuff."

Her head pops up. "Grandma?"

"Uh-huh. And since we became such good friends this morning, she said you could come to my clubhouse, and we could hang out. Would you like that?"

"Clubhouse? Like Mickey Mouse's?"

"Kind of." I pull my phone out and tap a quick message to Sly, asking him to get things fit for a kid. He replies immediately, saying he'll get Sissy and Tabitha on it.

Those two women are heaven-sent. In exchange for housing, food, and a paycheck, they keep that place running like mother hens tending to their chicks. Except their chicks are a bunch of unruly bastards.

Her eyes light up with excitement but only for a split second before the sadness returns. "Mommy had an owie. She needs a Band-Aid."

I try to tamp down the rage of knowing that bastard hurt Riley bad enough for Veda to know she needed first aid. I glance out the window, willing Loki to show up, even though it's only been minutes. I need to get my kid safe and then find my girl.

"Don't worry about that. We got her one before she went to Grandma's."

"Did you kiss it better?" Her cobalt eyes next to the tawny skin that matches mine melt me from the inside out. She's the perfect mix of me and her mom.

"Yeah, darlin', I did."

Her head goes back to my shoulder, and I rub her back as I take her into the kitchen. I should probably gather up snacks and shit that kids like.

That's when I see the back door. It's open, the glass window on the top half shattered, and dried up blood crusted on the shards of glass. My stomach turns, threatening to make me vomit. How wounded is she?

Veda and I gather her favorite snacks. It seems to perk her up a bit when I let her bring cookies and snack cakes that she says her mom doesn't let her have every day.

After that's done, I go back to Veda's room, standing just outside so she can't see in.

"How's he doing, Goblin?" I call out.

"Stable. In some pain."

"Can you gather up some clothes and shi—" I stop myself before I say the word. "Stuff."

"Books," Veda hollers, and it almost makes me smile.

"Got it. Clothes and books."

Minutes later, he hands me a backpack stuffed to the brim. "Didn't know how much."

"This works. Thanks, brother."

His worried eyes turn on me. "You handlin' this okay?"

"I'll be better once I can get out there and start looking," I say right before I hear tires crunching down the driveway. "Cavalry is here."

Truly and Loki are the first ones through the door. I point to the bedroom Ford is in, and Loki gives me a nod before heading that way.

"Who do we have here?" Truly asks with a warm smile. I chose her to help with Veda since she's a few months pregnant. Figured she'd have maternal instincts already.

"This is Veda. Veda, this is Truly," I introduce.

"God, Coyote. She's gorgeous."

"I know," I deadpan. Truly side-eyes me, but it's teasing. I set Veda down on the sofa and crouch in front of her. "Listen, Veda. I have some jobs I need to do, so Truly is going to take you to the clubhouse."

"But first, I thought we could go to the store and pick out a new toy to play with. Would you like that?" Truly asks.

Veda reaches her arms to me. "I want to go with you."

Unable to tell her no, I pick her back up. "I don't know what to do, Truly."

Truly rests a comforting hand on Veda's back. "Maybe come with us to the clubhouse and get her settled. You're the only one she knew before all this." She motions to the chaos of Goblin and Loki carrying Ford out the front door. "It makes sense she'd want a familiar face if she's going someplace new."

"Okay." I grab Veda's snacks and clothes before following Truly outside and placing Veda in the backseat of her car. We don't have one of those booster seats I saw Riley use. "I'll follow you on my motorcycle, okay?" She nods, and I open up a package of cookies. "A little treat for the ride."

After belting her in the best I can, I close the door and turn to Truly. She holds up her hand before I can speak, a knowing expression on her face. "I'll go slow. I won't make any sharp turns or even switch lanes. I promise."

"Thanks," I mutter.

We all leave at the same time; Loki in the van headed for Truly's mom's house and the rest of us for the clubhouse.

Now that I don't have a kid in my arms to take care of, I can try to figure this out. It would make sense for Crash to take her to his clubhouse. He has to know that the wrath of our entire MC is about to rain down on him, so he'll need the backup. And he's going to need a fuck of a lot of backup.

For the first time in my life, I have something worth protecting.

Chapter
TWENTY-ONE

Riley

My head. My fucking head. I think it's been crushed by a sledgehammer or something just as sinister. It's the only explanation for this pounding headache.

I will my eyelids to open, but they feel tight and glued shut. Reaching a hand up, I pat my face, panicking at what I feel. They're not tight; they're swollen. My whole face is swollen, and there's a thick layer of crust coating my skin.

Blood, I realize when I touch my forehead, and my hand comes back wet. Head wounds bleed a lot. At least that's what the doctor told me when Veda fell off the sofa and hit her head on the coffee table when she was two.

I thought she was going to bleed out with the amount of blood I saw. It was terrifying. But the doctor was quick to assure me she was okay. She didn't even need stitches, just some glue to hold the wound shut.

Even knowing this, it's startling when I feel the saturated fabric underneath my head.

I'm not in the car anymore. I know this because I'm

stretched out on what feels like a mattress. And it's quiet and still, no engine running or the feel of a bumpy road.

I pry my eyes open to slits using my fingers, which is better than nothing, and blink painfully, clearing my vision. Save for the cot I've been deposited on, I'm disappointed to find that I'm in an empty room.

Running through the chain of events, I try to piece my memory back into place. Crash took the news of Coyote and me badly, to say the least. I got banged up trying not to let him take me from the house, but honestly, I didn't stand a chance.

He shot the prospect and... Oh, God. The prospect. I wonder if he's okay. There was so much blood pouring from his arm. Then Crash hit him with the car. I'll never forget the look on his face right before it happened. It was a mixture of terror and disbelief that I hope to never see again.

And Veda. With tears falling down her face, she was so brave to do what I said and stay put. My angel girl. It was the hardest decision I've ever made to leave her behind. My maternal instincts were to hold her to me and protect her, but the rational part of my brain knew I couldn't fight off this enemy, so she was better left behind where the good guys were likely to find her.

I hope she's with Coyote. My already limited vision blurs with unshed tears. We'd just found our happy, and before we could enjoy it, it was ripped right out from under us.

Carefully peeling my face from the mattress, I lift myself up only inches before falling back down when a wave of dizziness and nausea hits me. This isn't just from the injury. I've been drugged. That motherfucker drugged me.

I close my eyes and take steadying breaths, but my nose is plugged. Knowing what I'll find but doing it anyway, I reach up and gingerly touch my nose. My previously straight bridge is crooked, swollen, and horribly painful.

He fucked up my adorable little nose. No way will heal

on its own, and I don't see Crash driving me to a doctor any-time soon.

The burning anger has me sitting up once again to get a better look at the room around me. The walls and floor are gray concrete, like a basement. There's a window near the ceiling, but I know by looking at it that it won't open. It's the kind of window strictly for light; there's no latch or slide.

He was prepared for this.

Across the room from me is a wooden door with a brass knob. If I can make it over there, maybe I can get out. I don't know where I am, but if I can get outside, I might stand a chance.

I push to my feet, but my knees are wobbly, and my muscles can't hold me up. Whatever drug he gave me is strong. But I'll be damned if my daughter grows up without a mom because I couldn't push away the effects of a drug. I'm stronger than this, damn it.

Willing myself to stand, I let out a battle cry until I get on my feet. Sidestepping to the left, I prop myself up against the wall and use it to brace myself as I make my way around the room to the door.

Unsurprisingly, it's locked. That doesn't stop me from jig-gling it over and over, frustration and disbelief coursing through me. But it's no use.

I rest my head against the door and scream. It's an ugly and pained sound, one that encompasses every emotion I'm feeling. I can't believe I allowed this to happen. If it weren't for that let-ter from Wrecker, I never would've trusted the bastard to get this close to me.

Slowly, I make my way back to the bed and lay down. Until Crash comes back, I'm stuck. I know I should preserve as much energy as possible so I'm ready when the opportunity for es-cape arises.

The mattress is worn and thin to where I feel the springs poking into my hip and shoulder. I close my eyes and do the only thing I can to make myself feel better. I think back to breakfast this morning.

Seeing Coyote with Veda was one of the best moments of my life. I was so worried she wouldn't like him or he wouldn't like her. It was stupid because they clicked right away.

I'm disappointed I never got to see Coyote at the water park. Despite my current situation, the thought makes me smile. If I get out of here—I stop myself—*when* I get out of here, our first family outing will be to the water park.

My thoughts slow, and I feel the tug of sleep. The last thing I want is to be caught off guard by Crash again, but I'm beyond exhausted, and I can't take being in this much pain. I'll sleep now and gain some strength to work on an escape plan.

There's no doubt in my mind Coyote is looking for me, but I can't count on the club to find me. I owe it to Veda to fight like hell.

The next time I wake, it's to the door being unlocked, followed by someone coming inside. It must be nighttime now because it's pitch black in here, but that doesn't stop me from knowing exactly who came into the room. Now that I've seen who Crash really is, I recognize why I was so uncomfortable around him.

That irritation under my skin when he was around, that niggling in the back of my mind that I couldn't pinpoint. I assumed it was because I never knew what he thought of me, but that wasn't it at all.

He's evil.

I shiver. The temperature has dropped with the setting sun, and I wish I had put on more clothes this morning. I wanted to stay in the same clothes I had on last night with Coyote. I wanted to remind him of all the dirty things we did. It seems so stupid now, and I'd give anything for a hoodie or even one of my oversized band tees.

"You awake?" Crash asks.

I don't answer, hoping if he thinks I'm asleep, he'll leave me the hell alone.

"I can tell you are because of your breathing. I can also tell that you're afraid." He inhales deeply, loudly. "I can smell it in the air."

He flips on a lantern, illuminating his face.

People associate trustworthiness and kindness to beauty, a mistake I'll never make again. Crash is one of the most beautiful men I've ever seen; he's also the cruelest.

"Looks like it hurts." He motions to my face, but I remain quiet. "Brought you some stuff to clean it up."

He tosses a bag next to the bed, then bends down and picks up a bowl. He sets that next to the bag and takes a seat on the edge of the bed, appraising me.

"You fucked up, Riley. This isn't how things were supposed to go. I laid everything out for you. Thought of every detail. All you had to do was walk the fucking line."

"What do you mean?" I whisper but don't need to because I don't think he even heard me. He seems to be lost in his own head.

"I prepared the will and got Wrecker to sign it. He's such an idiot. Didn't even look it over, just signed away. That's how much he trusted me. Made it so easy to kill him too." His tone turns mocking. "'Let's go for a ride, Wrecker. It's such a nice night.' 'The stars are so bright, Wrecker. Let's stop at this lookout.'" His eyes widen. "*A fucking lookout.* We were on our bikes and had the best view anyone could ever want. We didn't need to stop."

A lump rises in my throat, and I clear it before my words can come out. "You killed Wrecker?"

"You think that old bastard got to be his age running a

1%er MC by being dumb enough to get shot on the side of the road by some Nazis? Clearly, you got your mom's intelligence."

I swallow down the retaliating insult. Needing him to keep talking, I ask, "Why would you kill him?"

"All I ever wanted was to be Prez, to have all those men looking to me for guidance. I would've been damn good at it too. I waited patiently for him to hand it over. But Wrecker thought he was immortal. If I didn't take action, he would've held onto that title until the day he died. And I had plans. Plans he wasn't going along with."

"So you wrote a will?" I choke out because that damn lump won't go away, and my vocal cords sting something fierce.

"Had to make sure you ended up in his house all alone and needing some guidance." He chuckles humorlessly. "That must sting, huh?"

It does, but I don't have the luxury of unpacking those feelings yet.

"What about the letter?" I ask.

"I thought it was beautiful, some of my best work."

Fat, angry tears leak down my cheeks. "The things he wrote were private. How could you possibly know all those details?"

"Short answer is, he never stopped blubbering over the daughter he lost. But the long answer goes back much further."

"Tell me."

He takes me in for a long moment before responding. "My dad works at the Sons' shop. He's your everyday functional alcoholic. Gets through work, but when it's quitting time, he likes to drink and beat the shit out of things. Growing up, that thing was me. I think Wrecker knew, and I think that's why he sponsored me at eighteen. He took me under his wing, taught me everything I needed to know about being a biker. He became the dad I never had. The only downside was having to hear nonstop stories about his daughter, Riley." His nostrils flare. "I thought after all the years he put into our relationship that he thought of me like a son."

"He did, Crash." Wrecker told me many times that Crash filled the void I left when Mom took me away.

"No, he fuckin' didn't. Because the second you showed back up, he couldn't talk about anything else. He gave up time with the club to spend it with you."

"And you were jealous?" I ask.

"Hell no. I'm not jealous of you. I was worried he wasn't staying focused. We had a good thing going with the product we were selling, but he grew a conscience after one bad batch. He wanted to shut the whole operation down because he was worried he'd go away if he got caught and not be able to spend time with his precious daughter and grandbaby."

"Then why not kill me? Take me out of the equation." I sit up carefully, closing my eyes for a minute to let the dizziness subside. "None of this makes sense."

"I don't want to kill you. I want to be with you." He grabs my hands, his eyes wild with excitement. "You and me were meant to be together. I knew it from the first time I laid eyes on you. But I couldn't make it happen until I went through with the plan."

"Why not ask me out like a normal person?"

His head lulls back on his shoulders, and I feel his agitation grow. "I asked Wrecker once if I could take you out on a date. He was furious. Told me no club member would go near his daughter. Not even me." His spine stiffens and when he glances my way, what I see scares me to my core. It's a look of utter fury. "Me! The one he trusted everything with. All his secrets, all his plans, everything. But he couldn't trust me with his precious daughter? It was fucking humiliating."

If I thought I could talk my way out of this, I was wrong. I can see now that he won't let me go, and if my instincts are right, he'd rather see me dead than free of him.

"What happened to the plan to make you do all this?" I glance around the basement.

"The club started asking questions about Wrecker's death. They thought I didn't notice how they were separating themselves from me. But I heard the whispers. I saw the way they looked at me. They were planning something. I didn't have a choice but to take action."

"Why didn't you just leave? Why take me with you?" As much as I was hoping for answers, it's becoming clear that Crash isn't a rational person. His reasons will never make sense to me.

His face contorts into a look of disgust. "Them finding out doesn't change anything, Ry. Me and you make sense. The daughter of the man who raised me into the person I am. It's fucking poetic."

"I can't believe this." I bite into my lip to stop myself from crying.

"Don't be like that. As soon as things die down, we'll get out of here. I saved some money, and you have the money Wrecker left you. We'll find somewhere new to settle down."

He's delusional. Absolutely delusional. I don't know who I'm angrier with, him for being a psychotic asshole or me for falling into his trap so easily.

"What about my daughter?" I hesitate to ask.

"That bastard? Forget about her." His lip curls. "I nearly threw away this whole plan when I found out you got knocked up. I should've been the one to pop that cherry."

"Children aren't replaceable, Crash. You have to know that."

He stands. "It's better if you find a way, Ry. Maybe it'll be hard at first, but I'll put another baby in you. Make you forget all about her."

He's insane. Certifiably insane. And if he's right, and no one knows where we are, then I'm fucked. The only thing I can do is keep gathering as much information as I can.

"So, what's the plan now?" My voice cracks, and I don't know if I want the answer.

"Lay low until I can get us out of here."

"Go somewhere else?" I ask.

"Still not keeping up, Ry. So disappointing." He kneels in front of me. "Maybe we can go to California. I can learn the family business."

"You don't think my mom will notice we don't have my daughter?"

"We'll give her all the grandbabies she wants."

He's delusional, absolutely delusional, to think Mom would be okay with pretending Veda didn't exist. Not to mention allowing a biker in her home.

"Crash? It's time to let me go, okay? I'm sorry you've had such a rough life. I sympathize. I really do. But there's no way to make this work. It's better if you go find someone better suited to your mentality."

"No." His head shakes from side to side over and over. "No. I've already committed to you. I put too much time and effort into this." He moves to the door. "We need to adapt and adjust. Wrecker taught me that."

"Where are you going?" I ask when I notice him moving to the door.

"I'm adapting, Riley. We don't need to rely on your mom. We have money. Just need to find someplace cool to go." He shuts and locks the door behind him without another word.

I was scared before, but now I'm terrified. He's not a sane individual, so there's no reasoning with him. I was relying on my power of persuasion to get away. How do I do that with someone who's insane?

While I wash the blood from my face and dab antiseptic across my wounds the best I can without a mirror, that's what I'm thinking about.

How can I trick him? And if I can't, how do I get ahold of

Coyote to tell him where I am? Especially when I don't know where I am.

I stand on the bed, look out the cloudy window, and gasp when I see trees. So many trees. There are no distinguishing landmarks, just fucking trees. We're out in the middle of nowhere.

Screaming through gritted teeth, I lay down and close my eyes. The only peace I'll have until this is over is when I'm asleep.

So, I let the darkness overtake me.

Chapter
TWENTY-TWO

Coyote

We get back to the clubhouse, and I settle Veda in the backyard with Truly. Someone dug up a bottle of bubbles. Fuck knows why the clubhouse has those, but I'm grateful they do because my little girl is giggling like crazy, watching the dogs run all over each other to bite the floating circles of soap.

"Let's talk," Khan says, placing a hand on my shoulder.

I follow him inside, and we take a seat at the bar where I know Veda can see me in case she gets scared.

"How's Ford?" I ask.

"Aiyana cleaned and bandaged his shoulder up. She confirmed it was a through and through, and since he can move it and has feeling in his arm, she doesn't think it did any damage." He knocks on the wooden bar and looks around for a prospect. "Duncan!"

The prospect comes from running out of the kitchen. "Yeah?"

"Beer."

Duncan's quick to pop the tops of two cold ones and set

them in front of us. I'm thankful for the small dose of alcohol to dim the sharp edges of today's events.

"What about his leg?" I ask.

"That's a different story. Aiyana isn't equipped to handle that type of break, so she's taking him to the ER. They're gonna keep the gunshot hush-hush from the docs so they don't report it, and they made up some bullshit story about his leg."

"Fuckin' glad he'll be okay."

"Me too. He gave us a little more information on all that went down. Gotta say, brother. It's not good."

He tells me everything that happened, including how Riley looked when he shoved her in her car. I see fuckin' red. Crash better be praying for his sins because the second I find the bastard, he's going to Hades.

The front door opens in haste, and three bikers walk through the door. Loki, Dunk, and Mac.

"The cavalry is here," Loki says, motioning to the other two.

"What the hell are you two doing here?" I stand and give my nomad brothers a back-slapping hug.

"Loki called and said you got yourself into some shit. Hopped on our bikes and doubled the speed limit getting here," Dunk says. Everything about this man is overgrown. From his hair and his beard to his beer belly, he fits every stereotype there is for a biker.

"Thanks, brother. Appreciate that." For a long time now, it's been the three of us—traveling around, raising hell, and having a good time. It's good to know they have my back now that shit's gotten real.

"Let's gather in the chapel. We can figure out a plan," Loki suggests.

Biker after biker files into the room. Seeing everyone show up and knowing it's for me brings a lump to my throat. So fuckin' glad I patched in.

"I say we roll up to their clubhouse, locked and loaded," Khan says, leaning back in his chair, confident as ever.

"We do that, and some of us are guaranteed not to go home tonight," Loki says, always the voice of reason.

"I can try and tap into their phones," Sly says, his laptop already open in front of him.

"I'm sure I can slip onto the property without them noticing. Maybe get a visual on what's going on?" Moto suggests.

"I think—" I'm interrupted by Duncan yelling and an unknown voice yelling right back.

Nine chairs slide back from the table, and we scramble out of the room. Our guns are drawn before we can even see what the commotion is all about.

"Put the fuckin' heat away," a man as big as Khan but older says. He reminds me of a younger Hulk Hogan with a bright white handlebar mustache and a black bandana on his head.

None of us comply with his demand since he's wearing a Sons' cut.

"What're you doing here, Cyrus?" Loki asks.

"Came to talk about the girl Crash has. . . acquired." His words are carefully chosen.

"Riley," I supply.

"That's the one." Cyrus scours through the crowd until his eyes land on me. "You Coyote?"

I nod and fold my arms across my chest. "Yeah."

"Can we sit down and talk, son?"

"Not your son," I say. I don't know what the fuck he thinks he's doing showing up here like this, but if I have to take him downstairs and beat information out of him, I'm prepared to do it.

"It's not like that. An hour ago, the Sons voted to strip Crash of his patch. We don't got shit to do with whatever he's pulling, and to keep the fuckin' peace, I'd like to sit down and tell you what's been going on."

"You're not here to take revenge on the warehouse explosion?" I ask. "That had to hurt."

A flash of anger crosses his features, then it's gone. "Most of us wanted to get out of drugs, minus our legit weed shops. We had a bad batch get out recently. Killed some people and brought down the heat. We've been trying to get Crash to shut it down ever since." He motions to the men behind him, who nod in agreement.

"And the men who died in the blast? You're not pissed about that?" I'm not trying to start shit, but I need to make sure this isn't some kind of trap.

"All Crash's guys who didn't want to give up the money the drugs brought in. Good fuckin' riddance, if you ask me."

Loki glances back and gives me a subtle nod.

"Let's take it to the chapel," I say.

Before returning to the chapel, I look out the glass slider to see my girl still having the time of her life. Thank fuck for Roch's old lady.

"What's this about voting Crash out?" I ask once everyone is settled.

"Mind if I smoke?" Cyrus asks, pulling a pack of cigs from his pocket. Roch pushes an ashtray in front of him, and he lights up, taking a puff before speaking. "We think Crash killed Wrecker."

What the fuck?

"Why did you make him Prez, then?" Loki asks.

"Things went fast. Crash and Wrecker went on a ride together, nothing new. They were close, and it wasn't a secret that Wrecker was grooming Crash to take over. Hours later, Crash called and said they were ambushed, and Wrecker got shot and was on his way to the hospital. As you can imagine, we were pissed and ready for a war. We needed a Prez to lead us. Seemed like the best choice."

"Who shot Wrecker?" Goblin lights up a fat cigar, clouding the air with thick smoke.

"That's the thing. The description he gave us was vague as fuck. Something about some skinheads in a van. We've had problems with some neo-Nazis who don't like the way we conduct business, so we assumed it was them. Except they weren't taking credit, and those arrogant fucks would be the first to let us know if they killed Wrecker."

"Why would Crash kill the man who was setting out to retire and recommend him taking over?" I ask.

"I think the answer is with Riley."

"What do you mean?"

"We all knew he had a thing for her, but Wrecker was keeping him away. I don't know if Wrecker saw something in him that he didn't want around his kid or what. But I overheard a conversation where Wrecker told Crash he'd put him in the ground before letting him go after Riley. I assumed it was some fatherly overprotective shit, but after everything that's happened, I don't know."

My dark demon froths at the mouth, slowly taking me over like a fire burning within. I knew Crash was an asshole but didn't know just how bad. And I fuckin' let him stay in the same house with her.

"What do you think really happened?" I growl out.

"I think Wrecker saw something in Crash he didn't like and was rethinking his decisions. Crash couldn't let that happen, so he shot him."

"You really think he'd kill his Prez?" Loki asks.

"Hell yeah, I do. The kid has always been a little off, but Wrecker couldn't see it." The barrel-chested man stamps out his cig. "I don't know what else to tell you guys, except if you find him before we do, we'd appreciate you delivering him to us."

"Fuck no," I say.

"Thought you'd say that, so I have another request."

"What?"

"Let us help you find him. We don't have the resources you guys have, but we have a fuck more members than you, ready to do whatever's necessary."

Loki looks around at each of us, ready to send him packing if any of us catches a bad vibe about the guy. But no one does. He seems genuine.

"Okay."

"Appreciate it. One more thing."

Loki leans forward, resting his elbows on the table. "What?"

Cyrus meets his posture. "I want to be there when you kill the bastard. Wrecker was my best friend, my Prez, and was the best man at my wedding. I need to look him in the eyes when you send him to Hades."

"That can be arranged," Khan says.

"I need to make a call, get my guys here. Then we do an information exchange. Might piece together where he's hiding." Cyrus stands and pulls his cell phone out. "Be back in a minute."

While we wait for the Sons of Erebus to flock in, I go check on Veda again. There's a bigger crowd of women with her now. Sissy, Tabitha, and Birdie are circled around my kid, laughing and smiling big. Bexley's out there too, but she's sitting in a chair with sunglasses on, not joining in on the fun.

"How's it going?" I ask Truly.

"Oh my God, Coyote. She is adorable. Can we keep her, please?"

"That's what I'm trying to make happen," I mutter under my breath, but I'm smiling. I had nothing to do with how amazing this kid is, yet I feel so much damn pride. "Where'd the toys come from?"

"Oh, Bexley stopped by the store on her way over." Truly goes back to playing with dolls, and I sit next to Bexley.

"Thanks for that." I nod to the girl who is thankfully oblivious to what's going on around her.

"Not a big deal." She lifts her sunglasses to the top of her head. "Any news?"

"No, except the psychopath was working without the support of his club."

Her lips twist, and she stares at me long and hard for a minute before uncrossing her legs and shifting in her seat so she's closer to me. "I know I should mind my own business, but when I heard about Riley's dad's accident, I called up a detective I know who was assigned to the case."

My brows raise.

"Don't look at me like that. It felt off to me. I'm a defense attorney; I have a sixth sense for these kinds of things." She rolls her eyes.

"So?" I ask expectantly.

"They don't buy Crash's story. If it happened the way he said, Wrecker wouldn't have taken a bullet to the back of the head. When there's a revenge kill, they want the last thing the person sees to be the one ending them. Or something like that."

Makes sense. Matter of fact, I did that exact thing to Lucas Orton weeks ago.

"Thanks for asking about it," I say. Veda laughs, and it's deep and throaty for a little girl, making all the women swoon around her. "How come you're not going gaga over my kid?"

"No offense, but kids are dirty, smelly, and sticky. I doubt you'd understand this, but this dress is a Saint Laurent."

I nod even though I have no fuckin' clue what that means.

"Coyote," Loki says, popping his head out the slider. "The Sons are here."

"Better go back," I say to Bexley, who lowers her glasses over her eyes. Before I return to the chapel, I step between the gaggle of women and crouch in front of Veda. "You good, kid?"

"Look at my new dolls." She holds up a range of white, brown, and black dolls. I appreciate Bexley even more now.

"Pretty cool. You having fun?"

"Yes. Can we call Mommy and tell her about my new toys?" The way her pretty blue eyes light up is a punch to the gut.

"Later, yeah?"

"Yeah." Her excitement dims a bit, and I fuckin' hate it. Need Riley back and need her back right fuckin' now.

After hearing the info the Sons had, I realized finding a needle in a haystack would be easier than finding Riley because they have shit to contribute.

"So, what you're saying is you know abso-fuckin'-lutely nothing?" I ask, and four Sons jump to their feet at my tone. Cyrus holds up a hand, and they lower back to their chairs.

We had to move to the dining room since twelve Sons showed up at our door, with another twelve back at their clubhouse awaiting instruction. We have the manpower, but we don't have shit to go off of.

"He was one of you, your Prez, for weeks now, and you can't think of anything?" Loki continues my frustration.

"Hey, if it weren't for us, you wouldn't even know half the story," Cyrus says with his booming voice.

"Story means shit if we don't know where he is." Loki pulls his cigarettes from his pocket and glances out the back slider door at where Birdie is, then tucks the pack back in his pocket.

Time's ticking, and all we're doing is blaming each other and having a pissing contest. I need to fuckin' do something. My skin crawls, my dark demon scratching me up from the inside.

Looking around the room, I catch sight of Sly clicking away at the keyboard. I haven't been in front of a computer since tenth grade, the last year of school I completed before dropping out. But I understand the power of technology and have seen what Sly's capable of. He's damn impressive.

I also know that he's on the FBI's most wanted list for

194

hacking into government agencies, but they only know him under his old screen name. He's done with that phase of his life now and uses his skills to benefit the club. Still illegal but much less risky.

"You got anything?" I take a seat next to him and away from the shouting bikers.

"Maybe. Need a few more minutes."

I sit idly by, knowing I wouldn't have found Riley without him, so if anyone can find Crash, it's him.

"Because his dad works at the shop the Sons own, I got Crash's real name. Which is Landon James, by the way. From there, I searched county records to look for property he might own." He's speaking to me, but his eyes are fixated on the screen. "Except he doesn't. But I got to thinking his dad might."

"And?" I urge.

"He also doesn't, but Crash's grandpa does. A house in South Meadows and forty acres in NoCal near Portola."

"That's a long way away for a hunch. What's on the property?"

He clicks a few more times and brings up a map. "Looks like a dwelling."

I point to a different building. "What's this?"

"Probably a well house, or maybe an outhouse. Can't tell from this."

"It's the best lead we have so far. Guess we might as well check it out."

"I'll keep looking." He bumps me with his shoulder. "We'll find her, okay?"

"Sure as shit hope so. Not just for me but for the little girl over there."

"She's cute as hell. First kid I've seen around here since I got patched in. Makes this place feel more like a family and less like a frat house."

Outside, a giggling Veda's being chased by one of Roch's

dogs. Each time he catches her, he licks her face, making her laugh even harder. Sly's right. She brings an innocence and levity to a place I've only seen bathed in debauchery.

Soon, Roch and Truly's baby will be here, and I'm sure after Loki and Birdie's wedding, they'll add to their family too. Getting patched in came at the perfect time for the shift in the club.

But none of it will mean shit if we don't find Riley.

I stand and shout, "Need some volunteers to scout out a location in NoCal."

Goblin and Roch both raise their hand, along with two Sons.

Sly stands next to me. "It's forty acres of heavily wooded terrain, but I'll send you the coordinates of the dwelling to check out."

"Go in quiet," I add.

The four men nod and prepare to leave. Roch makes a stop outside to rub Truly's growing belly and give her a kiss. I'm surprised when my response is to think, *I want that.*

First thing I'll do when this is over is put another baby in Riley. Veda's no less my daughter because I wasn't around while she was growin' in her momma's belly or when she was a baby, but I regret I wasn't there, and I can't wait for the next one.

Fuck. I want that so bad.

Chapter
TWENTY-THREE

Riley

The next time I wake, it's to Crash standing over me. My eyes widen, and I suck in a sharp breath.

"What are you doing?" I ask.

"Checking on your wounds."

At the mention, the pulsing, throbbing pain comes back, no longer dulled by sleep. The only other time I've experienced this much pain was when I gave birth to Veda, but at least then, I had a newborn to snuggle when it was all over.

"I need a doctor," I groan.

"I think I can set your nose. Read up on it online."

"You're kidding me, right?" My brows bunch as he assesses my nose with a critical eye that frightens me.

"Not taking you to a doctor. It's me or nothing. All the other wounds are superficial."

"No." I shake my head and scoot back on the bed to sit up. "Absolutely not."

"You need me to do this. If left untreated, you could develop breathing problems or a nasal collapse." He tilts his head. "Not to mention your pretty face will be jacked up."

My throat plugs, and my eyes threaten to spill tears I don't want him to see.

When I say nothing, he tsks. "We need to build back our trust, you and me. We can't do that if you don't let me help you."

My only option to get out of here is to let him believe I've come around. I can't do that if I fight him at every turn. So despite my trepidation, I have to concede. There's no way around it. I can't sit around and hope someone comes for me.

"Okay." My voice is shaking, so I clear my throat and try again. "Okay. I'll let you try."

"That's better." He pulls a screwdriver out of his pocket and uses an alcohol pad to wipe it down.

My fear amps up a notch, and I'm second-guessing my decision. "What are you doing with that?"

"The doctor in the video had a tool with a flat end, but I couldn't find anything like that on the property, so this will have to do." He expels a breath and waves the screwdriver at me. "It'll hurt, but there's nothing I can do about that."

"Where are you putting that thing?" My imagination goes wild with a million possibilities, none of them good.

"This goes up your nose to provide counter pressure, then I'll use my fingers to bring it back into alignment." He readies himself by standing next to me. "Lie down all the way."

I scoot down on the bed and close my eyes. Maybe if I don't know what's happening, it won't be so bad. I can't imagine the pain being much worse than it is now, but that's probably naïve thinking.

"Ready?" he asks.

My heart races, and my breaths pick up. "Do it."

The cold metal of the screwdriver enters my nostril, and I feel his sweaty fingers grip the bridge of my nose. "One, two, three."

Searing pain shoots through my entire head, and I scream. Then I black out, letting sleep overtake me once again.

The next time I wake up, I'm in so much pain, I wish for death, pleading for God to take me away. But it doesn't happen.

"There you are. I was getting worried." Crash's voice tickles my ear, and I turn over, finding him on the cot with me, his body pressed up against my back.

I open my mouth to speak, but my tongue is stuck to the roof of my mouth. I'm parched. "Can I have some water?"

"Sure." He climbs over me to get off the bed. There's a rustle of a plastic bag, then he's back. "Here."

I guzzle the entire bottle without stopping. When I've downed every drop, I hand it back and ask the question I'm not sure I want to know the answer to. "Did it work?"

"I think so." He lifts up on an elbow and appraises me. "Won't know for sure until the swelling goes down."

It's crazy to think that a few weeks ago, I was actually worried about whether this asshole liked me. Now I can hardly look at him without wanting to throw up. My fingers curl into my hand, and my toes dig into the mattress to stop me from doing something stupid.

I've made it this far. I need to keep my head on straight until I can cultivate an escape plan.

"Can I use the bathroom?" I smile, hoping it doesn't come out like a sneer. "All that water is getting to me."

I need to know what's beyond that door. More importantly, I need to know where the exit is.

"I brought in a bucket." He at least has the decency to look sheepish at the suggestion.

"Crash, please. I'm covered in blood, and God knows what else. I'm disgusting. Can I please take a shower? Or at the very least, use a sink to clean up?" I'm also still on my period, but I'm not telling him that.

"There's no running water," he says.

"What? Where are we?"

"A cabin. There's a well, but the water pump went out a few years ago."

When he took me away from Veda, broken and bleeding, I thought that was the worst it could get. Then I woke up here and thought, no, this is the worst it can get. Now, I'm in some remote cabin after having my nose set with a screwdriver and no access to running water. Surely, *this* is as bad as it gets.

That thought is dangerous because, deep down, I know it's not.

I dig two fingers into my pounding temple. "So my only other option is peeing outside?"

I make it seem like that's the worst thing that could happen, but really, that's a best-case scenario. Maybe there are neighbors I can't see from this window, or maybe I'll find an escape route.

"No. It's too dangerous. It's dark out, and bears and mountain lions are out there."

Only now do I realize the room is lit by his lantern. "I'll be okay. It'll be fast."

He thinks long and hard before nodding. "Let me help you up."

Considering my body feels like I've been hit by a truck, I have no choice but to allow him to pull me to my feet. These dizzy spells are terrible, throwing me off balance and making me want to throw up the meager contents of my stomach.

Crash leads me up the stairs and into the main living area of this rustic cabin. There's a beat-up recliner in one corner, a wooden stove burning next to it, a basic kitchen with no appliances, and a wooden table with one chair pushed up to it.

To my left is a closed door that I'm assuming leads to the useless bathroom, but other than that, there's nothing else in here.

"This way." He reaches an arm around my waist to help me walk out the front door.

Much like what I've already seen, there's nothing here but woods. There might be neighbors but nothing I can see given the darkness.

"I don't have shoes," I say when I step down and am met with dry, sharp pine needles.

"Shit. I'll carry you."

I've barely tolerated his touch up to this point. Being in his arms would send me over the edge. I'm balancing on a proverbial thin wire here. If I go off balance even a degree, I might lose the facade I'm wearing. Then he'd see what I really think about him.

"No. I'm okay."

"You sure?"

"Yeah. Just tell me where to go."

He points to an area next to the house and hands me a roll of toilet paper. "Over there. There's a turned-over log."

Thankfully, he doesn't ask to escort me. I muster every ounce of energy I have to get myself over to the log. He turns his back to me, and the urge to run hits me. There has to be a house or another cabin somewhere close by. But it's pitch black out, I'm weak and injured, and I have no shoes.

I'm so angry and overwhelmed and exhausted. For the first time, I understand when Veda gets the same way and throws a tantrum. That's what I want to do. I want to throw myself to the ground, kick and scream, and get out all of this bubbling emotion. But unlike her, I don't have that luxury.

No. I'll hold myself together until I'm out of this hellhole.

I pull down my sleep pants, remove my tampon, and use the log to hold my ass up while I pee on the ground and wrap toilet paper around my panties. *Better than nothing.* It requires a lot of balance for my current state, but thankfully I don't fall on my piss. Especially since there isn't a working shower.

I thought Crash was looking away the whole time, but the second my pants are up, he's at my side, helping me back into the cabin and downstairs to the bed. Feeling like I ran a marathon—not just taking a bathroom break—I curl onto my side, ready for the blessed peace of sleep once again.

Crash leaves me. Thank God. I need some time without him

in my space. Seconds later, though, he returns, a crocheted afghan similar to the one I use at home in his hand. It makes me miss my log cabin with a view. Even if it isn't rightfully mine. The dull throb of disappointment over Crash's deception makes my chest ache.

Wrecker didn't have to die. None of this had to happen.

Crash tugs his shirt off, exposing his muscled torso that's covered in a chaotic scene of tattoos, and pulls his gun from the back of his jeans before removing his belt. Thankfully, he keeps his pants on.

"What are you doing?" Then it hits me. There's only one bed.

"Can't fuck you looking like that, so wipe that look off your face," he jokes, except it's not funny. Not even a little. "Been a long day, and we both need sleep."

I scoot as close to the edge as I can get and tuck the quilt around me. If physical space can't be a barrier, I'm sure as hell keeping layers between us. He climbs over me, gun in hand, and I nearly let out a choked sob when his arm goes around my waist, pulling me into him.

"Can't have you trying to escape while I sleep," he mumbles, pressing cold steel to my back. "This is just a reminder not to even try. You won't make it to the door before I shoot you in the leg."

The sleep I was so desperate for now evades me. His arm feels like an octopus tentacle, slimy and dangerous, and his comment about not raping me doesn't fool me. I doubt my injuries would deter him, and I don't want to be unconscious if he tries.

If I thought for one second I could escape, I'd do it. I'd wait until his breathing evened out and slip out of his hold. But right now, my only focus is staying alive. I need to get back to my daughter and Coyote. We deserve our happy ending.

Crash sighs, and I cringe. His touch disgusts me. The feel of his breath on the back of my neck makes my skin crawl, and the fact that he found the peaceful sleep I'm craving pisses me off to where I can't hold still.

"Hold fucking still, Ry. I can't sleep with you squirming all over the place," Crash says, his voice sleep roughened and his arm gripping me tighter.

My eyes close, and I chew the inside of my mouth until I taste blood. With nothing to distract me, the pain comes back full force. My head pounds, my nose throbs, and something passes through my body, a tingling, light, floating sensation. When it reaches my head, darkness clouds my mind.

Something's wrong. Really wrong.

"Fucking wake up!" an angry voice shouts near my face.

I didn't realize I had fallen asleep. I don't think I did. My eyes flutter open, and with no warning, I throw up. Forceful hands turn me onto my side, and I cough up the bile and residual contents of my stomach onto the floor next to the bed. When I'm done, I turn back around. The disgusting vomit and saliva trickle down my neck, making me feel disgusting, but I'm so weak I don't even have the strength to wipe it away.

"Jesus Christ. What the hell is wrong with you?" Crash asks.

"I don't feel so good," I slur. My head is floaty, and my entire aches in a way I've never experienced.

"You were shaking like you were having a seizure." He gets up, tucking his gun back into his jeans. "Are you sick?"

"I don't know, but—" My words are cut off by another round of throwing up, only this time I'm able to roll to my side.

"Fuck." He paces the floor, agitated.

"Need a hospital," I cry out but no tears flow.

"I can't take you to a hospital."

"Please, Crash. Something's wrong."

Crash freezes when a sound comes from upstairs.

"Shit. They found us." He reaches for his gun and moves to the door. "Stay here, Riley. I don't want to have to kill you."

He doesn't have to worry. I'm not going anywhere.

Chapter
TWENTY-FOUR

Coyote

I can't sleep, and I'm going crazy inside, so I step outside to meditate. Maybe the starry sky and cool breeze will give me perspective and focus for my scattered mind.

Pulling off my socks and boots, I wiggle my toes in the wild grass, feeling the wide blades crunch under my weight. After running through a series of yoga poses, I sit down cross-legged and rest my hands on my knees.

I don't know how long I stay there, eyes closed, listening to the sounds of nature, but when my cell rings, it's as though I'm pulled from a dream. Except I wasn't asleep. My mind is clear and calm, and I'm ready for the fight ahead.

"Yeah?" I answer.

"It's him," Roch says, short and clipped.

"Did you see Riley?"

"No."

I don't let that get to me. Crash wouldn't have gone through all this just to kill her. Plus, it sounds stupid, but I think I would know if she weren't on this earth anymore. I'd feel the planet shift with the loss of her life. My soul tie would be broken.

"Lie low. Be there soon." I rush to put my socks and shoes back on.

"Wait 'til mornin,'" he says in a shocking display of verbal skills.

"I can't, brother. Would you be able to wait to rescue Truly from that psycho?"

I know his answer before he says it. He went through hell to be with that girl, and he'd do it time and time again if he had to.

"No."

"Like I said, be there soon."

The line goes dead because Roch doesn't need things like formalities.

After the guys left on the scouting trip earlier, Truly reminded me kids need to be fed regularly, so Tabitha made macaroni and cheese. Veda gobbled that shit up like it was the best thing she'd ever had. Once it got dark, Truly suggested finding somewhere for her to sleep. Birdie stepped up and offered to take her back to her place. I was worried she wouldn't want to go without me, but she and Birdie were best friends by then, so she grabbed her backpack, gave me a hug, and left.

If I'm honest with myself, I was the one who had a hard time. I didn't want to let her out of my sight. I was already without her mom, throwing my world off its axis, so taking Veda away sent me into a full tilt. But I knew it was for the best. The more distracted she is, the less she'll miss her mom.

Loki stayed at the clubhouse in case he was needed, so my first stop was to his bedroom, where I rapped my knuckles on his door.

"Yeah," he calls out groggily.

"Found him. Gonna round up the guys and text the Sons."

"Okay. Be out in five."

I shoot a text to Cyrus, who replies like he was waiting by the phone. Which he might've been. No one's more pissed off than I am, but Cyrus is running a close second. His brother double-crossed his club and killed his president. There are few betrayals worse.

I pace from the dining room to the game room and back again for what feels like fuckin' ever, waiting for everyone to show. By the time they do, it's first light.

We file out of the clubhouse without much of a plan since we aren't sure what we're up against. Sly found blueprints for Crash's simple cabin, but other than that, we're playing it by ear.

The morning is peaceful and quiet until nine bikers start their engines. The ground vibrates with the rumble of bikes as we pull out of the gate and onto the road. Miles trails us in the van. We'll need a cage for after we rescue Riley since it's unclear what kind of shape she's in. Ford said her face was jacked, but her injuries could be more severe by now.

The air is chilly and bites against my exposed arms and face, but the sun will be hot in two hours or less, so I didn't bother with a jacket.

With few cars on the road, we're able to make it to Portola in just under an hour. We make the turn onto a dirt road and park. From here, we're walking so Crash doesn't hear us coming. We need to catch him off guard and not give him time to prepare.

"The cabin sits on this road, but we'll have to cut through the woods to stay hidden," Goblin says, pointing through the trees. "Riley's car is there, and we got a visual of Crash but not Riley."

"Let's load up." Loki circles a finger in the air, and we congregate at the back of the van to grab the long guns stored back there.

I also have my Glock tucked in the back of my pants; there's no such thing as too many weapons in this situation.

"Lead the way," I say to Goblin, and we begin our hike through the forest, leaving Miles and Roch behind to keep an eye on the bikes. They'll be on standby for when we need the van.

The hike there is quiet, save for our boots crunching the forest floor. My dark demon taunts me the closer we get, suggesting all the many ways I should murder this fool once we've caught him. I don't disagree with any of the suggestions.

Once we get close, Goblin raises a fist, and we stop. He points through the trees, and I get my first look at the cabin, if you can call it that. It's more of a shack that hasn't fared well over the years.

"Do you want to go scout it out?" Loki asks me. I appreciate he's letting me take the lead. It's a show of respect I don't take lightly.

I nod, and we creep closer. I'm in my element, at one with nature as my feet connect with Mother Earth. This is what I do, where I feel most at home.

It's still early, so I feel confident when I peer through a window on the east side. It's a small room with a kitchen and sitting area, nothing special, but no Riley. Or Crash. But there are things strewn about—an empty bowl sitting next to the sink, boots by the front door, and a half-full glass of water on the table.

Someone's here.

I walk around to the back of the cabin and peer into the other two windows. One is frosted the way a bathroom would be, and the other gives me the same view of the living room and kitchen, just from a different perspective, telling me there are no bedrooms.

So where the hell are they?

Then I look down and see concrete. I kneel and dig down a few inches, realizing it's not the footing; it's a basement.

"They're down there," I whisper.

"Shit," Loki curses under his breath.

Returning to the group, I fill them in on what I saw and where I think Riley is.

"I'm going in," I say, checking to make sure my Glock is locked and loaded.

"That's fuckin' stupid. You don't know what he's got going on down there." Loki places his hands on his hips.

"We have no other choice. We don't know how long he's prepared to hole himself up in here." My gaze returns to the ramshackle cabin.

"I don't like it," Loki says.

"I'm going with you." Cyrus removes his coat and pulls out his own weapon.

I nod. "The rest of you wait here in case he gets away."

Like a pack of wolves, we descend on the forest. He's outnumbered and surrounded. If he walks away from this, it'll only be because we're taking him to the kill room where he'll pay for his sins before I send him straight to Hades, where he belongs.

We creep onto the rickety wooden porch, and I try the door handle. No surprise it's locked. Since Cyrus is built like a brick house, he steps back and throws his shoulder into the door. The frame splinters, and the hinges give way, sending the door crashing to the ground.

"Good work," I say.

"Cover me." He lifts his gun and steps inside, looking to the left and right, while I follow behind, ready to fire at anything that moves.

We only make it halfway to the stairwell for the basement before there's a loud blast. At first, I think Cyrus fired his weapon. At least until he turns around to face me and I see the look in his eyes. His hands go to his chest, and I know he's been hit.

In a flash, I dive for the stairs, feeling the whir of another bullet whizzing past me. I nearly fall down the stairs but catch myself on the railing. Looking back, I see a lifeless Cyrus on the ground, blood pooling below him, soaking the wood floors.

Jesus fuck.

I can't go back out there; it would be a death sentence. Peering around the corner, I see Crash, shotgun aimed at me. He fires, and the plaster of the wall right next to my head explodes. I dig my phone out of my pocket and text Loki.

Me: Cyrus is down, Crash is armed. Going downstairs to find Riley.

I barely get the text sent before there's another explosion, this one much bigger and not from a gun. Some kind of bomb, maybe? I don't know and don't have time to figure it out. Rushing down the stairs, I open the one door at the bottom.

My dark demon roars when I see her broken and swollen face. Those owl eyes I love so much are nearly swollen shut, and her pale, creamy skin is marred with cuts and bruises. She's almost unrecognizable.

I can't wait to get my hands on Crash. That motherfucker just earned himself the slowest death known to man.

Rushing over to her, I sink to my knees, only realizing there's a pool of vomit on the floor after it's too late.

"I can't believe you're here." Riley falls into my arms, her body trembling. Whether from the trauma of the situation or shock, I don't know, but fuck, it feels good to be breathing in the scent of her patchouli and mint shampoo. It's faint, nearly covered up by the metallic scent of blood and the sour odor of vomit, but it's there.

"Need you to get up, Little Owl. We need to barricade the door before he comes down here." I help her up, noticing she's trembling. Not in fear, though. It's something else I don't have time to decipher.

It's then I notice she isn't wearing shoes, and the glass from the window at her house cut her feet. She leaves a footstep inked in blood with every step she takes away from the bed.

"Your feet," I say.

"It's fine. I'll be okay," she assures me in a shaky voice.

Goddamn, I'm proud of how she's handling all this. She's so

fuckin' brave, my girl. And when this is all over, I'll spend every day making sure she knows it.

I tip the bed on its side and push it up against the door. It's not a perfect solution, but it'll buy us some time to get the fuck out of here.

"You okay, Little Owl?" I ask, drawing her into my arms.

"I was so scared," she says, but her voice sounds off, slow almost, like she's drunk.

I'm about to get my phone out and figure out how to get us out of here when her body spasms and she falls limp in my arms. It's like nothing I've ever seen before. Like she's been struck by lightning.

Panicking, I lower her convulsing body to the ground. I keep her upper body pressed to mine and push my back against the overturned bed in case Crash tries to make his way in.

I brush her blood-stained and matted hair from her bruised face to get a look. Her eyes are open but unseeing, and her pupils are completely blown. She's having a fuckin' seizure.

"Come on, Little Owl. Come back to me. It's okay," I murmur as I rock her.

I know fuck all about seizures, so I'm forced to sit here while she works her way through it. After what feels like an hour but was probably only a minute or two, her violent movements slow. She blinks her eyes slowly, finally coming back to me.

"What happened?" she slurs.

"Think you had a seizure."

"I'm cold." It's then I notice her body is covered in goosebumps. I touch her forehead gently with the back of my hand. She's hot. Really fuckin' hot.

"Shit. You have a fever."

"I don't feel so good. I think I'm going to—" Her head turns, and I barely move before the contents of her stomach spill onto the concrete floor.

How the hell am I going to get her out of here?

I get my phone out and call Loki. "Riley's sick, bro. Like really fuckin' sick. She just had a seizure, and she's burning up."

"Fuck," he curses under his breath. "Crash tossed a bottle bomb out at us when we tried to breach the cabin after we heard the shots. You think Cyrus is dead?"

"Don't know. If he's not yet, he's headed there fast."

"Are you safe?"

"For now."

"Okay, sit tight. We'll work on getting you out."

"I'm worried, brother. She can't even stand."

He's quiet for a long minute. "We got you.

"Okay." I hang up and clutch her to my chest. "Hang on, okay? We're almost out of here, then I'll get you to the hospital."

"I'm okay," she says, her teeth chattering. I slip my cut and shirt off and drape it over her body, holding her close so she can absorb my body heat. "Where's Veda?"

"She's okay. She's with Birdie and Truly. They're spoiling her fuckin' rotten." I smile.

"I miss her." This time her voice shakes from emotion, and her lip quivers.

"Shh. It's okay. You'll be back with her before you know it."

"I had to leave her there alone. I had to. If I didn't, Crash would've hurt her too," she explains.

"You did the right thing. Ford got inside and sat with her until we got there. She was scared, but she's okay now." I brush my lips over the top of her head. "She asked about you constantly. Had to tell her you were with your mom running boring errands."

She lets out a quiet laugh. "That's the best lie you could come up with?"

"Hey," I tease. "I was caught off guard."

Her lips fall into a straight line, and her body goes into convulsions again. I've never felt so fuckin' helpless than to hold her while she shakes, eyes unblinking and mind off somewhere else.

I'm seconds from storming upstairs and taking Crash out myself just to get her to the hospital when I smell something burning. My eyes dart to the door, and sure as shit, smoke is pouring in from the gap at the bottom.

My dark demon claws at my skin, but I push him down. I can't panic. Not now. Not when Riley needs me. The walls are closing in.

Riley's body stops shaking, and I scoot us to the opposite wall, getting as far away from the smoke as I can get. She comes to and looks around like she doesn't know where she's at.

"It's okay. Had another seizure. We're going to be okay." But even I don't believe those words. Not when I'm on the brink of freaking the fuck out.

Her eyes dart to mine. "Smoke."

Chapter
TWENTY-FIVE

Riley

Coyote's hold on me loosens, and when I look up at him, his eyes are wide and wild with panic. Sweat collects on his brows and drips down his face, his chest moving up and down so fast he can't even take a proper breath of air.

It's the smoke.

"Need to get us the fuck out of here." He all but shoves me off him when he stands. Walking over to the door, he taps the handle with his hand. "Shit. The stairs are wood. That must be where he set the fire."

"It's okay. The guys will get us out."

"It's not fuckin' okay, Riley. Not fuckin' okay." He runs a hand over hair that's just beginning to grow in. He hasn't shaved his head in a while, and I briefly wonder if it's because he wants to match Veda. She's been surrounded by people who don't look like her all her life, but now she has someone who has the same skin tone and same hair. Her dad.

"Come sit down with me," I say, and he slows his pacing. "Please."

His eyes dart to the smoke and then over to me, like he's

debating what to do. I can see how hard this is for him. It's written all over his body language. From his rigid muscles to his clenched jaw, this is like a repeat of everything he went through years before.

"Please, baby. I'm freezing. I need you." I need to touch him, need to give him a reason to keep his thoughts here with me.

Eventually, he gives in and resumes his position. I curl into his warmth, thankful to feel his heat.

"I'm sorry." He kisses the top of my head, which I know must be disgusting, coated in blood, and who knows what else. It's for that reason the kiss means more to me than he will ever know.

"Don't apologize."

"When I was eight, my dad locked me and my mom in a closet and set fire to the house. We tried so hard to open the door, but I think he wedged it closed. Our house was built in the fifties, back when laundry chutes were popular, and we were in the closet with the chute. I didn't want to leave her there, but she made me, so I slid down to the basement and got out the back door. I ran next door and told the neighbors, but by the time the fire department got there, it was too late. My mom died of smoke inhalation."

"That's why you won't sleep indoors."

He nods. "And I don't like confined places."

I run a hand down his scruffy cheek. "You were so brave."

"I left her there," he says through gritted teeth

"Your mom would give up her own life for you over and over if she could." I cough through my next breath, my thoughts becoming fuzzy, and God, I'm so tired.

"She loved me. She was the only one who loved me."

My heart simultaneously aches and flutters for him because I'm sad for his loss, but also, I already know I love him. I don't know when or how it could happen. We're only now getting to know one another. But the love I feel hasn't been earned through time; it's deeper than that.

I hold in the words because when I say them, I want it to be special, and not when we're stuck in a basement with a literal fire outside our door.

"I'm sorry that happened to you. Where's your dad now?" I ask.

His brown eyes darken to nearly black. "Got sentenced to thirty years, served fifteen thanks to overcrowding and good behavior. Apparently, he found Jesus Christ in there." He laughs humorously. "Found *him* after he left too."

"What do you mean?"

"You really want to know what kind of monster you're involved with?" His lips purse.

I know right away what he means. He killed him. Surprisingly, it doesn't change my opinion of him in the least. "Good. He deserved it."

The shock and awe in his expression make my heart bubble over. "You're perfect, you know that?"

He leans in like he's going to kiss me, but I turn away. "I'm not kissable right now."

Another explosion sounds, and I cling to Coyote. I don't know what's going on, but I have a sick feeling that neither one of us will escape this alive. A thick layer of smoke has settled on the ceiling, getting lower and lower. Soon, it'll cut off our oxygen, and we'll meet the same fate as his mom.

I cough, and he lifts his shirt to cover my mouth and nose. "Keep this on."

We both jump at the *pop* of gunfire. It lasts for so long, each bang scaring me more and more. What are the odds of Crash killing all of them before killing us? I don't know.

"I wish I knew what was happening," I say.

Coyote's leg bounces along with his gaze. The door, the ceiling, me, the door again, over and over.

"Need to get up a second." He shifts me off of him. "Stay here."

This time I don't make him come back to me. He needs to expel some of his nervous energy. I get it. I curl into a ball on the concrete floor, too tired to hold myself up, as I watch my beautiful stalker pace around the room. Every now and then, he tests the door handle, like it'll magically not be burning hot.

His phone rings, and he nearly drops it in his scramble to answer it. "Yeah?"

I pay close attention to his expression, looking for a clue as to what happened upstairs, but he gives nothing away.

"Fuck," he curses, rubbing at the back of his neck. "No. It's too risky."

That doesn't sound good.

"I'll figure it out," he bites out and shoves his phone in his pocket.

"What did he say?" I reluctantly ask.

"We're on our own. They wanted to come down, but I told them not to."

"What are we going to do?"

"I don't know, but I swear to God, I'll get you out if it's the last thing I do." Then in a move I didn't see coming, he donkey kicks the door. It flies open as the flames lick their way through the door. "The ceiling will be the next to burn, then the floor will collapse into this room. We have to get out before that happens."

"Okay."

Coyote tries to lift me, but a coughing attack hits him, and he can't with spasming lungs. "Fuck. Hold on."

Again, he sets me down. I curl into a ball, holding his shirt up to my nose to block the smoke and letting me breathe in his woodsy, leathery scent. This is exactly the last thing I want to smell if I die.

Through painful sounding wheezes, he tries again. Then I'm back in his arms, and he's standing.

"Hold on, Little Owl. Don't let go," he murmurs into my ear before running out the door and up the stairs. The fire is all around, burning so powerfully hot it sucks the air from my lungs and singes my nostrils.

We make it to the main level with the fire still everywhere, though it must've been started on the stairs because it hasn't fully engulfed the room. Waiting at the front door is a behemoth of a man with majestic, flowing hair and the thickest beard I've ever seen.

"Jesus?" I ask, my fever taking away my grip on reality.

"Not Jesus, darlin'. Though I can't wait to tell my woman someone thinks so." He smirks and takes me out of Coyote's arms. "Glad to finally meet you. Name's Khan."

I hack in response, my lungs squeezing painfully. He turns and, with big strides, takes me away from the cabin.

"Wait. Coyote," I say, having lost sight of him.

"He's okay. He's—"

Another explosion detonates, and Khan ducks in response with me in his arms. I look over his shoulder and don't see Coyote anywhere.

"Shit," Khan curses and passes me over to another man with bright blue eyes.

I gasp, this time not from my lungs trying to clear themselves out. No, this time, it's because I'm looking at a man I recognize from the picture I found in my mom's things. I think this is my dad.

The picture was one Polaroid of them lying on a bed, holding the camera out to take a selfie. Mom was turned toward him, a hand covering her laugh, but he was smiling right into the camera. He was much younger, still a teenager, I think.

A window bursts, and the fire crackles louder, pulling me from my reverie.

"Where's Coyote?" I demand. "I need to make sure he's okay."

"Not safe to stick around. Coyote would want me to get you as far from here as possible."

A surge of adrenaline has me fighting against his hold. "No. I won't leave him."

He scrambles to keep me in his arms. "Okay, girlie. Chill out. But we're staying here."

He turns so I can watch as Khan runs into the trees. He disappears for way too long. Each second he's gone is like a year taken off my life. When he reappears, he has the limp body of Coyote tossed over his shoulder.

A blood-curdling scream rips from my chest. "No!"

"What the fuck?" Another man appears, this one Japanese, and runs to aid Khan.

I scramble to break free from the hold on me by the man I think is my bio dad, but he holds tight. "His brothers have him. Nothing you can do."

Khan lays him down and leans over his body. There are burn holes up and down his jeans, his forearms appear charred, and he hasn't woken up.

"Calm down," the man holding me whispers into my ear. Something about his tone and the absolute nature of his words settles me, and I stop struggling. "That's better."

Only now that I'm not working toward a goal, my broken body and fever overtake me. The last thing I see before I black-out are the blue eyes of the man holding me. Only this time, I don't want the peace. I try to fight it, but the dizziness and roaring in my ears are too much.

I wake up to an annoying beeping that won't stop. I try to slap my alarm clock but remember I don't own one, and I haven't since I was fifteen years old when I got my first cellphone with a built-in alarm.

I blink once, seeing a flash of white. I blink twice and see a TV mounted on a wall in front of me. I blink three times and finally manage to keep my eyes open.

The pain. Oh God, the pain. It's all-consuming and coming from every inch of me. I groan and turn onto my side, curling my legs up to my chest. The next time my eyes open, I startle at seeing a stunning blonde woman looking expectantly at me.

"Hey, there," she says.

"Hi." My mind scrolls through the list of people I've met in my life, but she's not one of them.

Seeing my confusion, she grins. "We haven't met. My name's Bridgette. I'm Loki's ol' lady." She uses air quotes around the last part. When she sees my confusion, she expands. "He's the club prez."

The club, the cabin, Crash, Coyote. It all comes back to me. Oh God. I scan the room. I'm in the hospital.

"Coyote," I say. My voice sounds like I'm talking through gravel.

She frowns and rests a hand on the bedrail. "He's okay, just banged up."

"I have to see him." I try to sit up, but my muscles won't cooperate.

"Just relax. You can't see him right now."

"Why?"

"Well, you're a fall risk for one." She points to the bright red bracelet affixed to my wrist.

I clear my throat. "Don't care."

"I know you're worried, but I promise he's okay. Just some smoke inhalation and a couple of burns. He wouldn't let the doctors look at him until he knew you were okay. Once you were stable, he agreed to go down to the ER. He'll be back, babe."

Knowing that helps calm me, and I sink back into the bed. At least until I think about Veda.

"She's okay too," Bridgette says. Apparently, she's a mind reader. "I knew that would be your next question."

"Where is she?"

"She's with Roch's girl, Truly. Took her to her mom's veterinary clinic to play with puppies." She sits up straighter, her brown eyes lighting up. "You have the cutest daughter ever. She spent the night at my place last night. We had a slumber party and watched Disney movies."

I smile. "Let me guess . . ."

"*Tangled*," we say at the same time and then laugh, which turns into a coughing fit for me.

"Drink some water." She holds a plastic cup with a straw out to me, and I suck down the cool liquid. It feels so good on my burning throat.

"Knock, knock." A voice draws our attention to the door. A woman in a white lab coat and holding a tablet walks in. "Miss Renna, glad to see you're awake. How are you feeling?"

"I'm okay." *Lies*. If I had been hit by a truck, I think I'd feel better than I do now.

"I doubt that." She taps something into the tablet. "Let's see. You have a severe concussion which explains the seizures and spike in temperature. You have multiple contusions, your nose is broken in two places, your feet have some nasty cuts, two of which needed stitches, and you have smoke inhalation, which we're treating with oxygen. And you feel okay?" She pauses for a reaction, but I'm too shocked to give her anything but wide eyes. "We cleaned up your head wound and set your nose properly."

I reach up to feel the bandage on my temple, then move lower to the hard splint covering my nose.

"All things considered, you're pretty lucky. We didn't find a brain bleed, and the plastic surgeon said your broken nose should heal without surgery. We're keeping you here for the next forty-eight hours for observation, but as long as there are no changes, you'll be free to go after." She taps out a few more things using a stylus, then holds the tablet to her chest and smiles. "Do you have any questions?"

"I don't think so."

"Okay. Well, if that changes, push this call button." She shows me the switch tethered to the bed. "And if you need a bump in your pain meds, push this button."

"Thank you."

"No problem." She almost makes it to the door before she turns back around. "Also, the friend you came in with?"

She must mean Coyote, so I nod, my ears perking up, desperate for more information.

"He was adamant about you knowing he's okay. He's having an X-ray done and getting some oxygen, but if all goes well, he should be back up here to see you in an hour or so." She gives me a knowing smile. "He's very worried about you."

"Thanks, Doctor," Bridgette says, resting her hand on mine.

"No problem." As she walks out, the best sight I've seen all day comes in.

"Mommy," Veda says, running toward me.

A beautiful woman with copper skin, a pregnant belly, and long black hair follows behind. "Remember what we talked about. We have to be gentle with Mommy."

Veda stops at the side of my bed, a look of concern etched on her features. "You have owies. We have to be sweet." She runs a hand up and down my arm.

"Hey, baby. I'm so happy to see you." Even knowing I shouldn't cry and worry her more, I do. I can't help it. Not that long ago, I was lying in a burning cabin, ready to succumb to a fire. Now I'm alive and back with my daughter.

"Don't cry, Mommy."

"They're happy tears. Very happy tears." I hold out a hand that she takes. "I heard you had a slumber party with Bridgette."

"Bridgette?" Her adorable head tilts to the side.

"Birdie," Bridgette intervenes. "Everyone calls me Birdie."

"Hey, Riley. I'm Truly, Roch's ol' lady." She rubs a soothing hand over my calf. "Thanks for sharing your girl with us. She was good practice for when this one comes." She rests a hand on her belly.

"You made so many new friends," I say to Veda. "You're so lucky."

"Truly works at a vet. She showed me puppies and kitty-cats." Her hands weave together under her chin, and her little nose scrunches. "They were so cute."

All three of us giggle at how adorable my girl is.

"How are you feeling?" Truly asks, lifting Veda to sit next to me on the bed.

"I've been better. Kind of embarrassed this is how we're meeting."

"Don't be. We're just glad you're okay." She turns to Birdie. "How's everyone?"

Birdie's face falls. "Coyote and Khan are in the ER getting some burns looked at. Still waiting for news on Cyrus."

My ears perk. "What's wrong with Cyrus?"

"I guess he got shot."

I gasp and look around for my phone, but I have no earthly clue where it is. Back home, I'd guess. "Char. I need to call Charlotte."

"Here's my phone." Birdie hands me her phone.

I stare at it, my fingers hovering over the buttons. "I don't know her number."

"Who's Char, Riley?" Truly asks.

"Cyrus' old lady. She's my friend." I hand the phone back to Birdie.

"When I leave, I'll find out if she's here. If she is, I'll send her this way, okay?" Truly offers, and I nod.

Another woman walks in holding a smart briefcase and wearing a dress that looks like something from my old life.

Expensive, tailored, and gorgeous. "Is this where the hen party is?"

"Riley, this is Bexley. She's the club's lawyer and Khan's ol' lady," Birdie introduces.

"I reject that term." She rolls her eyes, but I see the twinkle of humor. "But yes, I'm with Khan."

"Jesus," I muse, remembering what my fevered brain thought up when I saw him.

"Girl, don't get me started. Do you know how many times he's told me that story already?" She leans against the wall, crossing her ankles, the perfect picture of sophistication.

"What about Crash?" I ask. The three biker chicks share a look I don't understand.

Bexley pushes off the wall. "Best you don't worry about him. Which brings me to why I'm here. Like Birdie said, I'm the club's lawyer. Because of the nature of your injuries, Cyrus getting shot, and a fire that was reported at a cabin in Portola, you might get a visit from a police officer or two. I've prepared a statement. Don't say anything, just hand them this." She opens her briefcase and pulls out a sheet of paper.

"What does it say?" I ask, reading the legal-speak on the page but not understanding most of it.

"Basically, if they want to talk to you, they need to do it with me present."

"Okay."

"Is this going to be a problem?" Truly asks, her brows furrowed.

"Shouldn't be. After all, Coyote and the guys were merely hiking in the area when they saw a cabin on fire. They thought there was someone in there and went inside to rescue them. Unfortunately, the old loon who owns the place was storing illegal bombs, and the fire caused them to detonate," she says, her smile evil. "I think Crash's grandpa will face some pretty hefty fines, and honestly, he's lucky we don't sue him."

"You're bad," Birdie jokes.

"To the bone." Bexley slings the strap of her bag over her shoulder. "Hospitals make me itch. You guys need anything? I'm going to find my man and get him home. He has a mild concussion and a bruised tailbone that needs tending to."

"Nope. We're all good." Birdie waves her off.

"I think I'll go too." Truly looks at Veda. "Do you want to come feed the dogs with me or stay here with Mommy?"

"Can I?" she asks me.

"Are you sure? They say I have to stay for forty-eight hours. I don't know what to do with her," I admit. "I can call my mom—"

"I'll take her home," the deep voice of my avenging angel says.

Chapter
TWENTY-SIX

Coyote

"**Y**ou're here," Riley says, her voice sounding like she's a three-pack-a-day smoker. She's covered in bandages and has a metal splint on her nose, but she's still the most beautiful woman I've ever seen.

"Can't keep me away, Little Owl." I throw her a wink.

"I was just asking Veda if she wanted to feed the dogs with me," Truly says. "Do you want to pick her up from the clubhouse later?"

I keep my eyes on Riley when I answer. "Sounds good. Gonna hang here a while."

I lift Veda from the bed, and she wraps her little arms around my neck in a hug before I set her down. Riley covers her mouth with a hand, looking surprised. Me and the little squirt have gotten so close, so quickly. Kind of like me and her mom.

"We're best friends now," I whisper so only Riley can hear.

"We're leaving too," Loki says, appearing in the doorway, hooking a finger at Birdie.

"That's my cue," Birdie jumps up from her chair. "Riley, I

wrote my number down on a pad of paper on the nightstand. Call me if you need anything."

"Thank you." Riley's voice cracks.

Once everyone has cleared out, I sit down on the edge of the bed.

"You found new clothes?" she asks.

"Had a prospect bring them." I look down at my clean black jeans, black shirt, and black leather cut.

She gently runs a hand down each of the white bandages on my forearms. "Are you okay?"

"Little Owl, you're hooked up to a hundred different machines, and you're asking if I'm okay?"

She bursts into uncontrollable sobs.

"Why the tears?" I ask, crawling into bed with her, carefully avoiding all the tubes and wires.

"I thought I lost you." She fists my shirt, holding onto me with purpose.

"Never. Our story has just begun, Little Owl. It can't end yet."

"I was so scared."

"I know, but everything's okay now." I tip her chin up. "Can I kiss you?"

She doesn't wait for an answer. She uses her grip on my shirt to pull me to her. Not even her dry and chapped lips can stop the electrifying zing from racing through me when I press my lips to hers.

It's not the passionate beginning of something more like every kiss we've shared before. No, this kiss is a reminder that we're still here, that we still have each other.

I cradle the back of her head, holding her in position while I place small and meaningful kisses all over her face, willing them to heal all that's been damaged. Not the physical injuries—those will take time and rest—but the hurts we have on the inside.

Even though we aren't the cause of them, we're the only ones who can fix them in each other.

She pulls away. "I have a confession to make."

"Oh yeah? What's that?" I pull a piece of blood-crusted hair off her forehead.

"I knew about the fire from your childhood before you told me in the cabin."

"I know," I say.

"How?"

"I spend a lot of time in the woods, so I notice things like footprints. Not to mention I'm very particular about my things. Put two and two together and could tell they'd been gone through."

"I'm sorry I snooped."

I chuckle. "Only you would apologize for that after I went through your entire house, snuck in at night to watch you sleep, and peered through your window while you got yourself off."

If her face wasn't so bruised, I'm certain there'd be a blush. "I still can't believe I did that." She narrows her eyes. "Wait. You snuck in while I was sleeping?"

"Every night. Told myself I was protecting you, but really I did it to be close to you."

"You could've knocked on my door, you weirdo." She smacks my chest.

"Had to make sure I was ready for the whole parenting gig. I had a shit dad and didn't want to put Veda through the same thing. Had to make sure I was ready for you, too, though. Spent five years convincing myself it was my cut I needed back. The second I saw you again, I knew that was all bullshit. Don't get me wrong, I wasn't happy you took my cut. But you stole something else that night. My fuckin' heart."

She rests a hand on my chest. "I'm sorry I was too chicken to stick around."

"Don't worry about all that now. Just work on getting better."

"Okay."

I snake my arm under her head, and she snuggles into my chest. She fits so perfectly there, like it was always meant to be. Maybe it was. Maybe one night can turn into a family.

Riley falls asleep while I lie awake. I'm bone-tired, but my mind won't let me rest. Not while I'm inside this massive concrete structure, and not after being trapped in another burning building. Logically, I realize the chance of anything like that happening again, and in a hospital, is minuscule. But there's still a chance.

It hasn't gone unnoticed by me that Riley and I were the same age when our lives imploded. Hers, when her mom moved her out of the only house she's known, and mine with the fire. Parallel traumas, only separated by years and the lives we've lived since.

It's going to take some time for us to learn everything there is to know about each other, but now that Crash has been apprehended by us, we have nothing but time to figure it all out.

Fuckin' Crash. I think back to Loki's retelling of events while Riley and I were trapped. After I got off the phone with him, they charged into the cabin. A gunfight ended with Crash running out of ammo like the fuckin' pathetic asshole he is.

After that, he had no choice but to give up. Loki hogtied him, knocked him out cold, and threw him in the back of the van. Thankfully, he stayed unconscious back there while we drove Riley to the hospital. Wouldn't have been pretty for anyone if he woke up, but I'm sure he's finally come around as he waits in the kill room for me at the clubhouse.

I'm not in any hurry. I'll get to him once I feel comfortable leaving either of my girls alone for more than a moment.

Dunk and Mac left from Portola to head up north, leaving me behind for the first time in years. It was strange watching their bikes get smaller and smaller on the horizon and not being next to them. What was even more strange was not feeling the pull of the road.

Staying local feels right. Making me, Riley, and Veda a family feels right too. My nomad wings have been clipped, and the wanderlust I was consumed with no longer holds any importance. Damn happy about it too.

I stare out the window, stroking Riley's matted hair while she sleeps. I'm perfectly content staying here and keeping her safe while her broken body recovers. My arms and legs sting like a bitch, but it's nothing compared to the pain I felt when I almost lost hope of having a future with my girls. No burns could hurt worse than that despair.

Sometime later, the door opens, and a tall, curvy Black woman walks through the door. She looks wrecked with red puffy eyes and fisting a ball of tissue.

"Who're you?" I ask, probably too harshly, but I can't be too safe right now.

"Um, I'm Cy's ol' lady." Her voice pitches high like she's barely hanging on.

"Shit." I worm my arm out from under Riley's head. "How's he doing?"

"He's been in surgery for hours. No one's updating me."

I stand and move closer. "I owe Cyrus my life. If there's anything I can do. . ."

"I actually came to check on Riley. I was going crazy waiting for news, so I took a break to check on my girl."

My brows pinch. "Didn't know you were acquainted."

"Char?" Riley's scratchy voice sounds from behind me.

"Riley?" Charlotte's voice cracks, and she dodges me to get to her.

"How's Cyrus? I heard he was shot."

"I don't know how he is. No one will tell me anything, and he's been in surgery for too long. That's not a good sign, right?" She takes a seat on the bed.

"No, it is a good sign. It means he's still alive, and the doctors think he's still worth working on." The more I get to know the real Riley, the less I'm surprised that this optimism she's giving her friend is anything but bright as fuckin' sunshine.

"I hope you're right. How are you?"

"I'm okay. Happy to be alive."

"Fuckin' Crash, man. His punk ass better hope I never see him again." I don't bother telling her she won't. I feel like it's implied. "Don't worry about a thing, okay? As soon as Cy pulls through, the club will take care of you. They know they didn't take action fast enough once they found out Crash killed Wrecker."

"Thanks, but I've got her." I walk over and take my rightful spot next to Riley.

Char eyeballs me. "Wrecker was our family. That makes her our family too."

"She's my woman, which makes her mine," I say, realizing how stupid it sounds.

She rolls her eyes and takes Riley's hands. "I need to get back."

"Yes, go. And please tell me when you know anything."

"I will." She leans in and gives Ry a gentle hug. "Love you."

"Love you too."

She leaves without giving me a second glance, and I couldn't care less. Cyrus and the other Sons might not have known what Crash was capable of, and, yeah, they stepped up and helped us take him down. But they had their suspicions long before any of this happened and still let that psycho around Riley.

"You didn't need to be so rude to her," Riley says.

"That wasn't rude. That was me protecting you."

She shakes her head. "From my best friend?"

"She's your best friend?" I ask.

"Yes."

Not wanting to fight when we just escaped death, I drop it. We'll deal with it later.

"How are you feeling?" I ask.

"Pretty terrible."

"Let me go get a nurse so she can get you some more pain meds." I move to stand, but she stops me.

"There's a button." She reaches behind me to press the pump that dispenses meds into her IV, then settles against my chest. "I could sleep for a month."

"Then do it. I got you, Little Owl. Whatever you need."

And I fuckin' mean it. Never again will this woman have to deal with anything on her own.

Chapter
TWENTY-SEVEN

Riley

"**W**ell, this looks appetizing," I say, looking down at the meatloaf and mashed potatoes the hospital staff delivered for lunch.

"Glad I don't have to eat that shit." Coyote makes a face, then glances over his shoulder at the window.

I can tell being inside the hospital is driving him crazy. When he says he doesn't like to be inside, what he means is he gets anxious when he doesn't have quick access to the outside. And we're on the eighth floor of a ten-story concrete building. The unease is written all over his face and in his fidgety behavior.

"You should go. I'm sure Veda wants to be home with her own things." I absent-mindedly stir the potatoes with my fork. They're lumpy.

He keeps his attention on the window for long minutes until I think maybe he didn't hear me. I'm about to repeat myself when he turns back to me, hands tucked into his pockets and frowning.

"What is it?" I ask.

He clears his throat. "I can't sleep inside, Little Owl."

Of course. He doesn't want to take Veda home and leave her in the house alone while he sleeps in his tent. My instinct is to reassure him he can be inside, that nothing bad will happen. But that seems unhelpful. This fear is too deeply embedded for my words to make a difference.

An idea hits me, and I push my tray away. "You know what Veda would love?"

"What's that?"

"Camping." I smile, but it hurts my face, so I lower my enthusiasm to a grin. "She's never been."

He raises an eyebrow in question, but I can tell he's still not convinced. "You think?"

"I know. You could swing by the store, get a bigger tent, and if you camped on the property, you'd still have access to the house."

He runs his teeth over his lower lip while he ponders my suggestion. I'm sure Veda's fine where she's at, and I'm sure she'd be happy to have another sleepover with Truly or Birdie, but I think it's more important for her to continue to bond with her dad. Even if she doesn't know he's her dad yet.

"I could do that," he says. "Maybe she'd like to pick out her own sleeping bag?"

"Oh my God, she'd love that," I encourage.

He takes his phone out and types out a message. "Okay, we'll give it a try."

"Who did you text?"

"Duncan. He's taking first shift. He'll be here in fifteen."

"What?" I ask.

"Not leaving you unprotected."

"Is Crash still out there?" My question is rhetorical—there's no chance in hell he'd be so calm if they didn't have him locked up somewhere—but he answers anyway.

His eyes darken, and his jaw ticks. "No."

I'm a changed person after everything he put me through. The rose-colored glasses I had on are cracked and broken. I refuse to take them off completely, but there's no way I can go back to the way I saw the world before.

So while the new me wants to know the specifics of what's being done to Crash, the old me is fine just knowing he can't hurt me again. Ultimately, the old me will win this battle because the new me has been through enough today.

"Then why do I need protection?"

"I almost lost you earlier today, so until that memory fades, you'll either have me, a prospect, or, if it comes to it, one of my brothers with you. And I don't want to hear shit about it," he says, daring me to argue.

"Okay, sweetheart. If that's what you need."

He comes over to me, tilting my chin up and pressing a gentle kiss to my lips. "It is."

"Wanna play another round of War?" Duncan asks, shuffling the cards.

"Actually, I'm pretty tired," I say, yawning.

"Okay, no problem." He puts the cards back in the box and leans back in his chair. "Need anything?"

"No. I'm good."

"Well, I'll be right here if you change your mind." He crosses his arms over his chest and kicks his feet out.

"Are you going to sit right there all night?" I ask.

"Yep. Don't worry about me. I'm good."

Except I do have to worry about him. He's probably my age and intimidatingly good-looking. Not off-the-charts, burn-my-panties-off hot like Coyote, but handsome enough to make me nervous. And he's nice, almost too nice for me to think he's trying to get into a motorcycle club. But when hospital security tried to kick him out, telling him visiting hours were over, I got it. One sneer and some choice words later, and the security guard left with his tail between his legs. I finally understood he definitely has what it takes.

"Should I ask for a cot?" I suggest, thinking of anything to keep him from staring at me all night.

"Nope. I'm good right here."

Sighing, I turn on my side to face away from him and press the button for a dose of morphine. I've done my best not to use the pain medication, but my head is throbbing, and I'll absolutely need it if I want to get any sleep.

Duncan had been busy when Coyote had reached out the first time, so Roch and Truly showed up to stay with me until he was free.

While Roch stood outside the door, making the hospital staff nervous, Truly sat at my side, chatting away. I learned she's taking college courses to be a veterinarian like her mom. Then, in whispered hushes, she told me that Roch has PTSD, which is why he doesn't talk much and has a slew of dogs he rescues.

She also told me their love story, which had me swooning like a lovestruck teenager. I decide I like Truly a lot and make plans to get lunch with her after I get out of the hospital.

As the fuzziness kicks in from the morphine, I open the last text I received from Coyote. It's a selfie of him and Veda in their new tent. Their smiles say it all, but the text that followed warmed my heart to bursting.

Coyote: Sweet dreams, Little Owl.

When I wake up the next morning, it's to Duncan's grinning face.

Did he watch me like this all night?

"Good morning, sunshine," he says with way too much enthusiasm.

"Hi." I sit up and attempt to finger comb my hair into submission, but it's so matted and bloody, so I'm not sure it helps fix my appearance. They haven't let me shower or bathe yet, so I know I must look terrible, but there's not much I can do about it right now.

"Coyote texted already and said he was coming by with your kid. They should be here—"

His words are cut off when the door opens, and I hear the *pitter-patter* of tiny feet hitting the linoleum.

"Mommy!" Veda shouts excitedly with Coyote hot on her heels.

"Hey, honey."

Coyote lifts her up onto the bed, and Veda gives me a very gentle hug.

"Coyote said we have to be careful because of your owies," she says.

"That's very thoughtful of you." I cup her cheeks. "How was your first time camping?"

"I got a sleepin' bag with owls on it and we had s'mores." Veda rattles on, giving me every exciting detail of her night while Coyote speaks in a hushed voice with Duncan, both wearing matching serious expressions. Then they bump fists, and Duncan waves a goodbye.

After listening to ten straight minutes about their night, Veda finally gets bored talking and crawls off the bed to inspect the room.

"Finally, I can do this." Coyote leans in for a kiss that I quickly turn away from. His forehead wrinkles. "What's wrong?"

"I'm gross. I haven't brushed my teeth, and I still have dried blood in my hair."

He lowers the guardrail and sits down on the edge of the bed. "You may not think so, but you've never been more beautiful."

"Yeah, right. I'm wrapped in gauze, I have a splint on my nose, and my face is black and blue." The brief glances I saw while in the bathroom were horrifying.

"Maybe that's what you see." He runs a hand down my face, and despite myself, I lean into his touch. "But I see a badass survivor. Someone who went through hell and still is the sexiest woman alive."

"You lie so well," I joke.

"Not lying, Little Owl. I can't promise much, but I promise you I'll always be honest." The sincerity on his face gives me no choice but to believe that's what he sees when he looks at me.

"Well, thank you then."

"How are you feeling?" he asks.

"Not as bad as I should. Though the morphine is probably responsible for that." I watch as Veda climbs onto the window seat and plasters her face to the window. "How was she?"

"She's fuckin' amazing." He smiles, and it takes my breath away. "I still can't believe she's real."

It hits me that he never even questioned Veda being his, especially considering he wore a condom. He accepted her so easily, and she's nearly his carbon copy, but it's not fair of me to not even ask.

"You were so quick to want your name on her birth certificate, but if you want proof, I wouldn't mind getting a paternity test," I say.

He scowls at me. "You saying there's a chance she's someone else's?"

I take his hand and gentle my tone. "No chance at all, but I'd understand if you wanted hard evidence. That's all I'm saying."

"She's mine," he practically growls.

"She's yours," I agree.

"It was dark, things happened fast, and I don't know how old the condom was. So let's drop it, yeah?"

"Sure, sweetheart."

The term of endearment softens his expression. "She wants to go back to the clubhouse today, so Birdie's picking her up."

"That's nice of her." I turn my attention to Veda. "What are you going to do at the clubhouse?"

"Play with the doggies. And Goblin said I could watch cartoons on the big, giant TV."

"Which one is Goblin?" I ask Coyote.

"He's the one who's going gray, serious face, blue eyes. He's sweet on the kid. All of them are, actually."

Goblin. So that's my dad's name. Or at least who I think is my dad. I need to fess up; it's the right thing to do. But not yet.

"I come bearing real coffee and donuts." Birdie walks in, carrying a tray of coffee cups and a bag of food.

She's wearing a long, flowy white sundress with antique roses on it that dips low in the front, showing off her incredible cleavage. It makes me feel like an even bigger troll. Those nurses will let me shower today, like it or not.

"Birdie," Veda cheers, running over and hugging her around the legs.

"Aw." Birdie smiles and sets down the drinks and food before hugging her back. "My favorite little squirt."

"She's pretty fond of you," I note.

"Feeling is definitely mutual. I always thought I'd wait a few years to have a kid, but after being around her, I think I'm ready." Her head tilts, and her lips purse. "I wonder if there's a way to make sure my baby is as awesome as yours."

I laugh. "Maybe a deal with the devil?"

"Considering I'm engaged to the man himself, I might be able to work something out," she jokes, then crouches to Veda's level. "You ready to head out?"

"Let's go." She rushes to my bed, gives my arm a hug, then runs to Coyote and hugs him around the legs. "Bye, Mommy. Bye, Coyote."

"Bye, baby. Be good, okay?"

She takes Birdie's hand. "Okay."

They wave at the doorway, and then they're gone.

Coyote hands me a coffee that I greedily accept.

"I need this. These drugs make me foggy." I sip the hot liquid.

Before he can say anything, the nurse comes in to do her bi-hourly check. She runs through her checklist and takes notes on her tablet while Coyote and I patiently wait for her to be done.

"How's the pain?" she asks.

"Manageable."

"Good. I want to change your bandages but thought you might want to take a shower before then." She glances at Coyote. "I can help with that right now, if you want."

"I'll handle that," Coyote says.

"It's probably better if I—"

"Anyone sees my girl naked, it's me." His tone brooks no argument, and I melt into a puddle of goo on the inside. Yet the nurse isn't as susceptible to the alpha attitude as I am.

"Sir, this is a hospital. I assure you—"

"I don't give a fuck if we're in a convent. She's wounded and feeling like shit about herself. You think I'm going to sit around and let that continue? No, I'm going to help clean her up and get her feeling like the fuckin' queen she is. You feel me?" He pins her with a look that she takes in for a split second before whipping her gaze to me.

"Riley, is that what you want? Since you're the patient and all?"

I can tell she's expecting me to side with her as the professional, but when she sees I'm giddy and blushing, she frowns.

"It's probably better he does it," I say.

"Okay, but remember, she has a severe concussion and has had multiple seizures. So no excitement and no jarring motions. You can remove the bandages but keep the wounds as dry as possible. Towels are in the bathroom, and ring the nurse's station when you're done so we can redress your wounds," she says and then walks out.

Coyote flashes me a wolfish look. "Don't get any ideas, Little Owl. No jarring motions or excitement."

My smile is full-on cheesy, and I toss the blanket off my legs. "Let's go."

Chapter
TWENTY-EIGHT

Coyote

Since Riley's still unsteady on her feet, I sit her down on the bench inside the shower and hold the detached head away from her until I adjust the temperature.

She tilts her head back, and I carefully spray her hair while holding a washcloth over her forehead to keep the nasty-looking wounds dry.

Taking the bandages off nearly fuckin' killed me. Crash better be praying to whatever God he believes in right now because the longer I wait to deal with him, the more pissed I get.

"He slammed my head into the door. Twice, I think. I don't know. It's all kinds of foggy." She brings her knees to her chest.

"We don't need to talk about it," I say. My dark demon is raging, and this isn't the time or place for him.

"I want to." She removes the washcloth and looks me dead in the eye. "You should know everything for when you deal with him."

I don't like the tone of her voice. It's not her. It's anger and revenge and spite. That's not my little owl, and I fuckin' hate that she had to see this part of life. But I also understand her need for revenge, and if this is what she needs to do to let it go, then I'll take it in.

"Okay. What else?"

She runs through Crash's psychotic behaviors and the physical and emotional torture he put her through. I absorb it all, packing it away for when I need it. I had enough to go on before finding her, but by the time she's done recounting everything, I know I'll have to hold myself back from walking into the clubhouse basement and killing the fucker on the spot.

"You aren't saying anything," she says when I've been quiet too long.

I notice goosebumps on her skin, so I take the washcloth and run it up and down her back while I think of how to respond in a way that won't scare her. "There's nothing I can say to make this better for you. I shouldn't have let you talk me into leaving that day. This is all my fault, and I'll bear the weight of that for the rest of my life."

Her spine goes ramrod straight. "That's not why I told you. It was my choice to send you away. I didn't know he was so sick in the head."

"One thing you're not getting, Little Owl. I'm your man. I might not have learned what that means from my dad, but I sure as shit learned it from the club, and I broke rule number one, leaving you alone to deal with your problems. That's not happening ever again. You put your shit on me, or we take care of it together. But you'll never be alone. Not ever again."

Her big eyes peer up at me in the way she does that leaves me defenseless, breathless, and full of desire. Bruises be damned. "You're my man?"

"Guess I haven't made that clear. I get that we have a lot to learn about each other, but unless you feel differently, you're mine as much as I'm yours. And even if you felt differently, I'll spend the rest of my life convincing you to get on the same page. You feel me?"

"Yeah, sweetheart. I feel you." She's taken to calling me sweetheart, and I fuckin' love it.

"Good. Now let's get you out of this bath. The water's cold, and I don't want you getting sick on top of everything else."

She stands, and I watch every inch of skin come out of the water. Her small tits, her flat belly with the silver stripes, her bare pussy, and those thighs I love to feel wrapped around me. I haven't gotten nearly enough of those things, and I never fuckin' will.

"Goddamn, you're so fuckin' sexy." I reach for the towel and hold it in front of me to hide my raging erection.

"I don't feel like it right now. Not like this."

"Don't get used to that feeling. The second you're well, and I don't mean you telling me you're fine, but a doctor telling me because I couldn't bear to hurt you any more than you are, I'll prove to you how sexy you are every chance I get." The corners of her lips turn up, and I know that's what she needed to hear. "Come on. Let's get you back in a hospital gown and into bed so that nurse doesn't give me more shit."

"I don't think she likes you much."

"Yeah, well, not many people do."

"I do," she says as I wrap the towel around her, holding her in my arms.

"That's good because you're stuck with me."

She presses her lips to mine. "I hope so."

I walk down the stairs, pumping my hands into fists and summoning my dark demon from deep within. This has been a long time coming, and though it won't end today, it's time to start.

My brothers brought him here yesterday and locked him in the kill room. Last time I was here, I had to ask Khan for help since I'd been stabbed, not this time. It's just me and him and the Reaper.

Cyrus wanted to be here; I get that. But I don't know when he'll be well enough for that. Char came by earlier to tell us he made it out of surgery but is in the ICU, and it's touch and go. There's no telling when he'll be better, and this can't wait any longer.

I open the door and am hit with the scent of urine. "Jesus fuck."

Crash is lying on his side in the corner, hands tied behind his back. Before we left the cabin, a few of the Sons stripped him of his cut. When he was brought here, the guys removed his clothes, leaving him only in his underwear.

The left side of his body is covered in burns from the last explosion at the cabin. Layers of skin from his arm, shoulder, and face are peeled back and charred on the ends, leaving open wounds.

My arms have second-degree burns on them and hurt like a bitch, but I had proper medical care. He hasn't. I smile, thinking about how much pain he must be in.

"Just do it. I know it's coming. Please, just do it," he begs.

"You don't know shit about what's coming. And if you think it's gonna be a quick and easy death, you obviously have no fuckin' clue who you're dealing with." I use the winch to lower the chain from the ceiling. Dragging Crash to the middle of the room, I attach the grab hook to the rope holding his hands together and slowly raise him up.

Given his hands are behind his back, he struggles to stand. He cries out when the winch lifts him to his feet and tugs his hands up. It's almost enough to pull his shoulders out of place, but I stop right before that happens. I'm not ruling it out, but for now, I'll keep his joints intact.

I walk over to the cabinet of implements, admiring the selection. When you don't have a home, your weapons have to fit comfortably on your person. Having access to so many choices is a treat.

I pick up a cat-o'-nine-tails with razor blades affixed to the ends of the leather tails. I test its weight while Crash looks on, no doubt pissing himself all over again.

My dark demon roars in delight.

"You had your chance to be a man, to walk away. But you didn't." I swing the cat and hit his chest. The blades embed themselves into his flesh, so it tears cuts into him when I yank it back.

He screams in pain, and the sound feeds my hungry demon.

"You killed the only dad she's ever known, lied to her, and made her trust you." I aim lower, hitting his stomach this time. Yanking it away, I relish in the tug of his flesh opening and the spilling of his blood.

"Stop. Please stop!" he cries.

"Just getting started." I aim even lower this time, hitting his thighs and, with any luck, his dick, though I'm not looking to check. Bright red lines streak down his front, and his legs give out, pulling back on his arms even harder. "Careful, you might—"

I don't finish before I hear the pop and crack of his shoulders. He roars in torment as his arms raise higher now that the socket isn't holding them in place.

Damn, even my dark demon cringes a little.

His pained moans turn to sobbing whimpers. "Please. Please. I can't do this anymore."

"Then apologize. Say you're sorry for ramming my girl's face into a fuckin' door." I rage and swing higher, the razors digging into his face and neck this time. I jerk it back as hard as I can, lacerating his skin and leaving bloody open wounds.

"She's mine," he screams. "Not yours. She was never meant to be yours."

There it is. His truth. Despite his situation—his imminent

demise—he still believes he was in the right. Except he's never been more wrong, and I'm about to prove it to him.

"Fuck you." I lift the cat over my head and bring it down onto his scalp and dislocated shoulders.

When I'm done with him, there'll be no part of him left unmarred. He will feel my wrath on every inch of his body and his fuckin' doomed soul.

"She'd be in my bed right now, spreading those sweet thighs, if it weren't for you." The psychotic asshole smiles at me.

Maybe he really believes that, or maybe he's taunting me so I'll get it over with and kill him. Either way, the dark demon takes over completely, not giving me a say in what happens next.

"Shut the fuck up!" I toss the cat onto the ground and reach for an ax. Miles and Duncan will have an easier job after I get done here.

I swing at his leg, and the ax wedges itself in his femur, not quite making it all the way through the bone. Blood gushes like a faucet from the gash, and the sounds he makes are otherworldly, making my demon preen with satisfaction. Even more so when I place my boot on his stomach and yank the ax free.

Rearing back, I aim for his middle. There's no turning back now. This is a death blow, and I'm okay with it. I'll never get the apology I'm seeking, and even if I did, it wouldn't change shit.

Blood dribbles from his mouth, making him gargle and choke on it.

It's almost enough. I'm almost satisfied, but I need one more. One more good hit to appease my demon.

This time I hit his throat, damn near decapitating him. I watch as the light in his eyes goes out, feeling no regret. The fucker was off his rocker, literally insane, but that made him even more dangerous. The world is better with his absence, and though this manner of death wasn't necessary, it was so fuckin' satisfying.

My sweat and his blood drip down my body, and my lungs

heave from the exertion. Every muscle is taut and overused. But my mind is at peace, and revenge has been served. Crash is Hades' problem now.

Leaving the ax embedded in his throat, I release it and sit cross-legged and meditate, right there in a puddle of his blood. The murderous energy swirling inside me needs to leave my body and stay in this room.

Inhaling, I lift my arms above my head and draw in the sick, metallic stench of Crash, filling my lungs with it. Then I exhale slowly, letting it all go.

It's over. Done. And never again will anything bad happen to my girls.

Chapter
TWENTY-NINE

Riley

"**H**eard there was a fellow wounded in here." The prospect I now know as Ford hobbles in on one crutch, his other arm in a sling. His leg is in a brace that holds his wounded leg straight.

"Oh my God." I use the remote to lift the hospital bed to a more upright position and adjust my ugly hospital gown. "I can't believe you're here and walking."

"Well, sort of." He waves a crutch at me.

"Take a seat, brother." Khan pulls out a chair, and Ford limps his way over to it, collapsing like a sack of potatoes when he gets there. "I'll go get some coffee or something. You good?"

Khan has been here for a couple of hours now. He's good company and had me in stitches telling outrageous stories from some of the club's parties.

He promised to throw a rager once I'm out of here and feeling better.

"I'm good," I say.

Ford and I watch him leave, an uncomfortable silence

growing between us. We've never met, yet we both survived an insanely scary trauma.

I start with, "How are—" at the same time he says, "How's it—"

We laugh, and I try again.

"How are you?" I ask.

"All right. You know, all things considered." His head bobs. "What about you?"

"I got a free nose job and some epic war wounds, but I'm feeling better." My gaze falls to my lap, and before I can stop myself, I tear up thinking about what this stranger did for me. "Thank you for everything you did. You don't even know me, and you risked your life."

He grins. "Don't worry about it. You're part of the club, which means you're family."

"You were hurt and still went inside to protect Veda. I don't know how I'll ever repay you," I sob.

I've withheld my tears until now, choosing to focus on my anger. But seeing Ford conjures the memory of Veda's petrified face as she watched me drive away, covered in blood.

"Hey, hey. Don't cry." He rubs soothing circles on my calf. "Seriously, babe. I can't stand it when girls cry."

"You don't understand what it means to me. I was so scared. I had no idea if you were dead or alive or when and if someone would come for the both of you. It was the worst part of this whole thing." Snot drips from my nose, and tears drip down my cheeks. The memory of the fear I felt comes back full swing. It's going to be a long time before all these emotions get filed away in my mind.

He hands me the box of tissues. "It's all over now, and everyone's okay."

"You don't look okay." I blow my nose, forgetting it's broken. Now I'm crying for a whole other reason. Pain shoots down my face, and my tissue is blood-soaked.

"Shit. Should I get a nurse?" He reaches for the call button and whacks his leg on the hospital bed, making him wince.

"No, it's okay. I just forgot," I say, laughing through my tears. "We're quite the pair."

"Yeah, we are." He chuckles.

"What's the verdict on your leg?" I ask, trying to pull myself together.

"Got some fancy titanium rods and screws or some shit." He motions proudly to his leg. "I'm basically a bionic man now."

"That's a good attitude to have."

"Got to look at the bright side. And I'm pretty sure saving an ol' lady will get me patched in, so win, win." His eyes go wide. "I don't mean I expect to. Ultimately, it's up to them."

"I won't say anything," I assure him, then raise a brow and cup a hand over the side of my mouth conspiratorially. "I have it on good authority your wish will come true."

Coyote told me all three prospects will be voted in later tonight. Maybe I shouldn't have said anything, but this man protected my child and literally put himself in front of a car for me. I think he deserves the head's up.

"Thank fuck." He smiles. "How's the kid?"

"She's good. Really good. Coyote taught her all about camping, and now I don't think I'll get either one of them to sleep inside."

"Eh, that's good for kids. I grew up playing outside from sunup to sundown. Of course, I was doing it to avoid an alcoholic dad who liked to beat me up, but still."

I frown. "I'm sorry you had to survive that way."

"It's all good. Toughened me up or some shit."

"Still. Every child deserves to be loved."

"Maybe, but we don't all have moms like you. This world is full of monsters."

My mood sours. "I'm starting to see that."

I've spent a lot of hours thinking about this new life I

brought Veda and me into. Things like this never happened when we lived in California, safe behind an iron gate and far away from all the bad shit that happens in this world.

But we also weren't living. Not really. We were trophies, prizes for men to hang on their arms, and doomed to a life where we wouldn't have a voice or our opinions respected.

Ultimately, I've come to the conclusion that while choosing Coyote and his family of bikers might bring danger to our door, those moments in between the danger will be spent living. We'll be happy. And most of all, we'll be allowed to be ourselves.

I can't fathom making any other decision than staying in Reno.

"Didn't know how you liked your coffee." Khan walks in holding two Styrofoam cups.

"I like it when it's not from here," I say but accept the cup anyway.

"I better get going. The doc has me signed up for physical therapy downstairs." Ford gathers his beautiful golden hair into a low man bun, then stands.

"Need help getting there?" Khan asks.

"Nah. I got this. See you around, Riley."

"Okay. Take care of yourself."

"I will." He hobbles his way to the door awkwardly.

"Hey, Ford," Khan calls out, making Ford look over his shoulder. "Church tonight, and Prez wants your ass there."

I grin at Ford, who holds a straight face. "Got it."

I grimace, taking a sip of the brown water this place calls coffee. "This stuff isn't fit for human consumption."

"Sorry about that. Didn't want to leave the hospital and go somewhere decent. Coyote may be smaller than me, but that fucker's scrappy."

I look over at Khan, who is more giant than man, and gather the courage to ask him about an idea I had.

"See your mind spinning. What's up?" he asks.

"You're a contractor, right?"

"I am. Licensed and everything."

"I wanted to ask you about something. I know you're busy with Roch's house, your house, and the"—I wrinkle my nose—"strip club, but I have a project I want to hire you for."

Coyote told me about his new job for the club. Apparently, they needed another legit business, so they bought a strip club. Not the business most women want their men in, but they don't have a man like Coyote.

There's no chance of him straying when I'm the only woman he sees.

"You have my attention," he says, and I spend the next hour telling him all about my plans. He listens, adding his two cents when needed. By the time I'm done, we're both excited about the project.

I just hope Coyote is.

"Oh my God, I'm so happy to be home," I say, walking through the front door. "Forty-eight hours feels like a month when you're in the hospital."

"I'm happy too, Mommy." Veda swings our joined hands.

"Me three," Coyote agrees, dropping my bags on the ground.

I venture further into the house, not even thinking about Crash until my eyes land on the back door. Thanks to Coyote and Khan, the glass has been replaced, and my blood cleaned up, but the memories remain.

"You okay, Little Owl?" Coyote asks, noticing my change in mood.

"Yeah. I'm okay."

"Hey, Owlet. How about you go play for a bit while I get your mom settled? Then we can turn on a movie and order some pizza."

He's taken to calling Veda Owlet, and honestly, it's the cutest thing I've ever heard.

"I love pizza," she says.

"I know. We've had it twice in two days," he grumbles.

Veda hugs me around the legs. "I love you."

"Love you too."

She bounces down the hall to her room, singing the whole way.

"Do you think she's okay?" I ask.

I haven't spoken to her about what happened, mostly because I don't know what to say. But she doesn't seem bothered by it in the least.

"Yeah. Kids are resilient. At least that's what I hear." He pulls me into his arms, both of us still looking at that damn door.

"Has she said anything to you?"

"A little. She asked why you had owies."

"What did you say?" I ask, surprised he didn't tell me this before.

"Told her the truth."

I pull back and pin him with a look. "What truth did you give her?"

"I told her Crash was a bad man, and he hurt you, but she shouldn't worry because he's gone now, and that'll never happen again because me and all my brothers will protect her."

I gasp. "You said what?"

"Maybe it was the wrong thing, but she seemed to like that answer. Now she thinks of us as her personal protectors that she can boss around. She had Goblin playing Barbies with her. It was funny as hell."

Goblin. That's the next item on my itinerary.

"I need to tell you something. Can we sit down?" I ask.

"Yeah, Little Owl." He sweeps me off my feet and gently deposits me on the couch. "What's up?"

"The night we met, I told you I was at the clubhouse looking for my bio dad."

"Yeah?"

"Well, I think it's Goblin. The picture I saw was old, so he was a lot younger, but I'm pretty certain it's him."

"How old's your mom?"

"She's forty-six now but had me when she was twenty-four."

He lifts my legs up onto his lap, and it strikes me how easily and quickly we've become comfortable with each other. There was never a time I felt anything but secure with him. Mostly because there hasn't been time to relax in each other's company, but now that there is, I still feel like I've known him my whole life.

"You're twenty-two, and he's in his late thirties, so that would have made him seventeen or eighteen at the time. It's possible."

"He's been in the club that long?" I ask because he wasn't one of the people who came by the hospital to babysit me, so I didn't have a chance to grill him the way I did the others.

"He grew up in the club. His dad and Loki's dad are Originals."

"What's an Original?" As much as I know about MCs, some of the terminology is lost on me.

"Goblin's dad and Loki's dad started the chapter, so both of them grew up in that clubhouse." He inspects the bottoms of my feet that are littered with healing cuts.

"Do you think I should mention it to him?"

"Do you want to?" he asks.

"No. Yes. I don't know. I mean, it's not like I want anything from him. I'm grown." I reach for the afghan on the back of the couch and cover my legs with it.

"Why do you have so many of these grandma blankets?" he asks out of the blue.

"When I was pregnant with Veda, my mom didn't want me leaving the house because my bastard baby was an embarrassment. I got bored and taught myself to crochet. I couldn't make hats or sweaters or anything complicated, so by the end of the pregnancy, I'd made twenty-seven blankets."

The one time I brought up the fact that I'm a bastard too didn't go over well. In her mind, if she doesn't talk about it, it never happened. But I don't mention that. It's hard to understand her level of delusion unless you've lived in her world.

"Wow. You kept all twenty-seven?"

"Yeah. I mean, they're ugly. I couldn't exactly give them as gifts." I hold the blanket up so he can fully appreciate where I skipped stitches, stitched backward, and the millions of other mistakes I made. "I didn't say I was good at making them."

"Jesus fuck, you're adorable." His broad smile makes my heart pound in my chest, and butterflies swarm my belly. "I think you should tell him. He has a soft spot for Veda, and I think it'd make him happy if it turns out she's his blood."

"Okay. I think I will."

Chapter
THIRTY

Coyote

I hop on my bike and hit the freeway toward home.

Home.

I haven't used that word in so long I forgot what it meant. It's more than an address or the place you store your shit. It's having a place to make memories and a central place to gather.

The last few weeks flew by. Between helping with Veda because Riley is still in pain and tired, and working on Royal Treatment's renovations, I've been busy.

I was worried Riley would expect me to sleep inside with her, but she didn't even ask. Veda stays out there with me most nights too. The kid likes being outdoors as much as I do, and when she talks to me right before she goes to sleep? I fuckin' love that. She's smart and funny, the perfect mix of me and Ry.

Riley is healing slowly but surely. The doctor took the splint off her nose, and the blue and purple bruises are fading to yellow and green. I still catch her staring at the back door now and then, but I don't think I can fix that. She's got to come to terms with what happened on her own. I can listen when she wants to talk about it, but I can't take away the memories, no matter how much I want to.

Parking out front, I feel the same energy boost I get whenever I pull up. My girls are always waiting for me, and that's the best fuckin' part of my day.

When I walk through the door, I expect to be tackled by Veda, ready to tell me about her day, but she doesn't appear. The air in here smells good, like Thanksgiving dinner almost. It doesn't make sense, though, since Riley's a shit cook. It's something she's working on, and with Birdie in culinary school, she gets tips and tricks from her on the regular.

But no matter how much she tries, she fucks it up somehow, and I'm left trying to choke down a meal. Not that I'd ever tell her that. It's cute she wants to cook for me. It's probably out of boredom more than anything. She's talked about going back to work, but I convinced her to take some time off until she's healed.

And also because I need time to talk her out of going back to The Silo.

I follow my nose to the kitchen and stop short when I see Veda on the counter stirring a pot, and Riley bent over with her head in the oven. Her juicy ass is perched high, and it takes everything in me not to smack it.

If it were up to Riley, we would've picked up where we left off when she was released from the hospital. But that whole concussion shit scared me, and I didn't want to do anything to set her progress back.

"What's goin' on in here?" I ask.

Riley pops out of the oven. "We're making dinner. I think I actually did something right this time."

"Smells amazing." I hook her around the waist and bring her in for a kiss. "You look hot," I whisper after I pull away.

She's wearing her standard uniform of cut-offs and a

cropped tee. It's my favorite look on her because when she's wearing it, she's comfortable and happy. Just the way I like her.

"And you, Owlet. You look cute." I walk over and tug on her pink apron with owls all over it.

"I made stuffing." She holds up her wooden spoon full of chunks of herbed bread.

"Looks good. Why the fancy meal?"

"I thought we could have a special dinner." She pulls a roasted chicken from the oven, and I'm impressed that it's not burned.

"Oh, yeah?"

"Yeah. I thought we would tell Veda the big news tonight." She gives me the eye that says, "we're doing this, like it or not."

It's not that I don't want Veda to know I'm her dad, but I worry it'll change things. That she won't look at me like her fun friend. We have such a good thing going, I'm resistant to change.

"Okay. Yeah. Let's do it." I put as much enthusiasm as I can into my voice.

Veda and I set the table while Riley plates everything up, and then we take our seats around the small, round table. I take my first bite and hold my breath, ready for some obscene flavor to hit my tastebuds. But it doesn't. The chicken is juicy and delicious.

Riley has her elbows on the table, hands clasped, watching me expectantly.

"I'm impressed," I say, taking another bite.

"Really?" she squeals.

"Really," I mumble with a mouthful of food.

She wiggles in her seat, doing an adorable dance. So much of my life is spent on the dark side that it's nice to come home to two girls so full of light.

Riley dives in and grins like a fuckin' loon when she realizes I wasn't blowing smoke up her ass and her food really is good.

"I can cook," she declares with a fork in the air.

"Slow your roll, Little Owl. One dish doesn't make up for the thirteen others that I had to choke down."

"Jerk," she mutters lightheartedly.

"What did you girls do today?" I ask.

"We took a walk, and Char came over and let me do her makeup," Veda says.

My eyes close, and I exhale. Riley's friend, Charlotte, is a bone of contention. She's linked to the Sons, and although the threat with them has been extinguished, I'm still nervous about her being tied to them.

"I'm not going to stop being her friend, so you can huff and puff all you want, but it's still not going to happen."

"Just wanna keep you safe."

"Charlotte is not my enemy. She feels horrible about how things went down, and she needs a friend right now. Cyrus might be out of the ICU, but he's struggling."

I know this is an argument I won't win, so I'll have to compromise and stick a man on her whenever Charlotte's around. Even if I have to do it without her knowing.

"Okay." I hold up my hands in submission.

"Thank you," Riley says, reaching under the table and giving my knee a squeeze. Her touch makes my cock twitch, but I love the tease. The build-up is driving me wild, and I know she's going to rock my fuckin' world once we're able to.

"So, why don't we tell Veda our good news?"

"Are we going to Disneyland?" Veda asks, her head tilted.

"No. We're not going to Disneyland." Riley clears her throat. "You've been spending a lot of time with Coyote, huh?"

She nods.

"And it's been fun, right?"

Another nod.

"Well, guess what? Coyote isn't just your friend. He's your dad," Riley's voice cracks, and I know the waterworks are coming. I thought the residual trauma was causing her to cry nearly every day since she came home from the hospital, but she insists she's just a crier. No matter the emotion she's feeling—whether happy, sad, frustrated, whatever—she cries.

Veda's eyes shift to me, and I stay silent, waiting for her reaction.

"You're my dad?" she asks.

"Yeah, Owlet. I'm your dad."

"Awesome." She picks up her chicken leg and gets back to eating.

Riley and I gape at each other. That went much better than expected.

The rest of the night follows the same routine as every other. We clean up after dinner, then Riley props me in front of the TV with a beer while Veda bathes.

It's all so normal, but because nothing else in my life is, this little bit of simplicity is welcomed and appreciated.

Veda usually decides where she wants to sleep after her bath. I never encourage or ask her to sleep outside; I want her to love it because it's what she wants. But tonight, things are different.

"Give your dad a kiss goodnight," Riley says, looking pleased as punch that she can say that now.

Veda runs over, lips already puckered, and smacks me one on the cheek. "I want to sleep in the tent with you."

I'm about to tell her okay when Riley cuts in. "Not tonight."

"Why?" she whines.

"Because Mommy and Daddy have some talking to do."

I'd be nervous if I didn't see the playful lilt in her eyes.

Veda huffs and puffs, but Riley eventually gets her settled in bed.

"What are we talking about?" I ask, watching her hips sway as she walks over to where I'm sitting on the sofa.

Her cheeks pink up. "I know you've been holding back because of my injuries, but I'm all healed."

Her still yellow and green nose and forehead say differently, but I don't tell her that. She's been feeling down about how long it's taking for her to heal and worried each cut will scar. I told her she should be proud of her war wounds because they prove she's a fighter. But she's not hearing any of it.

She doesn't believe me when I say she could be covered in scars, and she'd still be the most beautiful woman I've ever seen. I'll just have to prove it to her.

"Oh, yeah?" I grab her hips, hooking my fingers in her belt loops and tugging her between my legs.

"Yeah." She bends at the waist and offers her lips for a kiss, and fuckin' kiss her I do. Sucking her lower lip into my mouth, I bite down and give it a tug before soothing it with another kiss.

She straddles me and grinds her cunt down on my hard dick. Jesus fuck, it feels good.

"Veda asleep?" I ask.

"Out like a light. I wore her out today so she'd be tired." She snakes her hands under my shirt and rubs up and down my muscled abs.

I wrap my arms around her and stand. She wraps her legs around me as I carry her to her bedroom, kick the door shut behind us, and flip the lock.

"My Little Owl needs to be dicked down, huh?"

"Yes," she breathes out as I set her down.

"Take your clothes off," I order.

Shyly, she pulls her T-shirt over her head, revealing a sheer, black lace bra. Her nipples poke through the fabric. It's so fuckin' hot, I have to adjust myself so I can enjoy the rest of her striptease.

Next, she pops the button on her shorts and shimmies them down her hips. My mouth waters at the matching panties and puffy pussy lips outlined through the see-through lace.

"This too?" she asks, reaching around her back to the bra enclosure.

"Everything."

The black lace is slipped down her shoulders and tossed to the side, exposing her tiny tits—perfect little plums, round and firm.

"And these?" She teases a finger along the hem of her panties.

"Turn around when you take those off."

A pink blush creeps down her chest, and she slowly turns. Hooking the fabric with her thumbs, she bends over and lowers them with her legs parted, giving me a view of that perfect puckered hole and her bare cunt. She stands too quickly for my liking and glances over her shoulder, her big doe eyes blinking innocently at me.

My cock thickens painfully, so I undo my belt buckle, toss it on the bed, and open my pants to give myself some room.

I stalk toward her and place a hand on the center of her back, guiding her to the bed. I push her forward so her front rests on the mattress and her ass is on full display.

"I've had a lot of time to think about all the things I want to do." I kick her legs apart and take both rounded globes of her ass in my palm, squeezing them and separating her cheeks. "And my imagination is just as wild as I am."

She gasps when I step back and slap a hand down on one of her ass cheeks. It turns the prettiest shade of red. But I need more, always more. I slap the other, making them match, then knead the tender flesh, loving how it feels in my hands. So soft and perfect.

Kneeling behind her, I spread her wide, groaning when I see her pussy glistening with arousal. I drag a finger from her cunt up to her asshole, loving the little whine she lets out, as if she's just as pent up as I am.

"I've been craving this pussy. Gonna lick you until you beg me to stop. But you need to be a good girl and keep quiet. Can you do that for me, Little Owl?"

"Yes," she breathes out.

With two palmfuls of her ass, I spread her open and bury my face between her cheeks. Her flavor bursts on my tongue as I lick and suck her juicy cunt. She mewls and arches her back, rocking and grinding against my face, taking what she needs. It's so fuckin' sexy and spurs me on even more.

My tongue finds her clit, and I flick it over and over with the tip of my tongue. I reach between her legs and up her body, finding her beaded nipple. Rolling it between my fingers, I continue to lick and suck her pussy.

Her thighs quiver, and she whimpers. "I'm coming."

I hook my arms around her thighs and press my face deeper into her, smothering myself in ass and pussy, not giving a shit if this is how I die. And if that happens, they better put it on my fuckin' headstone.

Here lies Coyote. Death by suffocation from the tastiest cunt in existence.

Don't shed no tears. He died doing what he loves best.

Her thighs quiver, and she lets out a muffled cry as she comes. I carry her through it until she jerks away, her sensitive clit needing a break. And I know just how to give her time to recover.

I slap her ass and stand. "How secure is that mirror?"

She eyes me curiously. "I tried to move it after we got here, but it's bolted to the wall through the frame."

"Good. Get out that dildo with the suction cup."

"What?" she asks, not expecting that.

"Get it out, Little Owl. You're gonna fuck yourself with it while my dick is down your throat."

Chapter
THIRTY-ONE

Riley

I t was one thing to put on a show for him when he was hidden. It's another to see the hungry look in his eyes as I stick the dildo onto the mirror. I should be embarrassed, but the salaciousness has me even more turned on.

"Get on your knees and impale that pussy," he demands, arms folded.

He's still fully clothed, and somehow, that's a turn-on too. Slowly, I get down on all fours and back up until I feel the silicone at my entrance. Reaching between my legs, I guide it through the folds of my soaking pussy. Before, I needed lube to make this happen. Not this time. I'm so wet for him.

I shudder as it fills me up. It's cold and not as big or solid as Coyote's cock, but it does the trick anyway.

He stands in front of me, and I kneel, adjusting my position to make sure the dildo stays inside, then looking to him for further instruction.

"Pull out my cock." His arms stay folded, making him look like a proud king about to be serviced by one of his concubines. I'm all too happy to oblige.

His belt is already off, and his jeans are unzipped. I reach into his boxer briefs and wrap my hand around his solid length before carefully pulling him out. No words other than beautiful can describe his dick. It's a warm shade of brown, the shaft velvety to the touch, and the head slightly darker but spongy and soft.

I hold it up to lick and kiss my way up the underside of him. When I reach his tip, I swipe my tongue to collect the pre-cum that's beaded there, moaning at the heady taste.

"Good girl, now suck," he commands.

The praise urges me to continue, and I take him in my mouth, slowly bobbing up and down. His girth stretches my lips almost to pain but knowing that I'm putting the pleased look on his face makes me not care in the least.

"That's it. Just like that." He reaches a hand down to rest on the back of my head, his thumb rubbing up and down encouragingly. "Keep fucking yourself on that dildo, Little Owl. Wanna see it."

I look up and see his gaze fixed on the mirror. God, the view he must have. Me on my knees with the silicone dick moving in and out of me and my head moving up and down on him. This is so dirty, and I love it.

Wrapping both hands around his base, I eagerly take him deeper. He likes it when I gag, loves it when I choke, nearly comes when my saliva drips down my chin and leaks onto my breasts.

"That's enough." He takes a step back, his dick bouncing as it pops out of my mouth. "Go get on the bed. Need to make you come on my cock."

I pull myself off the dildo and lie down on the bed, watching as he strips naked and removes the silicone toy off the mirror, tsking as he gets to the bed.

"You made a mess. Better clean it up while I fuck your

tight cunt." He climbs onto the mattress and kneels, handing me the clear dildo that's covered in my cum.

My eyes widen as I take it, not sure about this. The closest I've ever come to tasting myself is on his tongue. He places his hands on my knees and spreads them wide, all while giving me a look that says, "I'm waiting."

My face screws up as I lick the tip. I expect to hate it, but the taste is faint.

"Suck that cock while I fuck you, Little Owl. Show me what you can do." He positions himself at my entrance and presses in. He's so big and hard that I suck in a shuttering breath as he works himself deeper with each thrust.

I wrap my lips around the silicone and suck like it's his cock in my mouth. Surprisingly, I like my mouth busy while he works me up.

He reaches down and plays with my tits, strumming my sensitive nipples before pinching them hard, sending a jolt of pain that only serves to turn me on more. I'm so wet as he fucks me relentlessly that the sounds we make are obscene. I was worried he'd hold back, treat me with kid gloves since I'm still bruised. I've never been happier to be wrong.

"Jesus fuck, this pussy." He slams into me, his face pinched in concentration, his eyes glued to my mouth that's wrapped around the dildo. "So fuckin' tight, so fuckin' juicy."

Using my knees for purchase, he fucks me hard, pulling out completely before ramming back in. Each time takes my breath away and gets me closer and closer to coming. His brown eyes darken to nearly black, his chest glistens with perspiration, and every single one of his muscles is tensed as he works me over.

Oh my God, he's so sexy.

"That's it, Little Owl. Pretend it's my cock. Show me how'd you'd make me come."

I run my lips up and down the underside of the dildo

before sucking, pretending it's him in my mouth. Of all the things that have turned me on, I never thought this would be something I'd love. But watching him watch me is empowering.

"Need to taste those lips." He reaches for the toy and tosses it aside, then leans over me. The pressure of his body on mine, the base of his cock rubbing against my clit while he moves inside me, and his mouth on mine is the perfect erotic mix. I begin my ascent into bliss.

He rests his hand at the base of my throat and angles my head to the side so he can lick and suck the sensitive flesh of my neck.

He grunts into my ear. A feral and animalistic sound that sends goosebumps down my whole body as my pussy clamps down on his rigid length.

"You're squeezing me so hard. Gonna make me come. Right fuckin' now. Shit, yeah." The pressure around my throat tightens as he pumps his seed inside me. "Filling you up with my cum, Little Owl. Gonna plant another baby in that womb."

Baby? Is that what he wants?

Is that what I want?

It must be because his dirty words feed my orgasm and suck the air from my lungs. I claw at his slick back, unable to control myself. I've never felt this free, this seen, this exposed. Something drips down the side of my face, and when I wipe it away, I realize they're tears. I'm crying.

No, no, no, no. Crying isn't sexy.

The embarrassment has me crying even harder. I suck in a breath and hold it, not wanting to ruin the moment.

His thrusts slow, and he wraps his arms around me, rolling so I'm on top of him. Throwing his hands limply out to the side, his chest rises and falls rapidly. I bury my face in his neck and bite my lip to stop myself from blubbering.

"Are you crying?" he asks, his arms going back around me.

I can't speak. If I do, I'll give myself away. "Little Owl," he coos. "What's wrong?"

"Nothing," I say, my voice cracking.

"My cock's still inside her, my cum is leaking from her cunt, and she can't tell me why she's crying," he says to no one.

"I swear, nothing's wrong. I told you I'm a crier."

"Look at me," he says, trying to lift me up from where I'm hiding.

"I'm embarrassed."

"No need for that." He pulls out and positions me on his side. He kisses his way up my neck, then drags his tongue up my cheek, licking up my tears, taking my sadness into his body. It should be an odd thing to do, but nothing with him ever feels odd. It's just us. "You're so fuckin' beautiful, even when you cry."

My breath hitches, and I sob even more. He holds me through it all, stroking my hair and holding me close. He's been so good to me, even after everything I put him through. I kept his kid from him, took his cut, got him involved with Crash, and he nearly died saving me.

Yet he's still here.

When my tears dry up, he finally speaks. "You ready to talk now?"

"I'm sorry. I don't know where that came from." I wipe my nose with the back of my hand.

"It's okay. You've been through a lot and what we just did was pretty intense."

"I don't deserve you," I say.

"What are you talking about?"

"I've done nothing but put you through hell. I don't know why you're still here."

His hand settles on my bare hip. "You don't know what the fuck you're talking about."

267

"You missed out on almost five years of Veda's life because of me."

"Yeah, I did. But you had your reasons, and punishing you for that won't get us anywhere." He leans in to leave a sweet peck on my lips.

"I almost got you killed."

"You didn't do shit. Crash almost got me killed." His hand moves from my hip to my back, and his fingers skim up and down my spine, soothing my frayed nerves.

"I don't feel worthy of you," I admit my darkest truth.

"Fuck me," he curses and thinks through his response while gazing into my eyes. "I love you."

Three words. Three tiny words. But those three words bring me the clarity I've been missing. I love him. Madly, wildly, hopelessly love him.

"I love you too."

"I know you do." He smirks, and I slap his chest.

"How do you know that?"

"A connection like the one we have wasn't made through time and experience. It was made when our souls crashed into each other the night we met and then were pulled apart when we separated. You took a piece of me with you, and I took a piece of you with me. Whether or not we realized it, those pieces have been searching for each other this whole time." His hand skims up my side, breezes over my shoulder and neck, finally landing on my cheek. "We're meant to be together. Simple as that."

"You think?"

"I fuckin' know, Little Owl."

"You said you were going to get me pregnant," I say, needing to address that too.

"I will."

"You want another baby?"

"With you? I want a litter of 'em."

"Are we ready for that?" I ask. Getting pregnant isn't on my radar, yet we never use protection, so maybe I'm lying to myself.

"Not this second." A sly smile creeps across his lips. "But we could be in nine months."

"Things'll be so different with another pregnancy," I fantasize, the idea growing on me.

"I can't wait to see your belly grow, knowing I put a baby in you." His hand moves to my lower stomach, making my core clench with the need for him. "Matter of fact, I think we should try again right now."

He rolls me back on top of him and does just that.

"I'm nervous," I say, wringing my hands in my lap.

Coyote rests a hand on my thigh, his other hand on the steering wheel. "Don't be."

"Okay, thanks for the tip," I sass.

"My girl's begging for a punishment later."

My core warms. It's been a week since I made him give in and fuck me. Since then, we've had so much sex my pussy is sore. Nearly every time, he makes me get a toy out and show him how I use it before incorporating it into our lovemaking.

He's held a vibrator to my asshole while he fucks me from behind, placed a clit suction toy on me while eating me out, and threatened to fuck my ass with a dildo while drilling me from behind.

I'm looking forward to that one.

"Do you think we should've left Veda with a sitter? What if he responds badly?"

"You're overthinking this. Plus, we're not even sure he's your dad. There's a good chance he isn't." He pulls into the clubhouse, parks, and turns the key to shut off the car. It spits and sputters before the engine falls quiet. "Gotta get you a newer car. This thing is older than you are."

"No, it's not. And I can't afford a new car right now. I don't even have a job."

Coyote made me officially quit The Silo. Although they're on good terms with the Sons, he doesn't want me working there. And since he's backed off about Char and me being friends, I conceded. I didn't love the job anyway.

"I was going to talk to you about that. We need someone to manage the girls at the club."

"What do you mean, manage the girls?"

"Keep them happy, handle the drama, make sure they get on stage on time, feed them, that kind of thing. I think they call them 'house moms.'"

Could I do that? Strip clubs felt like such a seedy business at first, but the more Coyote talks about it, the more I realize it's a business like any other. It just so happens their product is skin. Everything else is the same.

"That actually sounds fun." I ponder the offer. "I think I'd be good at that."

"I think so too. That's why I'm asking."

"You don't need to clear it through Loki or anything?" I ask.

"No. He's handed the reins to me as far as management goes. It'll be a couple weeks still before the place is up and running, but even then, we'll only be open Wednesday through Saturday, so it's not quite full time."

"What about Veda?"

"We'll figure it out." He shrugs.

"Okay. Thanks."

"Now, can we go inside and do this thing?"

I take a calming breath. "Okay. Let's do it."

Hand in hand, the three of us walk inside. As promised, Khan is throwing a party to celebrate not only all of us surviving Crash, but Miles, Duncan, and Ford patching in. I wish I could've seen Ford's face when they voted, but Coyote said it was club members only.

I'll settle for being here tonight to toast his promotion, if that's what it's called. I have no clue.

We're early so we can sit down with Goblin before everyone shows up, so it's not surprising to see the guys lounging around while Sissy and Tabitha scramble to make food in the kitchen.

I spot Goblin on the sofa watching TV, so we make our way over there.

"Hey, how's my little rugrat?" Goblin asks, and Veda runs into his arms. She loves being here, mostly because everyone swoons over her and gives her all the love and attention she craves.

"I brought dolls we can play with," Veda says, setting her backpack on the ground.

"Can you go outside and hang out with the dogs for a minute before you get your dolls out?" I ask her.

She nods and runs to the backdoor. The dogs are another perk to coming to the clubhouse.

"What's up?" Goblin asks, his eyes narrowing with curiosity.

"I have something to tell you," I say, rubbing my hands down my jean-clad thighs and building the courage to say what needs to be said.

"Well, spit it out." He motions for me to continue.

"You might know my mom moved us away from Reno when I was eight, but I didn't tell you why." I glance over at Coyote, who jerks his head for me to keep going. "I was conceived after an affair my mom had with a member of a rival MC."

His head tilts. "Okay."

"When I was going through my mom's things, I came across this picture." I hand him the old, wrinkled Polaroid.

When he sees the picture, his entire demeanor changes. He scrubs a hand down his mouth and sinks into the sofa. "I forgot about this picture."

"So that's you?"

"Yeah. I was much better looking back then."

He was hot in the picture, but he's distinguished now. The hair on top of his head is longer but parted on the side and gelled back, the sides of his head shaved. He's average height and muscled, which would intimidate me if going off his size alone. But it's his stylish glasses, the graying hair at his temples, and his neatly trimmed beard that tells me he's more metrosexual than the other guys.

"The woman with you is my mom."

It clicks then, and his gaze shifts from me to the picture and back again as he takes it in.

"You mean to tell me. . ." his voice trails off.

"I think you're my biological dad."

"Well, shit," he says. "Sorry, I don't mean it like that. But it makes a whole lot of sense now."

"What do you mean?" I ask.

He blinks rapidly, as if coming out of a trance. "Your mom and I met at the coffee shop she was working at. I thought we were in love, but I knew she was keeping something from me. She could only see me on certain nights and wouldn't commit to any plans. Then, one day, she disappeared. Broke my heart. Years went by,"—he motions to me—"eight years, I'd guess. And she just popped up again, out of nowhere. Said she missed me and couldn't get me out of her head. I hadn't moved on either, so I thought that was a sign we were supposed to be together. That's when she told me her ol' man was Wrecker. It started a war between our clubs that hurt both of our businesses."

"Did she tell you about me?"

"No. Never said anything about a kid. Our clubs attacked each other back and forth until Wrecker and Loki's old man, Trucker, had a sit-down. Don't know what they decided, but it ended the war. Next thing I know, your mom disappeared, and I never heard from her again."

"That's sad," I say.

"It was whatever, but I was seventeen, and she was what, twenty-four?"

"She was," I say after doing the math in my head.

"Huh." He hands the Polaroid back to me, and his blue eyes meet mine. "I swear I never knew."

"I know you didn't. My mom is good at keeping secrets."

"I don't know what to say. Do we like, hug it out or something?" The poor man is visibly stunned.

"If you want to."

We both stand and embrace, but it's awkward and uncomfortable. I think we have some adjusting to do.

"That's some crazy shit. Your mom doing okay?" He pulls away and, if I'm not mistaken, is a bit misty-eyed.

"Yeah, she's good." I don't bother getting into what her life consists of these days.

An excited grin breaks across his face. "So if you're my kid, then Veda's my grandkid? Oh my hell, I'm a grandpa."

I laugh at how well he's taking this. "We can do a DNA test to confirm. I brought the kit with me. I just need to swab the inside of your cheek."

"Hell yeah, let's do this."

I get the kit out of my purse and swab his cheek before doing my own.

"That's it?" he asks.

"Yep. We'll have the results in eight weeks," I say.

"That long, huh?"

"Are you in a hurry?" Coyote asks.

"No hurry, just anxious. I think I'd like being a grandpa and even a dad. I know you don't need me butting in on your life, but I don't know. It'd be cool."

"Well, no one's stopping you from being that person, no matter what the results are," I say.

He stands. "Good. I'm gonna go play dolls with my grand-baby then."

We watch, dumbfounded, as he all but jogs outside. He stops when he gets to the door and turns to face me. "Will you tell your mom I said hi? And if she's ever around here again, that I think I'd like to take her to lunch?"

"Uh, sure. I can do that." I look at Coyote in shock. "What the hell just happened?"

"Told you not to worry, Little Owl."

Chapter
THIRTY-TWO

Coyote

The party is a fuckin' blast, but after the sun sets and the booze comes out, Riley decides it's time to take Veda home.

"I have something to show you before I leave," she whispers into my ear.

"Is it dirty?" I ask, pulling her into my lap.

She giggles as I pepper kisses on her neck. "No, it's not. But you have to come inside to see."

"Okay."

She takes my hand and leads me over to a table covered in blueprints that Khan is sitting at.

"What's this?" I take a seat next to him and look down at what I think are the blueprints of a house.

"I asked Khan to help me find an architect to draw up plans for a new house." Her smile is big and proud.

"Oh, yeah?" I'm still a little confused. She has a house. "For you?"

"For us." She pulls out a computer-generated mockup. "I added four bedrooms for the litter of kids you want."

"Smart." I smirk.

"But the owner's suite is my favorite part." She turns the page to a bedroom along the backside of the house, so it has a view of downtown Reno.

That's not the fuckin' incredible thing about it, though. The incredible part is that the room is all glass, like a sunroom.

She points to the longest wall of windows. "These are actually bi-fold window doors, so that entire side of the room opens to the outside." She shrugs. "Maybe it won't work, but I thought if you felt like you were outside, you could sleep in there."

I study the room and envision if sleeping there would ease the anxiety. Surprisingly, I think it will.

"You did this just so I can sleep next to you?"

"I love you for who you are, so if you need to be outside, that's fine. But winters will be hell on you, and if there's something we can do to make it easier, I think we should do it."

"Plus, her hiring the construction company for this job will allow us to clean up a shitload of our funds. It's a win, win. Though it won't help for this winter," Khan chimes in.

Fall is knocking at the door, and the nights are already cold. It's been weighing on my mind lately, but I keep putting it off to worry about another day.

"What do you think?" Riley asks.

"It's fuckin' awesome. Let's do it." I bring her into my side, planting a kiss on top of her head.

"Sweet. Looks like I get to hire more crew. The club alone is keeping us really busy." Khan rolls up the plans and inserts them into a protective tube. "You guys will have to move out for six to eight months."

"We'll figure it out," I say.

"Okay. I'll start ordering materials tomorrow." He leaves us to get back to the party.

"Where's Ve—"

I don't let her finish before drawing her to me and leaning in for a kiss. I sweep my tongue through her mouth, loving the little moan she lets out. She tastes like sweet tea, and I drink her down, relishing in every second we're joined.

Too soon, she's pulling away. "Does that mean you like it?"

"Fuckin' love it, Little Owl. Still can't believe you thought of it."

"I love you and want you to be comfortable in our home. I know you don't like leaving me at night; I see it written all over your face when you go. I also know it's not something you can control. Your feelings are valid, and I would never try to take that away."

"You're right, and I appreciate that."

She bites down on a nail, her face pinching. "You do have to help pay for it, though. I have some money but not build-a-new-house money."

"I have plenty of money," I admit. "I've saved nearly every cent I've made for years. And baby, I've made a lot of money."

"Oh yeah? Does that make you my sugar daddy?" She throws her arms around my neck.

"Only if you being my sugar baby means I get to bend you over my knee and spank your ass until it glows red."

She smirks. "I think I could get into that."

I groan and pull her closer so she can feel my erection. "Fuck the party. I'm coming home with you."

"Good." She spins in my arms and grinds her ass against my dick, then walks away laughing.

"Not fuckin' funny," I call out after her, adjusting my dick. "I wasn't kidding about the whole spanking thing."

She throws me a wink. "I was counting on it."

After getting an exhausted and grouchy girl to bed, I set out to find Riley. My palm has been itching all night, wanting to make good on my promise.

I look in her room and find it empty, as is the rest of the house. My girl loves to sit outside at night with a glass of wine, so I put on my boots and head that way. Except she's not on the patio either.

What the fuck?

The only place I haven't checked is the monstrosity of a tent Veda and I bought that's my new sleeping spot. We like to move it around so we never wake up to the same view, and right now, it's in the side yard.

I unzip it and stick my head inside, surprised to find the whole tent lit up with those fake flickering candles. Sitting on a sleeping bag in the center is a naked Riley. Her long dark hair is over her shoulder, and her knees are drawn up to her chest, keeping most of herself hidden in the shadows.

She smiles shyly, the way she does. No matter how much I defile her, she never loses her innocence, and it makes my dick hard as stone.

"What's going on here?" I ask, walking inside, zipping the tent back up behind me. The tent's tall enough to stand at my full height in the center. I only have to duck to go to either side where the makeshift bedrooms are.

"Don't worry, I have the monitor on, so if Veda needs us, we can go running." She holds up a small electronic box. "By the way, your singing voice is amazing. I didn't know that about you."

"Shit," I draw out. Veda talked me into singing the nursery rhymes in her book with her. Didn't know I had an audience.

"Seriously, you can sing."

"Don't want to talk about that. I want to talk about why you're naked in my tent." I remove my cut and set it down on a cot.

"I thought it was obvious." She stands, placing her hands behind her back and making her tits thrust out at me. The way the light dances across her creamy skin is beautiful. She's a god-damn work of art.

"You're somethin' else, you know that. You surprise me at every turn. Fuckin' love that about you."

"Good, because I have another surprise." She holds something out. "Take it."

She drops a plastic stick in my palm. "What is it?"

"A pregnancy test."

It's dark, so I hold it up close to my eyes to read what it says. *Pregnant.*

"Really?" I ask.

"It's either your super sperm, or I'm really fertile."

"Definitely super sperm." I toss the stick and lift her into my arms, swinging her in a circle. "How far along are you?"

"Four weeks." She sighs. "Super sperm."

I set her down and kneel in front of her so I'm eye level with her belly. "You saved your mama's ass tonight."

She swats my head. "Don't be dirty."

I run a finger down the silver stripes and then further to her pussy. "Oh, we're gonna get real dirty tonight. Hopefully, they don't have a memory this young."

"I'm pretty sure they're just a bunch of cells at this point."

"Good. Now sit on my face." I kick off my boots and lie down on the sleeping bag.

"Seriously?" she asks.

"Little Owl, if you don't smother me with that pussy in three seconds, I won't care that you got my kid in you. I'll make your ass glow."

She hops to it and straddles my chest, unsure of the best way to go about it. I snake my arms under her thighs and toss her up higher until she's hovering over me.

"Like this?" she asks.

"No, like this." I pull her down until her pussy rests on my mouth and chin, and my nose butts up against her clit.

The second my tongue enters her, she shudders and relaxes into it, her head falling back on her shoulders. Only bad thing is I can't talk when my mouth is full of pussy, and I fuckin' love seeing her reaction to my dirty words. But that can come later.

She grinds against my nose as I prod her hole, taking breaks to lick up and down her slit. She's silky smooth and has the best-tasting pussy I've ever had.

Sun-ripened tomato.

I cup her ass, kneading the flesh as she continues to use me to get herself off. Her hands move slowly up her body and stop at her tits. Turns me on to see her touching herself, seeking her own pleasure like the goddamn goddess she is.

Doesn't take long before her movements become erratic and her pussy spasms around my tongue.

"Oh, God. Coyote. Yes."

My cock throbs in my jeans at hearing her words. They're few and far between, something I hope she feels more comfortable doing in the future. But we moved at lightning speed, and some things take time. My super sperm isn't one of those things.

Can't believe she's knocked up already. I'm fuckin' thrilled, though. Thrilled to grow our family and thrilled I get to be around for this one.

Fuckin' thrilled for it all.

She falls forward, catching herself with her hands and worming her way down my body, panting and warm with afterglow and the flickering lights.

"You're beautiful," I say, pushing her hair out of her face.

"Not as beautiful as you." She kisses me long and deep, no longer shying away when she tastes herself on my lips.

I roll her over and take control of the kiss, exploring her mouth and relishing the way our tongues move together. Pulling away, I pin her hands over her head and kiss my way down her chest.

"Be gentle. They're tender already. It's what clued me in," she whispers.

With just the tip of my tongue, I flick each nipple, smiling when they pucker for me. "Fuckin' love these tits."

Moving back up her body, I release her to take my clothes off. With a hand splayed over her mouth, she watches me, her thighs rubbing together, already anticipating another orgasm.

"Spread those thighs. I want to see how wet you are."

Her legs fall apart, and I'm rewarded with her glistening cunt. Never seen a prettier pussy than hers. Delicate and dainty, the pussy of a lady. It makes it even more fun to dirty her up.

I toss my clothes in a pile and take one of her feet in each hand to flip her onto her front. She gasps and peers at me over her shoulder.

"What are you doing?" she asks.

"Want to play with that asshole while I fuck you from behind."

"I brought something that might help with that," she says, fluttering her lashes. "It's over there."

She points to where her clothes are folded. I bend down and find a thin, gold vibrator and a bottle of lube.

Hell yeah.

When I turn back around, she's already on her knees, her ass propped up high for me. Over the last week, I've worked her up to taking my thumb. This thing isn't much bigger than that, so I know I won't hurt her.

I bring the supplies back and kneel, regretting not having a mattress pad because the earth digs into my old knees. Not even that will deter me, though.

I drizzle some lube onto her hole and spread her open with one hand. I prod her back entrance with a finger from the other. She hums in approval, rocking back against me.

"Prettiest little asshole ever," I murmur, watching her accept my finger.

"You're so weird," she says, but her eyes are wide with excitement.

I pull out long enough to grip my cock at the base and guide it into her pussy that eagerly sucks me in. She's wet, warm, and slick, like fuckin' heaven.

"Feel good, dirty girl?" I hook my thumb in her ass, a move she loves.

"Oh my God, yes."

I fuck her like that, getting her used to the fullness before lubing up the vibrator and working it in her slowly, stopping now and then so she can adjust. Once it's all the way in, I turn it on, and she bears down on my dick, crying out. A sound that's music to my ears because it means I'm doing something right.

"Such a greedy girl, needing both her holes filled up."

I feel the rigid device through the thin barrier between us, the vibration making my balls draw up, nearly ready to explode. Goddamn, this is the best idea she's ever had.

Despite what I said, I slap a hand on the fleshy part of her ass. The way it bounces and jiggles is a feast for the eyes, so I do it again and again.

"Oh my God," she says under her breath. "I'm coming."

If I thought she was tight when it was just my dick inside her, it's doubly so with the vibrator. Her inner walls squeeze as I pound into her while circling the vibrator to stimulate the nerves around her asshole. It's too much, and I come along with her.

"Fuck yeah, baby," I roar as the tingles make their way up the base of my spine.

I flip the vibrator off when the orgasm wanes and slowly work it out of her before pulling out. My cum glistens in the candlelight as it drips out of her. If she weren't already pregnant, I'd shove it back in and make her close her legs.

"Come here, Little Owl." I help her to her feet and use my T-shirt to wipe between her legs, then bring her over to my cot. I lie down and pull her on top of me. We worked up a sweat, so despite the chilly air, I'm hot.

"That was amazing," she coos, running her nails up and down my chest.

"Maybe next time I'll fuck your ass and use a dildo in your pussy," I say.

She laughs. "We'll see."

"That's what you say now, but I know my dirty girl. If you didn't just have an orgasm, you'd be creaming yourself."

"You're so crass."

"You love it."

"I do," she admits. "And I love you."

"Love you too, Little Owl. And I'll keep loving you for forever."

"Forever," she repeats.

"Gonna marry you someday."

Her hand freezes in place, and she lifts her head off my chest. "You want to get married?"

"Hell yeah, I do. Need all the other Crashes of the world to see my ring on your finger." I tuck a strand of hair behind her ears. "But I'm waiting until I meet your mom. Figure it'll be hard enough to tell her you're pregnant again by a man she's never met. Don't want to add being engaged to the mix."

"You want to meet my mom?"

"I'm living in your house, you're pregnant with my second baby, and I love you. I should meet your mom."

"She won't like you."

"Don't give a shit."

"She'll probably say some awful things to you."

"Don't give a shit about that, either."

"Okay." She rests her head back on my chest.

"Forever means forever, Little Owl. You're my soul tie."

"What's a soul tie?"

"Five years ago, when we made love, it tied our souls together and made a connection that can't be broken. No matter where I went or what I did, I felt that tie to you. Tried to ignore it, tried to move on, but you can't move on from your soul tie. The second I saw you again, my life felt complete, and my soul settled."

"I felt the same thing. No matter what I did, I couldn't forget you."

I kiss the top of her head. "Soul tie."

"Soul tie," she repeats sleepily.

I hold her close as she falls asleep, thinking about my life's progression. Never thought I'd ever be where I am today, and honestly, it scares the shit out of me. But I got my kid—soon to be kids—my woman, and my club. I went from a boy with nothing to lose to a man with everything to lose.

And I'd die to protect it all.

EPILOGUE

Riley
One year later . . .

"**Y**ou've got to be fuckin' kidding me." Coyote walks out of our bedroom in a pair of swim trunks I had specially made. They're black with the RBMC logo across the ass.

I double over laughing. He looks so uncomfortable. This man is either completely naked or in his jeans, T-shirt, and cut. There's no in-between.

"Laugh it up. I'll just get even later tonight after the kids are in bed."

Kids.

It's still hard for me to believe Veda has a three-month-old brother. Huxley is every bit his dad, reserved and introverted. He hardly cries, hardly ever even makes himself known. He just watches, taking everything in.

He has my light skin, dark hair, and, much to my dismay, also my eyes. But Coyote is always quick to remind me it's his favorite part about me.

Coyote moves behind me and wraps his arms around my

middle. "I'm not going to the water park with you. This shit is embarrassing."

"You are going," I insist. "Goblin will need you. He's not excited about this either."

The last year has taken many twists and turns, none more surprising than Goblin and Mom reuniting. After the first time we had them over, whatever they shared was rekindled the second they saw each other.

They have a lot of work to do to get to a place where they can be together. Mom isn't ready to walk away from the life she built in California, and there's no chance of Goblin leaving the club. So right now, they're just enjoying each other's company whenever their schedules align.

It's fine by me because, honestly, it's really weird to see them together. Mom in her expensive slacks and blouses, and Goblin in jeans and T-shirts. They're a strange pairing, but love doesn't discriminate.

He releases me and lets out a huff of irritation. "This is the worst thing you've ever made me do."

"Worse than being there when Pup was born?" I ask.

Since Veda's nickname is Owlet, it only made sense to call Hux, Pup. He might hate it when he's older, but for now, it suits him.

"So fuckin' worse." He pulls a black T-shirt over his head, covering up all his delicious muscles. "If I have to do that each time, we might be stopping at two kids."

Nothing puts Coyote in more distress than to see me in pain, and my labor with Pup came on so fast and furious we didn't even make it to the hospital. He was born on the side of Veteran's Parkway in the back of my Mercedes G Wagon, a gift Coyote gave me a month before my due date.

Coyote was forced to play doctor with nine-one-one on speaker as I pushed Pup out. While it was traumatic for him,

I wasn't worried at all. I knew Coyote would be there for me, and he was.

"Next time, I'll know not to wait to head to the hospital when I feel the first stirring of a contraction." I tug my sleep shirt over my head and push my panties down before pulling up my bikini bottoms.

"Goddamn," Coyote says, his voice husky.

I turn to see him watching me. "I think I should find my one-piece suit."

"Hell no. You're wearing that." He stalks over to me and palms one of my tits.

"Might not want to do that," I murmur, feeling the stirring of arousal.

"Why? We have time."

And then it happens. Breast milk leaks through his fingers and down his arm. "Oh."

"Sorry." I wince and grab my shirt, wiping up the mess.

"Don't be sorry. Proud of your body for giving me a family and feeding my son." He tips my chin up and kisses me long and deep. When he pulls away, he smacks my ass. "Wear the damn bikini to the water park, then later, I'll peel it off you with my teeth."

My eyes flutter open, still stuck in a Coyote lust-fog. It's been more than a year since we reunited, yet we still can't keep our hands off each other. I hope that never goes away because the things he makes me feel and the love he surrounds me with are intoxicating.

"Get going then," he says. "Let's get this over with."

I slip my bikini top over my head and adjust it into place. Something catches my eye outside, and while I pull my swimsuit cover on, I step out through our new bi-fold window doors and onto the back patio. Our newly renovated house was finished just in time to bring Pup home.

I was nervous that my vision wouldn't work and Coyote

wouldn't be able to sleep in this room. But not only can he, but he also loves it in here. We spend hours each night gazing at the stars through our glass roof, talking and making love. It turned out so much better than I could've hoped for.

Looking up into the trees, I see an owl perched high on a branch.

"What are you doing out in the day?" I ask, and he gives me an answering *hoot*.

His eyes are big and wide, taking me in as much as I'm taking him in. So much happened after the first time Coyote called me Little Owl that I feel connected to the bird in a weird way. They have integrity, serenity, and wisdom. All things I aspire to be and all things Coyote tells me I am.

He blinks at me, then turns his head, distracted by something, and takes flight, soaring over my head and out of sight.

"Little Owl, let's go," Coyote says, walking outside with Pup in his arms.

Seeing him with our baby makes my heart swell and my pussy clench. This man as a dad is the most beautiful thing I've ever seen, and I hope I get to see it over and over again. I never wanted a big family until he came into my life. Now I want it more than I can express.

"Okay."

We gather our things and walk to the door. Veda and I slip our feet into our flip-flops before Coyote passes the baby over to me so he can tie his boots and put on his cut.

His boots and his cut.

"Sweetheart, you can't wear boots, and you don't need your cut at a water park." I nearly laugh at how ridiculous he looks.

"I don't have any other shoes." He folds his arms across his chest, looking every bit as confident as he always does.

"Okay." I shake my head.

Once everyone and everything is packed into the car, we head out.

"I need to go shopping later so I can make dinners for the girls," I say, pulling my phone out to make a grocery list.

"Any new drama I should know about?"

I love my job as house mom at Royal Treatment. After I gave birth to Pup, Coyote asked if I wanted to quit working for a while, to which I responded with a definitive, "No." The girls are part of my extended family now, and giving that up is not something I want.

There's so much more to it than keeping the girls happy. I'm in charge of costumes, I help them create new routines, I'm a listening ear and amateur therapist, and I make sure they have healthy meals. The list goes on and on.

During the remodel, I suggested adding a bedroom for Veda and now Pup. It's unconventional to take your kids to a strip club, but it works for us. At least until Veda starts school this fall. Then we'll have to reassess.

"No. Kelsey is graduating medical school after next semester, so we'll need to look for a replacement, but other than that, things are stable."

"Good." Coyote parks, and we all get out.

"Daddy, will you ride the toilet bowl with me?" Veda asks, taking her dad's hand.

"I don't know what that is, but sure."

The teenager taking tickets eyes Coyote suspiciously before placing a wristband on him. It's a common occurrence. Everything about him is intimidating, and the Royal Bastards have a reputation around town. One they've earned, sure, but it's not all bad.

Since the club has become more family-friendly, they've organized charity rides and become more involved in the community. They probably won't be invited to ribbon-cutting ceremonies or anything, but they aren't shunned as much as before.

We rented a cabana since we have a baby who'll need the shade and some quiet, so we follow the cement path to our assigned area. Mom and Goblin are waiting for us, sitting very close to one another, involved in a deep conversation.

Mom's wearing a sheer floral coverup over her sensible one-piece. And Goblin's wearing swim trunks and his cut, with no shirt. Oh, and boots.

These men.

"Hey, guys," I say, setting down the diaper bag.

"There you are." Mom makes grabby hands for Pup, and I hand him over.

Goblin gives Pup a kiss on the head and stands to give Coyote a fist bump.

"You two look ridiculous," I say.

"What?" they ask in unison, glancing down at their attire before looking at each other.

"Will you at least take the cuts off while we're at the park?"

"Hell no," they say, again, in unison.

I roll my eyes, but I'm smiling. I'm giving them shit, but really, I wouldn't have it any other way. They're Royal Bastards, through and through.

"Grampa, come ride the toilet bowl with me and Daddy," Veda chirps.

Goblin's face screws up. "The toilet bowl?"

"Yeah!" She takes his hand and pulls him to his feet. "Let's go."

Coyote strips himself of everything but his trunks, and Goblin follows suit.

"Nice shorts," Goblin compliments. "Where'd you get those?"

"Riley," Coyote says.

"I'll order you a pair." I take a seat next to Mom.

"Cool."

The two men each take one of Veda's hands. It melts me from the inside to see two unconventional angels care so much for such a sweet and innocent little girl.

"Just thought of something. When I finally marry Riley, you'll be my father-in-law." Coyote chuckles.

"Shut the hell up, man."

"No swearing," Veda says in her stern voice.

"You tell them, baby girl," I call out.

Mom and I giggle as they walk away. I pick up the menu from the table and glance at the food selection. I'm starving, and weirdly enough, this place has the best French fries.

"I think I'm in love with Sloane," Mom blurts out.

Mom refuses to call him Goblin. I think it's her way of detaching him from the club.

The menu falls from my hand. "Really?"

"Actually, I don't think I ever stopped loving him." She pushes her Chanel sunglasses to the top of her head.

"Do you think he feels the same?"

"I don't know."

Pup fusses to tell me he's hungry since that's the only time he makes a peep. I slip off my bathing suit cover and take him from Mom before lifting my bikini top and shoving my boob in his mouth.

"I'm sure he does. I see the way he looks at you."

"We don't agree on anything. Not where to live, not the club. We can't even agree on where to go to dinner." Her arms fly wildly into the air.

"Sounds like you have some talking to do."

"Are you happy? I mean, being so close to the club?"

I smile. "Wildly happy. Nothing can save me from bad things happening, but I have an entire family ready and willing to go to war for me when they do. I have a man who loves me and his family with everything in him, a job I adore, and a house I'm in love with. What more could I ask for?"

Laying it out like that has tears welling in my eyes. This isn't where I thought my life would go, but goddamn, I'm lucky fate took the wheel and led me down this path.

Tears fall down my cheeks, and Mom wipes them away. I could blame them on the hormones, but I'm coming to terms with the fact that I'm a crybaby. Always have been, always will be.

"I fought this union so hard, but seeing you this happy is all I could ever ask for."

"I leave for ten minutes, and you make my girl cry?" Coyote stalks over and kneels in front of me.

"They're happy tears," Mom clarifies, stiffening her posture. She and Coyote have had a bumpy relationship. He holds a grudge against her for how she treated me while I was growing up and when I was pregnant. He's protective of me in a way she'll never understand.

"They are." I sniffle and move Pup over to the other side.

He leans over and gives me a kiss, dripping water on Pup and me. He looks good wet, and his shorts cling provocatively to his body, showing the outline of his manhood. He's limp now, but I know what it looks like when he's aroused, and now I can't get the image out of my head. Coyote notices where my eyes are zeroed in and smirks.

No, no, no. I can't get turned on at a family water park.

Pup stirs from the cold water and pops off my nipple. He grins up at his dad as I cover myself.

"Hand him over. We'll take the kids to the lazy river," Mom says with outstretched arms.

I release him into her hold, and the four of them leave us alone.

"Little Owl, are you aroused?" His hands go to my hips and drag down my outer thighs.

"No," I lie.

Coyote stands, his cock now at half-mast. He zips all four sides of the vinyl canopy closed and takes a seat on a chair. He pulls himself out and strokes lazily. "Come sit on my dick."

"We're at a water park."

"I know. Better hurry before they get back."

I saw my lower lip between my teeth for roughly two seconds before I jump up and rush over to him. He releases his dick long enough to turn me around so I'm facing away from him. Pushing my bathing suit to the side, he drags a finger through my already sopping pussy.

"Always so wet for me, Little Owl," he says, and I glance over my shoulder to watch as he sucks my juices off his finger. My head goes light, and my pussy throbs with need. "Gonna have to keep quiet."

"I will. Just please," I whine.

He fists his cock with one hand and tugs on my hip with the other. I sink down on him, my head lulling back at the delicious fullness.

"Bounce on me, baby. Make me come." He reaches around and palms my breasts roughly before skimming down my body and placing both hands on my hips.

My thigh muscles work overtime as I work him over. It feels so wrong to be doing this with people walking around, just inches from where we're seated, but the voyeuristic side of me I didn't even know I had comes to life, egging me on.

"That's it, baby. Fuck. You're such a good girl, giving it to me so good," he murmurs so only I can hear. "Your cunt is so greedy, needing my cock in the middle of the day, out in public."

His praise and filthy words have my toes curling and my pussy spasming around him.

"Oh God," I say on an exhale.

He takes over, standing and bending me forward. His fingers dig into my hips as he thrusts in and out, prolonging my orgasm until I'm positive I can't take one more second.

"Where do you want my cum, Little Owl? You want it in your pussy so it'll leak out of you all afternoon? Or do you want to drink it down?"

I can't think right now; I'm too blissed out and enjoying the aftershocks.

"Need to know right now, or else I'll decide, and you know how I love trying to put babies in you."

I know breastfeeding isn't the best method of birth control, but it's the only one we're using right now. Since I don't want to be pregnant again already, I pull off him and turn around before sinking to my knees.

"My queen, kneeling before me. I'm a lucky fuckin' man."

I take him in hand and wrap my lips around his cock, tasting the erotic mix of him and me. It doesn't take long for a burst of his cum to land at the back of my throat. And like the good girl I am, I swallow every drop, pumping his cock until it goes limp in my hand.

Placing one last sweet kiss on the tip, I tuck him back in and stand, adjusting my bathing suit bottoms.

He grips the back of my neck and kisses me like his life depends on it. When he pulls away, he rests his forehead on mine, both of us panting.

"Love you until the day I die, then I'll love you again when our souls reunite in the stars," he says softly.

"The nomad and his little owl. We'll make our own constellation."

"Damn right, we will."

The Fuckin' End

* Turn the page to read the prologue from *Petra's Biker*, the next book in this stand-alone series.

PROLOGUE

Petra

The club's music pounds a steady beat that flows through my body as I move. The people dancing around me are just as lost to the music as I am, and our combined energy is nearly palpable. God, it feels good to let everything go and pretend I'm a carefree twenty-something like almost everyone else here.

I close my eyes and lift my hands in the air, letting every ounce of stress I felt earlier go. I feed off the smell of perfume, sweat, and alcohol, a combination that equates to freedom and joy.

As a third-year resident at UMC, I'm surrounded by so much death and sickness. I need this reminder that people are thriving in this world. Some of them are even happy.

"Let's go get some water," Mia yells into my ear.

My eyes open, and I find my best friend and co-worker at my side. She grabs my hand and tugs me toward the bar, where we find one open stool. She takes it, and I slide between her and the man in the seat next.

"The vibe is amazing tonight," I say as I wave to get the bartender's attention. She gives me a nod and finishes the drink she's pouring before making her way over to us.

"It really is." Mia tugs on the neckline of her sparkly, champagne-colored top. She's a true ginger, so she wears every emotion on her skin. And right now, her bright red cheeks tell me she's overheated.

"Two waters, please," I say.

"You got it." The busty bartender grabs two plastic bottles and sets them on the bar.

I set a ten-dollar bill in front of her and smile. "Keep the change."

"Thanks, babe. Let me know if you need anything else."

Both Mia and I twist the caps off the bottles and chug. The cool liquid re-energizes me, and by the time I reach the bottom, I'm already scouring the dance floor for the crowd that looks like they're having the most fun.

I catch the eye of a tall man with long hair, a beard, and dark, sultry eyes. Just my type. I send him a flirtatious smile that he returns right back to me.

"Oh, he's hot," Mia says.

"Delicious." I bite into my lower lip, my gaze still firmly on him. When he walks toward me, I grab Mia's hand and lean into her. "Oh my God, he's coming this way."

"Get it, girl. He looks like he'll be fun to grind up against for the night."

As he struts his way to the bar, he drags a hand through his hair in a montage moment usually reserved for movies. Yes, this is what exactly I need tonight. As the crowd parts, his body comes into view, and it's every bit as tantalizing as the top half of him. He has on low-slung jeans and a gray, acid wash T-shirt that somehow looks both trendy and casual.

I straighten my slinky tank top and tug on the hem of my corset-style leather skirt. Since my day-to-day uniform is a pair of scrubs, I go all out on the rare occasions I get a night off.

"Hey," he says, tucking his hands into his pockets. "Can I buy you a drink?"

"You sure can," Mia chimes in, hopping off the stool. "I was just leaving. Take my seat."

"I don't want to break up the party."

"Not at all. I need to pee." She pats the stranger on the arm as she brushes past him. "She likes tequila."

"Noted." He offers me the stool, but I decline, so he sits down. "I'm Tyler. What's your name?"

"Cameron." I shake his hand, noting his callouses. Definitely not a doctor like the last three men I dated. "Nice to meet you, Tyler."

"It's really nice to meet you, Cameron." He flags down the bartender and orders us tequila shooters. I don't drink often, but I have a day off tomorrow and nothing better to do than recover from a hangover.

"Cheers." I tap my shot glass with his and toss the liquid down. It burns, and my face screws up, but Tyler is right there holding a lime to my lips. I smile and bite down, letting the sour flavor erase the liquor.

"Thanks."

"No problem." He runs his thumb along the bottom of my lip. "Lime juice."

My cheeks heat, but I shake the nerves off. I'm not about to be bashful. "What do you do for a living, Tyler?"

"I'm an acquirer of goods."

My brows knit. "What does that mean?"

"Wealthy people hire me to find very specific merchandise." He rests an elbow on the bar. "What do you do?"

I could be honest, tell him I spend a hundred hours a week at the hospital where I don't even have time to pee, let alone shower, but that feels like too much. I'm not that girl tonight. Nope.

"I'm a go-go dancer at a club downtown."

"Really?" He flashes me a wolfish grin. "I need to see those moves in action."

Standing, he takes my hand and leads me out to the dance floor, where I show off my best moves. The liquid courage helps, but so does this fine as hell man watching me like I'm giving him a private show.

"You're fucking beautiful," he shouts over the music, gripping me by the hips and tugging me into him.

"Thanks." I toss him a wink and wrap my arms around his neck. He smells expensive, like citrus and oak. His clients must pay him well.

After another shot of tequila and a full hour on the dance floor, I'm parched. The twelve-hour day I had before getting ready to go out is catching up with me. Tyler probably thinks I'll be going home with him tonight, but I need to have a connection with someone before I feel comfortable enough to get naked. If he wants to see me again, I'm down for that, but otherwise, this is where it will end.

I hook a thumb over my shoulder. "I should go find my friend, but I had an amazing time with you."

"Party's over, huh?" He pouts, but there's no pressure behind the statement, which I appreciate.

"I'm afraid so." I search through the crowd, trying to find Mia, but since the club doesn't close for another three hours, it's still popping.

"Can I give you and your friend a ride home?"

"You've been drinking," I remind him. I've seen too many people come through the ER busted up from drunk driving accidents. There's no way I'll let that be me, or worse, Mia.

"I'd never drive drunk," he says solemnly. "I have a driver in the lot waiting for me."

"A driver? Maybe I'm in the wrong business."

"I do okay." His confident smirk is all-telling. This guy is loaded.

"Let me find Mia, and I'll ask her what she thinks."

"Okay. I'll be at the bar." He leans down and kisses me on the cheek. "Whatever you decide, I hope I'll leave with at least your phone number."

My insides do a dance. "Only if you plan to use it."

"Oh, I'll use it. This isn't the last time you'll see my face."

I walk the perimeter of the club twice, not finding Mia, and send a ridiculous amount of texts, all of them unanswered. The buzz I had fades quickly, and an uneasiness settles over me. This isn't like her. At all.

I find Tyler right where he said he'd be. He's on his phone and nursing a glass of brown liquor.

"She's not here," I say.

He tucks his phone away. "Is this something she does often?"

"Never. We always come together and leave together."

"Did you try to call her?" he asks.

"I texted her. All of them are sitting at delivered." My shoulders sag.

"How about this? I'll have my driver swing us by her house so you can see if she made it home. If she's not there, then I'll help you call hospitals or the cops, or whatever you decide." His genuine concern puts me at ease.

I could take an Uber to her house, but it would take an hour to get a car on a Saturday night in downtown Vegas. And with the way I'm feeling right now, this can't wait.

"Okay. Thank you."

He places a hand on the small of my back, leading me outside. A black, tinted-out limo pulls up the second we step up to the curb.

"This is me," he says, opening the back door.

Looking back, I'll see all the signs I missed, all the red flags that were flying right in front of my face. But at this moment, I'm too worried about my friend to pick up on any of them.

I duck into the car, sliding along the buttery leather. The last things I remember are Mia, duct tape across her mouth and hands tied on the seat in front of me, and the sharp sting of a needle being pushed into my neck by someone who was waiting for me inside.

I wake up with my head pounding and every muscle in my body aching. Whatever I'm lying on is hard, cold, and unforgiving. As my brain registers everything that happened, I bolt upright.

I'm in a pitch-black room. No, not a room, a metal box, maybe because every move I make echoes against the walls and roof.

A grunting noise comes from my right, and I blink to adjust to the dark but can't see shit. There's someone next to me, so I crawl that way, my knees scraping against the steel as I go. She grunts again, and I know it's Mia. My hands skim up her shoulders until I reach her face and feel the slick duct tape still stuck across her mouth.

"Oh my God, Mia." I grimace as I rip off the duct tape. "What happened?"

The second she can, she lets out a pained sob. I hug her to me while she collects herself.

"There was a-a-a guy," she stutters, her green eyes wild with fear. "We were dancing, and he asked if I wanted to go smoke a joint in his car."

"Mia," I scold.

"Don't *Mia* me. You're here too."

I sigh. "Fair point. What then?"

"He took me to that limo, and the second I was inside, he attacked me. Oh my God, Cam. Where are we? What's going on?"

I fall back on my ass. "I don't know. I couldn't find you at the club. Tyler, the guy I met, offered to help me find you. Then I saw you and"—my hand flies to my neck where I feel the sore spot from whatever I was injected with—"another man drugged me."

"They drove us to the middle of fucking nowhere, Cam. Seriously. Nowhere. Then they put us in here without saying a word."

"Give me your hands. Let's find a way out." I work the tape

off her wrists, and we hug for a long moment. "How did this happen?"

"I have no idea. I thought we were smarter than this," she says.

"Apparently, we aren't, but let's be smart now. Come on. Feel around for a latch or something."

The second we stand, a loud clattering comes from the far end of the container, and artificial light spills in. Two shadowy figures walk inside. I know from the silhouette that one of them is Tyler. I spent all night admiring his frame and beautiful, flowing hair.

"You're awake," Tyler says.

"What the fuck, Tyler. What is this?" Venom drips from my words.

He ignores me, turning to the other man. "Go take a look. You'll be happy."

A flashlight clicks on, and he aims it at us. I wrap my arms around Mia and squint at the bright light.

"Very nice," an accented voice says. Italian, maybe?

"I told you. Doubt they're virgins, but they're pretty enough to make up for it." Tyler tucks his hands in his pockets casually, like this is normal. Is it normal for him? When he said he acquired goods, did he mean—oh, God. He meant women. He acquires women.

The man I don't know walks closer and caresses the side of my face with the back of his hand. I flinch and jerk away. "Don't touch me, asshole."

He ignores my outburst and glances over his shoulder at Tyler. "Very nice. I'll give you twenty for the meek one and forty for the feisty one."

Mia whimpers, her whole body trembling, but my mind is stuck on what he said. Twenty? Forty? Is he talking dollars?

"She's worth fifty, at least. She's a dancer."

Why did I make up that stupid lie? Would it have made a difference?

The stranger's attention returns to me. "A dancer, huh? Okay, then. Fifty. She'll be fun to break."

Tyler claps his hands. "Great. Let's go finish our business, and then they're all yours."

"What are you talking about? You can't sell us. We're human fucking beings," I spit out.

The stranger clucks his tongue, not at all bothered by my outburst. "That's where you're wrong, sweetness. Your country, your constitution, your government make you think so. But all of those things mean shit when you cross the path of men who have enough money and power to override your freedom. Men who have money, like me? We're the ones who are free. We have no laws, no rules, no one to tell us what we can or can't do."

I squeeze Mia's shoulder, drop my arm, and grab her hand, hoping she'll follow my lead. With no plan other than to run, I knock the flashlight from his grip and run, dragging Mia behind me.

Tyler blocks our exit, but I've taken self-defense classes. I shove the base of my palm into his nose. A sickening crunch echoes off the steel walls, and he grunts in pain. It's enough to get me past him but not enough to save Mia. He grabs her wrist and yanks her backward, out of my hold.

I pause, looking out at the empty parking lot we're in, and then back to Mia, who's full-on sobbing now.

"Even if you get away, and that's a big *if* because we will catch you, you'll never see your friend again. I'll make sure she pays for your mistake." Tyler ignores the blood trickling down his face.

What do I do? Try to run for help? Or go back and wait for another chance? Really, there's no choice. I can't leave Mia here to fight alone.

I double over and scream out my frustrations.

"Good choice." The man with the accent approaches me and jerks me upright with a tight grasp on my upper arm.

With the light from the streetlamps overhead, I get my first look at him. His face is littered with pockmarks, his nose is round like a drooping balloon, and his eyes are dark as night. It's July in Vegas, so the temperature is sweltering, yet a chill runs up my spine.

"What do you want from me?" I whisper.

"Do you want the truth?" he asks, his tone playful and light.

"Yes."

"Everything. I want to use you up until that fire behind your eyes is extinguished."

"What then?" I don't want the answer, but I need it. I have to know what this is.

He fists my hair and jerks it back so I'm looking him square in the eye. "Then I'll kill you, and this will all be over."

ABOUT THE AUTHOR

 Misty Walker writes everything from dark and delicious, to sweet and spicy. Most of her books are forbidden in some way and many are age-gap, because that's her jam.

She's lived quite the nomadic life, never staying in the same place for long until she met her husband. They've recently settled in Reno, NV with their two daughters, two dogs, and two hamsters, because everything's better in pairs.

Misty is fueled by coffee and the voices in her head screaming for their stories to be told. Which is why the coffee is necessary, because there are only so many hours in a day and who needs sleep anyway?

If you'd like to keep up to date on all her future releases, please sign up for her newsletter on her website. You can also order a signed paperback of this book, or any of her releases, there.

Connect with Misty:

www.authormistywalker.com
authormistywalker@gmail.com
Instagram: www.instagram.com/authormistywalker
Facebook: www.facebook.com/authormistywalker
Twitter: @mistywalkerbook
Tiktok: www.tiktok.com/@authormistywalker

Turn the page for a list of all of Misty Walker's books.

ALSO BY MISTY WALKER

Standalones:

Vindicated

Conversion (also available on audio)

Cop-Out

Crow's Scorn: Diamond Kings MC

Royal Bastards: Reno, NV:

Birdie's Biker

Truly's Biker

Bexley's Biker

Riley's Biker

Petra's Bikers

Brigs Ferry Bay Series:

Kian's Focus

Kian's Focus (also available on audio)

Adler's Hart

Leif's Serenity

Doctor Daddy

Brigs Ferry Bay Omnibus

ACKNOWLEDGMENTS

Kristi, I didn't think I could love you anymore. Then 2021 happened. Thank you for being there for me when I needed someone to trust through all the dark and ugly. You're the best work wife and best friend I could ever ask for.

Ty-bot, remember when we were twenty-one, working for the weekend? Friday and Saturday nights were spent out on the town. Now, we're fucked up for a week if we sleep wrong. But there's no one I'd rather grow old with.

Ariadna, thank you for putting up with my bullshit and false alarms. I'm shocked you haven't fired me (Please don't ever fire me).

Diana, I didn't know how much I was missing by not knowing you. Every author needs someone on their team who gets as excited as they do about their books and you're that person for me. You're amazing and I'm so grateful to you!

Elizabeth, Lauren, Sarah, Rhonda, and Jayce, my BETA team, thank you so much for valuable feedback. You have no idea how much it means to me that you take the time to read my books in their most raw form.

Sarah Goodman, thank you for never judging my misplaced and absent commas. I love you to pieces! You are so talented and I'm lucky to have you.

Molly Whitman, without your attention to detail, my books would be a disaster. I thoroughly enjoy working with you and you're not allowed to ever leave me.

Stacey Blake, the pages of this book are so important, and you make them look magical. Thank you, thank you, thank you!

Renita, thank you a million times over. You were so quick to help this newbie author and your feedback and thumbs up gives me the confidence I need to confidently write the characters of my heart.

To my Street Team, it's an incredible feeling to know I have a group of amazing women who love my work so much, they'd devote their time to helping me promote. There are no words to tell you how much I appreciate you.

To my Thirsty Readers, you guys rock my world and motivate me to keep writing. I love nothing more than to get your messages and read your reviews. It's a great big book world, but you choose to read my books, and that means everything.

Lorelai and Mabel, don't ever read this book. I love you.

Mom, 2021 was downright cruel to us. I wouldn't have made it out to the other side without you. You're stronger than you know and more beautiful, inside and out, then you'll ever see for yourself. I love you.